WISH ME LUCK

Sgh De Blake

WISH ME LUCK

A story of second chances

Gayle De Blake

Wish Me Luck by Gayle De Blake
Published by PublishMyBook.online
© Gayle De Blake, 2023

1st Edition 2023, pbk.
ISBN: 978-0-6456338-7-0
Designer: Amanda Greenslade, typeset in Alwyn New
Contact: gayledeblake@gmail.com

Dedication

For my husband Mark and the wonderful 20 yrs we've
shared together.

Author's Note

I'd like to thank Erin Rosen for her tireless research and
Ann Tinkham, for editing and elaborating on my story.

Thank you both, Gayle

Chapter 1

Dusk, May 2nd, 2019

David Stern slumps in the driver's seat of an eight-year-old BMW that represents everything he despises about himself. The car is neither old enough to be considered a classic nor new enough to signify the status he so desperately yearns for but hasn't been able to achieve. He grips the steering wheel and stares blankly. *How did I get here?*

Outside, the evening sky blackens. The county road is deserted. He's parked on a gravel path that leads below the bridge in front of him. He glances at the front passenger seat strewn with unpaid bills, delinquent notices, letters from collection agencies—an avalanche of bad news enough to make anyone drink. The pint of cheap vodka resting in the cup holder of the car's center console calls to him, mocks him, emboldens him. David grabs it viciously, presses it to his lips, and throws back a long drink. Winces. Then does it again. Tears stream from his eyes and tinsel his cheeks as he chokes back a sob. *Pitiful.* He slams the steering wheel so hard he hurts his hand. *Goddamn it!*

David doesn't remember opening the driver's side door or climbing out. When he gains awareness, he's beneath the bridge, standing on a concrete abutment between rusted columns, the Fleming River raging below. The dark water is like a black hole willing him forward, promising a quick end to his months of anguish.

Do it, just do it. He blinks. Did he say the words or only think them?

David sees that he still holds the bottle. Disgusted with life, disgusted with himself, he hurls it, watching it sparkle with reflected moonlight as it arcs over the river. It shatters against the opposite abutment, exploding in a spray of shards that disappear into the water.

The act of throwing the bottle and hearing it smash has vented his anger and he's at a loss for what to do next. He notices the steel stairway to the bridge and starts upward. Within a few steps, he feels winded and stops to grasp the handrail to catch his breath. The air rasps the back of his throat. He swallows painfully and waits a few minutes for his pulse to settle.

Another wave of anguish flows through him. His inability to climb even this short distance without feeling like he's inviting a heart attack underscores how much he's let himself go. Years back, he was a collegiate athlete, a champion. Now he's a doughy mass of failure and self-pity.

Too fraught with anxiety for exercise or healthy routines, he drinks and eats too much. A thick gut flops over his waist. Red-rimmed eyes stare from the flabby-faced man in the mirror, pretending to be him.

David starts up again, this time by hauling himself along the handrail. As he proceeds step by labored step, self-recriminations heap upon him. He was the one most likely to succeed. He married the prettiest girl. He was the one everyone invited to parties to bask in the radiance of his confidence and optimism. Even now, many of his business associates still consider him a winner; that's how well he'd been living this lie.

For two years he has been juggling the books and borrowing to pay for his gambling addiction. They don't call it EZ credit for nothing. Now he has liens on everything with his name.

Most nights he awakens in a cold sweat from night terrors. Stress eats at him like a tumor. His insides feel scrambled like when an elevator drops too fast and you get the fleeting sensation that it's going to crash against the bottom. But that sensation of certain doom is no longer fleeting, it's a constant presence.

His days are a whirl of ignoring phone calls, answering others, and when he's cornered, stoking his charm so hard it's a steam engine of bullshit that he hopes keeps him going another day, another chance for Lady Luck to save his ass.

But it wasn't the lack of luck that buried him. It was his arrogance, his pride, his unwillingness to compromise, and his delusions that he always knew best. And his gambling.

Once on the bridge, he inches along the narrow edge of concrete, the steel railing against his back. It's a drop of fifty feet to the river frothing below. He sways as he walks, and he tells himself that he's not drunk even as he burps vodka.

He halts and looks down past the toes of his shoes, the swells beckoning him, inviting him to end it. David takes a deep breath. Closes his eyes. Opens them. A watery grave is seconds away. Nothing has changed.

Panic overtakes him. He clutches the handrail with both hands, suddenly aware of the danger. He scoots along the edge of the bridge, fear wiggling along his spine and down the back of his legs.

A moment later, he reaches the top landing of the stairway, hands trembling, knees threatening to buckle. He wipes sweat from his face and lifts his gaze to the sky. A thin overcast sky obscures the stars and the moon; the effect is like the universe is oblivious to his torment.

Like he doesn't matter. *But I do matter.* Defiance pushes aside his despair. An electric rage burns along his nerves, and the hopelessness consuming him suddenly evaporates. The veins in his temple throb.

A renewed strength energizes him, and he bounces, stumbles down the stairs toward his car. He collapses in the driver's seat and gulps air. He gropes for his keys, and they hang from the ignition where he had left them. A quick twist and the engine growls to life.

He looks back to the bridge, to the trough of river water sloshing between its banks. *I could be a fucking dead man, a corpse sinking to the bottom of the river. Or do dead bodies float? Who the hell knows? But what the fuck was I thinking?*

He opens the glove compartment and swipes at the pile of bills and legal papers, knocking some to the floor and crumpling others in his fist. He shoves them all back into the glove compartment and slams it shut. With the heel of his right hand, he blots one eye, then the other. He takes a deep breath to cleanse himself of this spell of bad juju, throws the car into gear, and speeds off.

***

That same evening, Lissa Benton sips herbal tea in bed and settles in to watch a YouTube video. She's transfixed as the screen opens on an ethereal panorama of the earth as seen from 150 miles in space. A quote is superimposed over the view. *Twenty years from now, you will be more disappointed by the things you didn't do than by the things you did.*—Mark Twain

Lissa wonders, *Twenty years from now I'll be in my late fifties. What will I regret? Am I not living my best life?*

The narrator begins in a deep, resonant male voice. "We all experience joy. We all experience pain, success, failure, love, and heartbreak. It is all part of the cycle of life. Part of the amazing journey that opens up to us every day."

As he speaks, the view from space descends, the geography of the earth taking shape. Continents. Oceans. Mountain ranges. Deserts.

Closer now. A montage of human activity: cities teeming with life, suburbs sprawling, endless beaches, deserts sands rising like tidal waves, countryside filled with farms and forests.

The narrator says, "It's not what happens to us, but what we do when things happen. How we respond. How we grow and evolve."

Lissa coaches herself. *Yes, I must remember not to be a victim of my circumstances but rather see growth opportunities in the difficulties that arise.*

Closer, the everyday cycle of life and a juxtaposition of cultures and ethnicities, people working, cooking, jogging, dancing, crying, celebrating, arguing, laughing. People in love. People at war. People living and dying.

The narrator asks, "Do you look back with regret, or do you rejoice in your journey? What would you do differently if you could go back in time? Would you choose a different course or stay steadfast in the flow of your life as you know it?"

Oh, now those are loaded questions. I mean, who doesn't have regrets? Oh, and what if you go back and things are worse than before?

"The future is ours to shape. How we shape it begins with the decisions we make today."

When the screen goes black, Lissa smiles. "So true." With that, she places the iPad at her bedside, flips off the light, and tries to sleep, but the questions posed by the YouTube video whirl in her mind.

***

Kate Stern sits in the office of Dr. Stanford. His degree in general surgery from the University of Michigan Medical School hangs prominently above his cherry desk. Like Lissa, Kate is about to turn forty. But unlike her slim best friend, Kate is a solid twenty pounds heavier than she was in college. Years back, Kate had a figure that could really turn heads.

The door opens and Dr. Stanford walks in dressed in sage green scrubs still creased from the laundry. He's a slender, light-skinned black man with silvery hair and a gleaming smile who looks like he's straight out of central casting for a medical soap opera.

As the doctor sits, he hands Kate some paperwork. She anchors her elbows on his desk and smirks. "So, can

I get a tummy tuck as a gift with the purchase of the mastectomy?"

Dr. Stanford laughs, shakes his head. "Oh, please. You don't need one of those. Besides, I'm focused on the task at hand."

Kate sighs. "True." She can't argue with that.

"We'll get you all fixed up when you return—okay?" He leans back and crosses his arms.

"Sounds like a plan," says Kate. "I'll try to forget about it all while I'm poolside, soaking in the Mediterranean sun."

"Now you're making me envious. Family trip?"

"No. David and I are traveling with my brother, Todd, and his wife. We're leaving the kids at home." She looks left and right as if others might be eavesdropping and in a hushed voice, says, "I love my kid, but I can't wait to be free of him. Does that make me a bad mom?"

Dr. Stanford chuckles. "No, that makes you human."

Kate dramatically wipes her brow. "Phew. Because I was going to ask you if there's a cure for that."

Dr. Stanford chuckles again, then discusses the procedure and post-surgery instructions he gave her. "Now, get out of here, and have a fabulous time. Doctor's orders."

Kate pops up from the chair. "I don't know what I'd do without you, Dr. Stanford." She reaches across the desk to tap his arm. She says, "Thank you for giving me peace of mind," and slips out of the room.

***

Todd Benton measures his breathing. He swipes one hand over his buzz cut, the remnants of what once was a proud mop of blond hair. The stride of his Nikes is a muted *slap, slap, slap* on the pavement. He passes a distance marker and checks the time and his heartrate on the wrist monitor. *All good. I'm right on pace for a personal best. Pretty damn good for a man in his early forties.*

Then he hits the dreaded wall. Just like that, his legs feel like lead weights. The effort to move them saps his resolve. His confidence wanes and he second-guesses his decision to run this marathon. *What was I trying to prove?*

As he passes the twenty-six-mile marker, he recalls an argument with his father. It ended in name-calling—the kind of words that leave scars that will never heal. When his father challenged his dreams for his future, Todd spoke the searing words, "God forbid I end up like you!" Todd shivers and shakes off these thoughts just as he spots the red, white, and blue balloon arch. This sight always lights a fire under his belly. *What a sight!* He powers towards the finish line, amazed he has anything left in the tank.

As he strides across, a young woman exclaims, "Congratulations!" and hands him a chilled water bottle and a foil blanket to help regulate his body temperature.

Todd tries to say thank you, but no words come out, only a low moan. Spent, he shambles from the finish line, feels his legs at last give out, then props himself on his knees and gasps for breath. He waits for his body to recuperate. He's not sure how long he's in that position—a few minutes or maybe even ten. Racers stagger and collapse around him, but he hardly notices.

The victory of the marathon fades and regrets burden his mind. Anguish replaces his physical pain. Tears sting his eyes. He begins to sob. Shamed by his loss of composure, he gathers the foil blanket over his head, hiding his face. The weight of some memories is too heavy a burden.

Was I an awful son?

***

"Hut, hike!" Jack, a star quarterback on the Austin High varsity team, throws a long, elegant pass. The ball arcs and spins perfectly toward an imaginary agile wide receiver. But it's just his dad. "Run! Oh, come on, Dad, faster."

David leaps for the ball, misses, and lands hard on the sod in their back yard. "Oof." Jack runs to help him. David struggles to his feet, his beer belly interfering with his balance, but pretends he doesn't need help. He still sees himself as the fit, speedy running back he was in high school over two decades ago.

Waving his finger, David says, "When I was your age, I could run past any defender. I had four touchdowns in one game."

Laughing, Jack replies, "I've heard that fairytale so many times."

Every time his son teases him about his glory days, David feels the sting. Jack sees him as a washed-out, middle-aged has-been living in the past. David struggles with Jack's success. On the one hand, he's proud as hell; on the other, he doesn't like that Jack is more of a football star than he was. *My best days are behind me, while Jack's are only just blooming.*

In his time, David was the center of attention. He has heard of Eastern teachings and the need to get rid of one's ego, so he repeatedly tells his to go to hell. So far, it hasn't; it's still wounded by all the attention and accolades his son receives, and he's only fifteen. Hell, his wife Kate has devoted an entire room to all Jack's trophies. David only goes in there if he's had a few too many drinks, and he feels petty and small for being jealous of his son's success.

Kate appears on the patio of their mid-century home. Although a fine structure, the rotting wood and faded paint cry out for refurbishing and updated windows.

"Guys, I hate to break up the party, but we have a plane to catch. David, you need to finish packing. Jack, you too. We're dropping you at Marty's on the way," says Kate. David wonders if she likewise lives in the past, wearing a fitted red dress that's way too tight.

"On it, Mom." Jack palms the football and sprints into the house as if in pursuit of a winning touchdown. He is so athletic; he always looks as though all his moves are choreographed.

"I think I might have cracked a rib." David breathes heavily as he shuffles into the house.

"You need to get cracking!" Kate ushers him inside.

Todd sits in his home office and squints at his computer, grimacing. He hasn't left his desk for five hours. Conveniently, he has a coffee maker next to his computer. Today, he has gone through the whole pot. His wife, Lissa, encourages him to cut back, but he's convinced it fuels his success.

They live in a large two-story modern home in a swanky Austin neighborhood. It's a custom-designed home built with solar panels, repurposed wood, and other recycled materials to create an ultra-contemporary look. Large picture windows and an enviable rooftop deck make the house perfect for hosting foodie cocktail parties. Lissa always tells her friends that the party will be nothing fancy, and then she wows them with her well-honed culinary skills.

Todd worked his way through college as a bartender and had gone to mixology school, so he's in charge of the beverages. His friends call him Mr. Mix. Though he keeps the drinks flowing for his friends, Todd prefers to maintain a clear head and rarely over-indulges.

Miles stands by his office door, biting the nubs of his nails and gnawing at his cuticles. According to Lissa, his hands are a fright. But that doesn't stop him from chewing on his fingernails. Miles has a subtle goth aesthetic about him. A long fringe of hair hides his face and perhaps a secret? He clears his throat. Todd waits until the third throat clearing to look up and see Miles give him a disapproving look.

Miles and his friends are part of a growing group of backlash Gen Zers who self-consciously reject the digital realm. Todd secretly wishes for a computer gaming son when his friends complain about theirs. Miles prefers painting on real canvases with real paint. Todd considers Miles's painting as quaintly antiquated and has said, "It's so Renaissance." Todd often warns his son that he'll have to transition to graphic design with computer tools to ever be marketable.

Todd rolls his chair back from the keyboard. "Miles. What's up?"

"Um, did you and Mom talk about the Griffin Art School?"

"She told me about it—after it was booked—if that's what you mean."

"And?"

"Thirteen hundred dollars a week for a summer program at an art school? How about an MIT course, something that applies credits?"

Miles rolls his eyes. I'll research tech courses while you're gone," he says, his tone laced with the usual sarcasm.

"Yes. Do that," Todd quips to end the conversation.

As Miles walks away, Todd turns back to the computer. His attempt to sink back into work is interrupted by his sixteen-year-old daughter, Stella. While Miles cloaks his emotion with layers of gloom and feigned ennui, Stella is a cheery ball of teenage exuberance. She prances in wearing an abbreviated tank top that shows off her bare midriff and even more abbreviated shorts that border on revealing as much as a thong.

"Put some clothes on, sweetie."

Stella mouths, "Thong Nazi" before kissing her dad on the cheek. "You drive me crazy, but I love you anyway. Have an awesome trip!"

"Love you too, sweetheart. Now, listen. You need to be good for Grandma."

"Da-ad," she sings, "I'm not a child."

Todd looks back to his computer. "Well, actually, yes, you are until you're eighteen. If you break your curfew while we're gone, that brand-new iPhone is going back to the Apple store."

"Whatever." She throws him a cheeky smile. "Looooove you." With that, Stella slips away, and the room goes quiet.

Todd chuckles. He's not worried about Stella because she mostly shows good judgment. Miles spends his time brooding. He's most worried about leaving Leo, his diminutive, sweet-faced boy with cerebral palsy. In fact, he worries about Leo even when he's home; he feels helpless in the face of his boy's disability. *If only I could magically go back in time and give my boy a strong, healthy body instead of a broken one that limits his potential. If only.*

When he brings his attention back to his computer, it's in screen-saving mode, reading *Benton EHR Systems*. After glancing at the wall clock, he decides he's done for the day. He saves his work and powers off his computer. Before heading out, he studies the framed photo on the desk. It's his wife Lissa holding Leo as an infant, with Miles and Stella as toddlers, all of them beaming for the camera. The image makes Todd smile.

Todd walks into the kitchen to see his mother, Elaine, and Leo icing a vanilla cake with chocolate icing. As Todd enters, Leo moves awkwardly on leg braces to hug his dad.

"I'm gonna miss you, Dad."

"I'll miss you too, buddy." He gives his son a hearty bear hug. He always hugs Leo extra-tight to infuse his little fragile body with strength. Today, he feels extra-fragile in his arms.

"Somehow, I think Grandma will take great care of

you. Oh, and maybe not too many sweet treats," Todd says pointedly to his mother.

"Oh, Todd, a little cake never hurt anyone." Elaine rolls her eyes at her son.

Lissa appears with her suitcase and places it by Todd's at the door. Her brunette hair is now styled in a topknot, and stylish black travel clothes hang elegantly on her petite frame.

She turns to Todd and says with contained excitement, "Your sister called. They're headed to the airport."

Todd pans the kitchen, nods like he approves of what he sees, and then reads a checklist on his iPhone. Miles, check. Stella, check. Leo, check. House, tickets, passports, luggage, reservations, check, check, check. Only one thing left to do. "I'll book the Uber."

Leo licks the chocolate frosting off his fingers. "Mom?"

"Yes, my love?" Lissa gently touches his shoulder.

"Can you bring me back a luzzu? It's a fishing boat. But not one with a motor. That's for tourists. I saw online hand-painted wooden ones. More my style."

"I'll do just that." She kisses him on his head and appears to inhale her beloved boy.

***

The couples planned to spend a night here in Amsterdam, celebrating Lissa's and Kate's fortieth birthdays before heading to Malta.

Kate tries to keep her cool as they make their

way to the VIP section of a thumping night club. It has expansive, comfy leather couches, sheer curtains, sparkling candlelight, chilled champagne resting in ice, and Mediterranean-themed appetizers. On the dance floor below, couples shimmy and shake to techno house music.

The birthday girls are both decked out in black dresses and bling. Kate squeezed herself into Spanx so she didn't bulge in her little black number. Her hair falls in loose, sexy curls while Lissa wears hers silky and straight.

David and Todd sing "Happy Birthday" to Lissa and Kate, who can barely hear them over the noise.

"Forty and fabulous," Todd toasts. They cheer, clink their glasses, and sip the bubbly.

Lissa leans over to Todd and doesn't just give him a peck on the lips but a long, intimate kiss.

"Oh please, you two, get a room," Kate scolds, teasing. "Forty and fabulous indeed. As for me, I'm like forty pounds too heavy."

"Every ounce and pound of you is de-li-cious," coos David, nibbling at her ear.

Everyone at the table laughs and they raise their glasses for another toast.

David secretly cops a feel of Kate's bottom.

"Cheers," Lissa says. "To the best year of our lives… and to the next forty."

Kate smiles and hugs her friend. "Let's dance!" She reaches for Lissa and drags her to the crowded dance floor, everyone trancing out to the high-energy techno music with a vibrating base. There was no point trying to get their husbands to dance. The guys would only consider it when buzzed. And then they were such terrible dancers,

Lissa and Kate would pretend they weren't with them.

Kate is both amused and flattered as three different guys hit on them on the dance floor. She suspects these dudes have eyes only for Lissa.

After fending off an eager twenty-five-year-old, Lissa shouts to be heard over the music, "How do they know we're not lesbians?"

Kate answers, "They don't. But they're so arrogant, they probably think they can convert us."

Back at their table, David pours Todd another shot.

Todd glowers at him. "Clearly, you're out to destroy me."

"You got that right, buddy. This is our last night to party in Amsterdam. We're going out big!" They clink their glasses and down their shots. "Thanks, man. I mean, we wouldn't be here if not for you, hosting and all." David gets almost weepy. "I really appreciate it."

"Bro, I got your back. Always will," replies Todd.

David gives Todd a huge bear hug. They look over at the girls as David pours another round.

***

Lissa rolls her eyes as her husband leads the way down the international concourse, searching for their gate. His pace is brisk, and he doesn't notice that the others aren't keeping up. David gazes at glistening goods in the window of a duty-free, looking decidedly off-color. Lissa smiles at him as he saunters toward a bar.

"Hair of the dog, here we come," says David, tiredly triumphant.

Kate lags behind them, chowing down on a chocolate croissant.

"Here's the gate, seventy-two." Todd halts and points to the sign before realizing the others aren't right behind him. "C'mon, Lissa. Flight boards in twenty."

Lissa's heartbeat quickens. She places one hand on Todd's shoulder and glances back.

Kate finishes her chocolate croissant, licking the crumbs off the paper. "I'm still hungry."

Lissa points at a vendor. "Fresh juice bar over there."

Kate grimaces. "Seriously? Of course, you'd suggest that you waif, you. It's all very mathematical, I guess... Nope. I am looking for a double latte, extra whipped cream, two sugars."

"The carrot kale is so good, and so good for you."

Kate smirks at her and heads toward the nearest café. "Kale and I broke up. Actually, kale and I never dated."

Lissa shakes her head, but the side of her lip lifts. Her phone rings. "Hi, Stella!" Lissa's face drops as her daughter speaks.

"Mom, Leo is being a little shit about PT."

"What's that? Leo refuses to go? Please put Grandma on the phone."

Todd beckons for Lissa to sit next to him as close to the gate as they can get. He hands her a drink bottle from home.

"Hi, Elaine. Sorry to hear Leo is giving you a hard time about PT. Call the office, ask James to send someone to the house."

Todd grabs the phone from her. "Hi, Mom. Please tell Leo he will lose his Xbox and his iPad for the next week if he doesn't shape up. He will go to his session today. Okay? We'll call you tomorrow. Bye."

"Really? Can't cut him a little slack? That kid faces each day like a warrior," says Lissa, her eyes in angry slits.

"He does, but why spend one hundred and twenty dollars for an in-home session when the office visit costs seventy? You have more money than sense?"

"Not taking the bait. I'm on vacation." Lissa has been looking forward to this trip for over a year and is determined not to let anything or anyone ruin it for her—especially not Todd and his relentless penny-pinching ways. It is more her style to lead with her heart, not her pocketbook. Todd says if it were up to her, she would beggar their bank account just to make life a bit easier. *You're teaching our kids they can get out of their commitments and have anything they want...* blah, blah, blah. This lecture is most annoying and leads to her accuse him of mansplaining.

"Oh, and I forgot to ask, how are you feeling?" She pokes him.

"Ouch. Not nice. I'm not looking forward to this flight." He rubs his temple.

David returns victorious with a short drinking glass, clearly holding a spirit and a large cube of ice. He raises his glass. Kate joins him, sipping her latte. Boarding announcements come over the speaker.

Todd jumps up. "Let's go, guys."

"Valletta, here we come!" Lissa rejoices.

As a child, Lissa enjoyed pictures of Malta on the

24

wall calendar next to the breakfast nook. The local gas station, owned by a friendly Maltese man, gave them to customers each year. Lissa loved it when her mother told her to change the month and she'd open it to a new picture. She loved the architecture and colors of this small country island, especially those depicting the city of Valletta. *You'll see. I'm going there one day...*

Chapter 2

Todd's head bobs and jerks as the plane begins its descent toward Malta. His mouth ratchets open and closes as he snores.

Kate leans from her seat. "Psst, Lissa. Does Todd always snore so loud?"

Lissa elbows him, just as she had throughout the flight to get him to stop snoring.

Todd cracks his eyes open and works his mouth, then grumbles and goes back to sleep.

Kate settles into her seat. "He's louder than the engines."

She, David, and Lissa share a laugh.

Lissa had insisted on the window seat so she could have the best vantage point of Malta as they flew in. She loves the bird's eye view from the plane, peering down on the world and all its beauty and wonder. She gazes upon the dotted archipelago floating in a stunning sea of deep blue-green. As they approach, a castle with ramparts, a harbor, and red-tiled roofs come into view. She loves visiting Europe for the rich history America lacks. It is worlds away from home and her children. She is thankful to have a break but also concerned about how Leo is doing. It's a worry that never lets up, his disability making his life so much more difficult than it should be. *Life's not fair!*

She instructs herself not to think about it as they approach the Hotel Phoenicia. Lissa comments on the lovely old-world grandeur. They check in and while they wait for their rooms to be ready, they wander the grounds and inspect the rooftop patio, which blends classic architecture with modern touches. An infinity pool meets the horizon and leads the eye to a breathtaking panorama of the port, the ancient city, and the Mediterranean.

Kate says to Lissa, "Will you take a pic of David and me in front of the pool?"

"Really?" David complains. "That's so touristy."

Kate yanks him toward the pool. He grabs her arm and whirls her toward the water. She squeals in protest and when he freezes, she whips an arm around his waist, striking a pose.

David says, "Bo-ring. Let's try this," and he dips her in a dance move. He wiggles his eyebrows. "That's a little something I learned in those tango classes you made me take."

Todd applauds while Lissa snaps pics with her iPhone.

David and Kate hold hands and venture toward the gardens on the other side of the rooftop.

"Come with," Kate says to Lissa and Todd.

Lissa replies, "Todd and I are going to stay and take in this view."

Kate waves and admonishes playfully. "You kids behave."

Lissa smiles and kisses her husband. "This place is spectacular. Even better than the photos."

"The view alone is worth the price of admission," says Todd. "I may never leave the poolside."

A hotel bellhop, dressed in a crisp white and black

uniform with a matching pillbox cap approaches and asks with a British accent, "Mr. and Mrs. Benton?" Todd and Lissa turn to him. "Your room is ready."

"Thank you. We're ready for it," says Todd.

He grabs his wife's hand as they saunter toward the hotel elevator.

"After we unpack, let's head out to sightsee," says Lissa.

"Actually," Todd replies, "a nap is my first order of business."

Lissa pouts. "Really, the way you were sawing logs on the flight over here? You got enough sleep for a hibernating bear."

"I need to recharge, sweetheart. But you go, I'll unpack for both of us." They follow the bellhop into the elevator and the doors close.

A few minutes later, Lissa tingles with anticipation as she waits outside the Hotel Phoenicia for a tour of Malta's Hypogeum. This was one of the big draws for her when researching their travel plans. The Sterns also declined the tour, saying they'd rather have umbrella drinks by the pool than hang out with spirits in a tomb. Lissa disagrees. *You can hang out by a pool anytime. How often can one explore ancient relics?*

Lissa reads a pamphlet on the Hal Saflieni Hypogeum as tourists gather for an exclusive tour of the 6,000-year-old underground burial chamber. Archaeological evidence suggests that around 4,000 BCE, the people of Malta and Gozo began building the Hypogeum for the purpose of ritualizing life and death. The builders expanded existing caves and, over the centuries, excavated deeper, creating a temple, cemetery, and funeral hall.

Her fellow tomb explorers load onto a bus, chattering with anticipation. She hears a cacophony of French, German, Japanese, and other languages she can't make out. Her seatmate is a chatty Australian surfer dude with curly golden locks who's doing an around-the-world tour to the best surf spots in the world. He shares photos on his iPhone of him surfing Nazaré in Portugal, his most recent stop. Lissa lets her attention wander to the historic vistas they pass on the way to the Hypogeum.

After the bus arrives at the Hypogeum, Lissa follows the single-file line of tourists as they enter a chapel-like stone structure. A female guide leads the way. She's a tall, elegant woman with thick curls of brown hair that fall past her shoulders. Because of her appearance, she could be from Eastern Europe, but then again, she could also be Greek.

"As you venture down into this hand-sculpted temple," her accent is an indeterminate European, "you'll note it is a spiral labyrinthine structure of chambers." The tourists are in awe as they pad down the steps. "This is, in fact, an underground burial site for 7,000 souls." This fact ignites a chorus of exclamations.

"Will we be seeing any ghosts?" asks an American tourist with a Southern twang and a Crocodile Dundee hat.

The group erupts in giggles while Lissa winces. *It's not Ghostbusters. Americans abroad can be so embarrassing*, Lissa thinks, vowing to never be that American.

The guide ignores him and announces to the group,

"Let's stop for a moment of silence." It takes a minute for the chatty tourists to quiet. As a hush overtakes them, the guide continues, "Close your eyes and imagine the thousands of souls before you who have been down here. Some buried here. Take in the sanctity of the stone walls and the history of this underground temple. You may very well feel like you're entering the womb of Mother Earth."

The guide then glides to face the American tourist as he meditates, eyes shut. "Boo!" He jumps. Everybody laughs. The guide, satisfied with her payback, asks, "Any questions?"

"I've heard there's another chamber below—you get to it through a secret passage—where people enter a vortex of time and space," says the Australian surfer with trippy eyes. He looks ready to surf the vortex.

The guide replies, "Ah, yes, of mystical happenings that occur under brilliant light. I've heard the same. If you find that passage, do tell. Let's continue."

"I'd buy a ticket to time travel!" says the loud American tourist.

The group erupts in giggles again as the guide, who throws a stern look at the American, continues to lead them further down to the middle level of the Hypogeum, where she explains that archaeologists believe that most of the ritual activity occurred thousands of years ago. The temperature has dropped, and the dimly lit chamber cools with each step downwards.

Another visitor whispers to her husband, "It's eerie down here."

Lissa disagrees. She's enthralled by this ancient place and as she slides her hand across the cold stone walls, she wonders what stories this passage could tell.

***

It's late afternoon, and Lissa window-shops as she strolls through the street market. After spending even that short time deep underground within the Hypogeum, the urban landscape blooms wide and inviting. Compared to the earthen walls of the subterranean chamber, the street scene is lively and colorful, a kaleidoscope of hand-crafted items, weavings, lavender, and rose soap, floral bouquets, and edible treats like fig cakes and glazed almonds. Children run underfoot and older folks barter with vendors. She wonders what Todd, Kate, and David are up to. Probably washing down cocktails by the pool; something they could do at home. What's the point of traveling if you stick to the same routine?

Lissa comes upon a store that intrigues her with its display of antiques in the windows. When she enters, the scent is musty with a touch of sweet, earthy incense.

A lean, elderly Arabic man with a headscarf and a scruffy, silver beard putters about the store. Thick eyebrows arc above his warm eyes, which exude a calm yet confident, gentle, and wise demeanor.

He tracks Lissa as she enters and bows his head in a humble gesture. "Welcome. I am Yusaf, beholder of fine treasures." His accent is a blend of British English and Arabic, his voice soothing.

"I'm Lissa. Nice to meet you." She reaches out to shake his hand—his grip is warm and dry—and he bows his head again before placing his hand over his heart and doing a unique gesture Lissa has never seen before. His formality intimidates her so when she retracts her hand, she bows awkwardly, not knowing how deep to go or how long to hold the pose. She laughs to hide her discomfort. He smiles, exuding kindness.

As Lissa browses, checking out the furniture, sculptures, wall hangings, and rugs, Yusaf attends to a small gas stove at the back of the store. Out of the corner of her eye, she notices how carefully he turns a valve along the front of the stove. There's a slight hiss, followed by the odor of gas, then a muffled *whoosh* as he lights the burner. He sets a much-used kettle on the ring of blue flame.

Lissa is drawn to a statue of a woman and carefully picks it up. The winged figurine, carved in marble with golden accents, is sleek and slender. It feels smooth to the touch.

Yusaf says, "You have a good eye. I found her in the northern region on a hike, lying on the ground like a discarded toy. I named her the 'Goddess of Life.'"

Lissa examines the statue's face. She sees herself in its features, as if she was the model. Maybe the jetlag is making her imagine this. But one thing is certain—she must have this antiquity.

Yusaf glances at the figurine and then at Lissa. He raises his eyebrows. "She looks like you."

Lissa holds his gaze. "Really? I was just thinking the same thing. Is she for sale?"

Yusaf pauses, making Lissa think he doesn't want to part with her. Then he says, "Well, yes. I've enjoyed her company for many, many years. Besides, my goddess appreciates that I hold on to nothing. Belongings do not, after all, truly belong."

"I guess you're right. We can't take them with us. How much for your goddess?"

Yusaf smiles his approval. "Forty dollars, U.S. I should charge more, but I can see you two are meant for each other."

"Perfect. Thank you. I'll take her."

The kettle rumbles and steam plumes from its spout. Yusaf turns off the gas and then selects a glass jar off the shelf beside the stove. From the jar, he scoops loose-leaf tea into a teapot. He then pours in hot water, quietly whistling an exotic tune.

He turns to Lissa. "Would you like a cup of tea? It's tghanniqa. A special blend of Ceylon and Maltese carob."

"Why, yes. Thank you." She can't wait to show her goddess statue to the others back at the resort. She continues to look around while Yusaf sets two teacups on a platter.

She continues to browse and notices a box on a corner table, sitting under another statue of a megalith. She opens the box. Lissa pulls out a glass orb about the size of a tennis ball. Inside, a golden light revolves, captivating, mesmerizing. "This is… amazing. What is it?"

Yusaf approaches. "May I?" She nods, and he takes the orb. He holds it up to the light. "It's the energy of life. Past, present, future."

"Wow! That sounds intense. But what does it mean?"

Yusaf invites her toward an alcove to one side, to a wrought-iron café table with matching chairs and red velvety cushions. He returns the orb to its box and sets them in the center of the table. He then brings the platter with the teacups and the teapot, and arranges them on the table. "Sit, please, and I will explain while we enjoy tea."

Lissa eases into one of the chairs. Yusaf fills the teacups, ornately decorated in a Moroccan design with specks of gold and silver. Vapor feathers from the tea, bringing a heavenly aroma.

She lifts a teacup and blows on her tea, and then takes a sip. "It's lovely tea. Thank you."

Yusaf gazes intently at Lissa and begins, "I ask you," his tone is serious, dramatic, "if you could go back and do it all again, what would you change about the past twenty years?" He sits back and slurps his tea, waiting.

Lissa reflects on the question. "No one has ever asked me that." She sets her teacup on the table and gazes toward the sunlight beaming through the window. "I mean, it has all been pretty good, actually. Oh, wait, I'd stay in college and not drop out to become an actress. That didn't go so well." She laughs, remembering, then becomes wistful. "Truth be told, I still dream of becoming an actress, but I know it's not practical. Some dreams are meant for the cutting room floor. You know?"

Yusuf nods but Lissa is not sure he understands her. She continues to mull over the idea. "I'd plan my third pregnancy a little differently... and I would, oh, never mind. Why do you ask? Are you a fortune teller?"

Yusaf leans in, his eyes narrowing. "Not exactly. But I can send you back to relive your life with the knowledge of what is to come."

She smiles incredulously, hoping to prompt him to admit he's kidding, but his face is solemn, unchanged.

"Seriously?"

He nods. "Indeed."

"I get to redo the last twenty years? How is that even possible?"

"Through the Deheb Orb." He reaches into the box and palms the golden glass ball. "Those who find it, as you did just now, get the chance to relive." He lifts the orb. "This gift comes with great responsibility. Most people are content to fix their own mistakes and live better lives. Some want to change the world. Either way, it's not as simple as it seems."

"I'll bet it's not." Lissa stares at the orb, entranced. She imagines her life going in so many different directions. Although intriguing, it's also a bit overwhelming. She struggles to accept the idea of going back in time.

"You don't believe me?" he asks, a grin peeking through his beard.

"I'll need a little convincing."

"Then return tomorrow. Noon." He's serious.

"Can I bring anyone with me?" She wonders which of her travel companions, if they had the chance, would join her.

"If they're here in Malta, bring them along."

"Okay." She puzzles over Yusaf and the orb and his incredible offer. *What have I got to lose?*

She finishes her tea and pays for the goddess statue. He carefully wraps it in crinkly light-blue tissue paper and tucks the figurine into a brown paper bag with handles.

"Thank you. I'll be back tomorrow." As she walks out into the balmy afternoon air, her thoughts spool over what just occurred. Yusaf acted as if the Deheb Orb had the power of time travel. In his quaint and mysterious store, anything seemed possible. Now that she is back outside, not so much. Still, on her brisk walk back to the hotel, Lissa lets her imagination range over the changes she would make, the regrets she would undo, and the dreams she would chase—the ones she'd given up in this lifetime. The fantasy leaves her almost giddy with excitement.

***

Kate relaxes on a lounge chair, texting and sipping an iced tea. David hauls his bulk out of the pool, water cascading from the deep navel in his beer belly. He grabs a towel and dries off.

"I love vacations." Kate waves a hand in glee. "Nothing on the agenda but having fun."

"I love you, babe," David says unexpectedly, plunking onto an adjacent lounge chair. He reclines with his hands behind his head.

A server arrives with a tray of appetizers, which he places on a cocktail table between the lounge chairs.

David says, "Bulleit bourbon on the rocks. Thanks."

The server nods and walks off. David sits up and digs into the food. Kate plucks a prescription pill bottle from her bag.

David eyes the bottle. "Only two more weeks of those little chemo bastards, right?"

"Yup. Let's hope I get the all-clear when I get home. Doctor Stanford reminds me it's better to battle stage one than four."

"Damn straight."

Kate pops her pills and sips iced tea. David takes her hand, kisses it, and smiles lovingly at her. She's relieved to be worlds away from their mounting financial woes back at home, at least for now. She knows it weighs heavily on David's mind, and it stung when he had to accept that Todd was paying for their holiday. Kate, on the other hand, is comfortable with her big brother's generosity, in view of her recent diagnosis. Inhaling deeply, she brings her thoughts back to the poolside and vows to make the most of the trip and not think about the future.

***

Todd and the Sterns are seated at an outdoor dinner table of the hotel restaurant, the magenta sky aglow, wispy clouds painting the horizon. An uncorked bottle of white wine rests in an ice bucket. On the table, small bowls with dip and olives flank a basket filled with a variety of freshly baked breads.

Kate basks in the view, sipping Chardonnay and popping olives into her mouth. "I think I might just stay here forever."

"For that, my dear," David teases, "you'll need a sugar daddy."

Kate laughs. "I saw a few candidates today." She looks at the stairs. "Where is Lissa?"

Todd answers, "On her way. She got back just as I was leaving to come here. She wanted to freshen up first."

"Speak of the devil." Kate spots Lissa heading

towards their table, appearing trim and elegant in an evening dress.

She lowers herself onto the vacant seat. Her hair is moist and glossy, and she smells of fragrant soap and scented shampoo. "Sorry, I'm late. What a day!"

David pours a glass of wine and hands it to her. She raises the drink and they all clink their glasses. "Cheers."

Lissa says to the group, "I toured the Hypogeum, which you must do. It's an underground temple built 6,000 years ago."

"Imagine if you could go back in time and see how people lived back then," says Kate.

"No, thanks." David dips a piece of bread into the olive oil and balsamic vinegar. "No bourbon or barbecue, that I can tell you."

The group laughs. Todd notices that Lissa is leaning forward, eyes alight, looking from one to the other.

"You have to see this!" she exclaims. She pivots toward the setting sun and raises a hand to shade her eyes. "Wait for the green flash."

"The green flash is a myth," says Todd even as they all study the horizon.

"Ah, did you see it?" asks Lissa.

"I did!" Kate replies. "So cool."

Todd and David exchange skeptical glances.

Lissa sips wine and regards the other three with a serious expression. "Actually, I'm glad you brought that up... the past, I mean." She leans over the table and whispers, "I'm about to blow your mind."

Kate raises her eyebrows. "This better be good."

Lissa proceeds to tell them about a man named

Yusaf, a funny old antique store, something called a "Deheb Orb" and Yusaf's claim of time travel to the past. Todd's chest restricts as a wave of embarrassment threatens to overcome him. *She's being serious.*

David guffaws, chokes on his bread, then thumps his chest to clear his throat. Kate hands him a glass of water, which he gulps. His reddened face fades.

"Are you better?" she asks.

He nods and takes another drink.

"Good," she explains in a playful tone. "Because I don't remember how to do the Heimlich. So, if you were really choking, and it was up to me to save you, you'd croak."

David sits straight and composes himself. He notices Lissa's glare and replies, "What? I thought it was funny. Maybe that tea that guy gave you—"

"His name is Yusaf," Lissa shoots back.

"Yeah, him," David says, nonplussed. "Maybe Yusaf gave you ayahuasca, a psychedelic tea. That's obviously what he gave you."

Todd exchanges a knowing look with David. Lissa rolls her eyes and thankfully does not see it. "Like you were there. It was Ceylon and Carob."

David starts to answer when Kate cuts him off by waving a napkin. "Honey, remember how you asked me to give you asshole alerts? You're being one right now." She waves the napkin again.

Todd purses his lips thoughtfully. "Lissa, with all due respect, I love you, but David makes a good point. How can you expect us to believe this? This Yusaf can take us back to the past, essentially 'time travel,'" Todd makes air quotes, "which sounds crazy. Sorry, sweetheart, the dude just wants your money."

Lissa ignores Todd's remarks as she counters, "Yusaf said if we're interested, we should meet him tomorrow at noon, and he'll explain all. Come on, where's your sense of adventure?"

Kate pans the table. "I'm in. Why not hear more about it? What do we have to lose?" She pours herself more wine.

"I'll go along for the ride," says David, "especially if there's ayahuasca involved."

Todd picks up a menu. "It'll be a waste of time." He feels the weight of the gazes from around the table. Resigned, he puts the menu down and sighs. "If that's the majority vote, I guess I'm going."

This vacation is ostensibly for Lissa's fortieth birthday, and Todd paid for the Sterns to come to make it more fun. He's not about to let things go sour between him and Lissa over a crackpot from some back alley on day one.

David raises his glass of wine. "Let's see what this time travel guru has to say." He clinks glasses with Kate and Todd as they merrily toast, "To time travel."

Chapter 3

Lissa leads Todd, David, and Kate to Yusaf's store, feeling both nervous and excited. They pass stands of freshly cut flowers, sweet-scented baked goods, and other sundries as they go. Tourists wander aimlessly through the marketplace while locals haggle with vendors.

Over breakfast earlier that day, the foursome speculated how Yusaf's time travel occurred. Kate talked about zipping through a wormhole but admitted she didn't really know what they were. Todd explained that wormhole theory predicted connections through space-time that are shortcuts for long journeys across the universe. He cautioned that wormholes bring with them the dangers of collapse, high radiation, and dangerous contact with exotic matter.

David, always ready to joke around, liked the idea of a plutonium-powered DeLorean like the one featured in *Back to the Future*. Todd, ever skeptical, also wanted to discuss the predestination paradox but speculated that Yusaf had a time-travel machine and his store was a front. Lissa could practically see the tongues in their cheeks.

Lissa doesn't want to think about their suspicion and disbelief anymore. The cutting feeling of being belittled, for believing in Yusaf, only makes her want to go back in time even more. *This is something I can do. I can change my future... my present.* She reflects on the process: go to the past to change that future, which will change this "now." If she thinks about it too much the idea ties her thoughts in knots. She has a moment of doubt, though, wondering if Yusaf had, in fact, given her ayahuasca tea and this whole thing is a misguided cosmic scam but shakes it off as they approach the store. He didn't ask for any money.

Yusaf is outside speaking in hushed tones to a rotund, silver-haired heavy-set man who's dressed in business-casual attire. He has the air of an influential man. As they approach, Yusaf notices Lissa. He greets her with that cryptic hand signal and a nod. "Welcome back, Lissa."

"Yusaf, meet my husband Todd, his sister Kate, and her husband, David."

"Meet Howard," says Yusaf with a sparkle in his eye.

Howard politely smiles but it's obvious he doesn't care for the introduction.

Yusaf says to Howard, "I will see you back here promptly at dusk."

"Very much looking forward to it." Howard shakes Yusaf's hand and then turns to the group. "Nice to meet you all." He strolls down the street with a bounce in his step that belies his age and size.

David, watching Howard leave, whispers, "I thought I recognized him. That's Warren Buffet's son."

"What? Really? No," says Todd, turning around to confirm David's claim. *He always has to decide for himself*, Lissa reflects. Howard has turned the corner and is out of sight.

"Scout's honor." David poses stiffly and earnestly, holding up three fingers.

Todd scoffs. "You were never a scout."

"But that was definitely a buffet. I can sniff out the money." They both muzzle a laugh.

Yusaf invites the foursome into his store. He locks the door and guides them toward the wrought-iron table. Kate, David, and Todd glance at all the antiquities and knickknacks on the way to their seats. Lissa remains standing.

Yusaf waits on the opposite side of the table. He squares his shoulders and sweeps the group with a gaze. "I'm the caretaker of the Deheb Ethereal Orb. It is an awe-inspiring transversal sphere of light and energy. Some call it a wormhole, others a ball of cosmic strings. Call it what you like; I just know what it can do." With little ceremony, he pulls the glass sphere of brilliant gold light from his pocket, cradling it like a delicate bird egg. "I have a piece of it encased in glass, something my great-grandfather gave me decades ago."

All eyes are drawn to the orb, captivated by the light pulsating within the glass.

"May I?" Todd asks, reaching toward Yusaf.

The old man hands it to him.

Todd holds the orb, staring. "Wow. It's a little like touching a lightbulb, but it feels alive, as if it's pulsing. I've never experienced anything like this."

Kate leans close, her eyes fixed on the light. "It's mesmerizing." Her voice is breathless.

David reaches toward Todd. "My turn?"

Todd acts as if he doesn't hear. David nudges him and only then does Todd reluctantly pass the orb along.

When David clasps the magical sphere, his face lights up almost as brightly as the intense glow coming from the orb. "Holy shit! This is awesome." He delicately turns the orb over as if looking for clues about how it works. "What is it, exactly?"

Yusaf intones slowly and with solemn conviction. "It is now. It is the past. It is the future. It is the essence of existence."

David and Todd exchange skeptical glances but there is no denying the mystical attraction of the orb.

Kate furrows her brow and extends a finger to touch the sphere. She holds still, a wave of emotions playing upon her face. When she pulls her hand back, her eyes flame with astonishment.

Lissa stands on the periphery, arms crossed, and although she has yet to handle the orb and feel firsthand its miraculous effect, her lips curve into a "told you so" smile.

"This is impressive, but how is it possible to travel back in time through this orb?" asks Todd, trying to mask his cynicism.

"There are many things we don't understand about our universe," Yusaf replies, then with technical acumen, adds, "Simply put, science today accepts travel to the past as theoretically possible, although they have yet to prove it. Certain general relativity space-time geometries permit traveling faster than the speed of light. Backward time travel through the Deheb Orb relies on the elusive counterpart known as positive energy versus zero-mass particles, which are found throughout its traversable realm."

Todd wiggles his eyebrows as he tries to comprehend, but the blank faces on David and Kate show that the explanation went over their heads. Lissa is beyond caring about the technicalities, instead dreaming of a future where she is in control of everything. That would be a new experience for her. Maybe the others don't realize they will still have the wisdom of the past twenty years during their do-over.

Lissa chimes in. "Yesterday you said we keep all our memories when we go back. Yes?"

Yusaf nods. "And should you go back together, you start your new journey together."

"That would put us all back in college!" David shouts.

Yusaf raises a finger of caution. "You must be wise." He then addresses Kate. "Careful what you say."

"Okay, this may be a dumb question, but could a person entering it just like, get fried? You know... die?" asks Kate, wincing.

"You don't die; you relive," Yusaf says patiently.

"But how do you know it works?" asks Todd.

"I send twenty to thirty guests back a year. I hear from some later. They are alive and well." Yusaf turns to Kate. "I went back myself." He pats his clothes. "Do I look fried?"

***

That night, the hotel pool bar glows, illuminated by the pattern of lights along the bottom, and from the electric bulbs twinkling in the swaying palm trees. A warm breeze blows ripples across the pool's surface, causing the reflected light to undulate.

Lissa and Kate relax on bar stools in sundresses. Lissa sits cross-legged while sipping iced tea from a tall skinny glass. Kate sips a flute of champagne and scarfs peanuts from the bowl at her elbow. After finishing this bowl, she reaches for another. Lissa watches and suppresses a giggle. Knowing that peanuts pack a caloric punch, she allows herself a ration of exactly six. She wishes she could let go of the calorie-counting Nazi in her head, but she revels in her slender body.

She plays with her straw, twirling the ice and gazing into her glass. Her thoughts return to the orb. Later this evening, they are to meet Yusaf again and begin their big adventure. "If Warren Buffet went back, that would make sense. Makes you wonder who else."

Kate whispers, "I bet Donald Trump!"

"Oh, God. You may be right. If so, he's taking full advantage." Lissa hails the bartender. "I'll have what she's having."

The bartender, a black man with short dreadlocks and diamond stud earrings, expertly fills a pair of clean flutes on the counter. He pushes the flutes to the women.

Lissa takes one and empties it halfway with one quick pull.

"Look at you go," Kate teases.

"I needed that. I'm feeling really anxious. You're not worried?"

"Please, you're fine. Yusaf was like, 'You two will do great.' Then did you notice? Waving his finger, he said to David, 'You must be wise.'"

"Yeah, I heard that."

"And to me, he said, 'Careful what you say.'" Kate

waves her finger.

"He does have a point, you know. Sometimes you should be more careful about what you say."

"Nah," Kate retorts. "Where's the fun in that?"

They laugh and sip champagne.

Lissa ponders aloud. "Yusaf said his family has been the guardians of the Dehab for eight generations and that it's the honor of his lifetime to protect and facilitate its 'magic.' When he said, 'No payment required,' Todd said he felt it was a privilege. I needed to hear him say the kids would still be in our future, and thankfully, he did. That would have been a deal breaker."

Lissa wonders if she can do anything different to ensure Leo is free of his disability. Thing is, the cause of cerebral palsy can be genetic. She didn't have any infections during the pregnancy and Leo suffered no brain injuries as an infant. He was born premature and in the breech position, but what can she do to prevent that?

"Our kids will still be our kids as long as we stay on track!" adds Kate. "Staying on track won't be hard. We simply redo our lives but make fewer mistakes." She pans the poolside patio. "Where are the boys?"

"In the business center Googling the last twenty years."

"Clever, although my wish list doesn't require Google. There are pretty much three things I want to change. One. Keep my figure." Kate kneads her paunch. "This roly-poly shit ain't happenin' next time." She extends two fingers. "Two, I'm for sure having a second child. Even if I have to adopt. And three, I'm getting mammograms on a regular basis." She cups her breasts.

"Let's hear it for boob smashing." Lissa chuckles. "But seriously, can't they come up with a test that's less like a medieval torture device?"

"God, no kidding." Kate plucks peanuts from the bowl.

"And good luck with the diet."

Kate, feigning offense, says, "Just watch me."

The girls laugh again. Lissa adores Kate, despite her love affair with snacks. *Will knowing the consequences of overeating help her in her re-do?*

"Oh, and four," Kate's tone flattens. "I will not burn through my granddad's inheritance. David is in for a rude awakening. That money stays in the bank!" Kate's lips are pursed in all seriousness. She raises her glass. "To no money woes next time around."

***

Todd and David sit, side by side, at computer terminals in the hotel's fully equipped business center. Todd is glued to his screen while David gleefully sips his bourbon. The sign above reads in several languages, including English: *Please do not bring beverages into the business center.* But there's no one around to enforce it.

Meeting Yusaf and becoming acquainted with the Deheb Orb has not convinced David that Yusaf's claim of time travel is legitimate, but there is no denying that the sphere projected something supernatural. So what if they followed up on Yusaf's offer and nothing happened? At the very least, it would make for a good vacation story.

David is on his second bourbon and is willing to daydream that every word from Yusaf is true. "No more working for the man. When I go back, I will work for yours truly and yours truly only."

"Huh," Todd replies, half-listening. "You know the Oklahoma City bombing was in '95? I thought for sure it was in the last twenty."

Perplexed, David glances at his friend. "What are you searching for?"

Todd, engrossed in skimming search results, replies, "World events, terror attacks, disasters."

David cocks his head to scope out what is on Todd's screen. "Why the hell are you searching for that?"

"You never know. We might be able to change fate," Todd answers, his voice sincere. "Imagine if we prevented some of the worst we've been through as a country, as a world."

David almost starts singing "Kumbaya" but thinks better of it. "You're much nobler than me, man. How about we do this? You focus on saving lives, I'll focus on our bank accounts."

Todd laughs. David returns to his screen, tapping keys. "I'm checking the best time to buy stock in Apple, Amazon, Nike."

Todd asks, "Your plan is to take over Wall Street?"

"Dude, see this?" David shows six numbers he's Sharpied on his arm: 5, 10, 12, 20, 40, 3. "Powerball jackpot, June 30th, 1999. Some chick won 151 mil and complained it ruined her life. So, I plan to take some of the load off and split the win with her. After cash payout and taxes, that's a cool twenty-five mil to me. Nice, right?"

"Are you sure those numbers will be there when we go back?"

"If not," David taps his temple, "I've got them memorized."

Todd furrows his brow. "Karmically, that worries me."

David shrugs, careful to not spill his drink. "I'm not worried. Like I said, you change the world, I'll conquer it. I'll give you ten percent. Deal?"

"If I'm going to change the world, I'll need more than that. Twenty percent?"

"How about fifteen percent?"

"Deal."

They high-five and return to internet surfing. There is so much to remember. Though he tries to etch specific details and dates in his memory, David decides the best strategy will be recalling broad events and trends.

Todd, suddenly serious, adds, "And you might not want to be driving on Route 135, New Year's Eve 2009."

David pauses and pushes away from the computer, turning somber. "Fuckin' A. That, or call a cab."

***

Yusaf leads Lissa and the others up a hillside trail carrying hand-held lanterns that flicker like fireflies in the growing darkness. The trail meanders through cypress, palm, and Aleppo pine trees. A blanket of bright yellow daisies lines the trail at their feet. The city below sparkles in its ancient yet modern elegance, the urban landscape punctuated by church spires, towers, and domes. They pass a crumbling archway and other ancient ruins overgrown with purple bougainvillea—nature reclaiming its bounty.

David and Kate lag slightly behind. Lissa notices

how out of breath they are. This do-over might enable them to be more responsible about their bodies. Howard trails them, also puffing and red-faced. The group is uncharacteristically quiet, as if they are engrossed with the possibilities of creating a new past.

Doubts begin to plague Lissa. *What if everything goes wrong? What if the others make choices that pull us apart? What if I never see them again? What if I can't change Leo? Or have different kids entirely! Would their souls be the same but in different bodies?*

Her stomach clenches, and she resists the urge to run down the hill toward the hotel, retreating to her room. She now regrets ever having ventured into Yusaf's universe, and she wrings her hands in trepidation.

They arrive at the base of a megalith set back on a wide shelf. It's part altar, part giant boulder—a mystical cluster of limestone. A middle-aged man and a teenage boy wait at the entrance. When Yusaf nods, they pivot a stone slab to one side, revealing a low, narrow passageway into the megalithic temple, lit by votive candles tucked into the walls but still a very dark space.

"Follow me." Yusaf enters, the flickering light of his lantern throwing dancing shadows on the walls and floor. The others step after him. The man and boy remain outside, guarding the entrance.

If Lissa were just a tourist here to snap pictures, she would've reveled in the mystical experience, imagining the ancient people who worshipped in this temple. But knowing this is a portal to the past that she may or may not want to revisit, she is filled with dread, her heart pounding.

"Watch your step," cautions Yusaf.

The group descends single file into a tight, winding staircase with slippery worn steps. They run hands against the smooth walls to keep their balance. The passage underground reminds Lissa of the Hypogeum tour, yet she can't help but feel it's a longer, colder, and intimidating journey. She trembles as she walks, her pulse beating against her temples, but says nothing.

The staircase empties into a narrow hall hewn through the stone. Continuing perhaps seventy feet, Yusaf approaches the end of the hall. His lantern illuminates a door made of rough wooden planks. He halts and everyone shuffles close around him.

"We have arrived," he says dramatically. The lantern's candlelight plays over his face, sparkling across his silver beard, his bright eyes, and the pearly crescent of a toothy smile.

With his free hand, he clasps the wrought iron doorhandle and twists, rotating a simple bar free of the latch. He pulls the door open and muted squeaks emit from the iron hinges.

Golden light spills across the threshold and bathes the group in a yellow glow. Each face beams with awe. Words cannot describe the sight: amazing, magical. Despite her trepidation, Lissa feels her soul quiver reverently before the orb.

"Holy cow," exclaims David.

Lissa expects the orb to be the size of a basketball, but it is huge, about ten feet in diameter. At first, the orb resembles a harvest moon brought to the earth, but unlike the moon, the orb is featureless, just golden light contained within a sphere. It hovers inches above a stone pedestal, itself not higher than a stairstep. The orb's light reaches out into a room of indeterminate size but everything past the orb's glow of light is lost in darkness.

Yusaf leads them through the door and they cluster around the orb. They stare as if expecting the ball of light to make a sound, an ethereal hum, but it only shines, silently, majestically, expectantly.

Kate reaches for the orb. "Can I touch it?"

"No!" Yusaf snaps. His voice softens. "Not until you all are ready." Yusaf gestures with the lantern. "Howard will go first. Are you ready?"

Howard nods and moves toward the orb. "It's exactly as my father described. Thank you for this opportunity, Yusaf. Let's do this." The anxiety in Howard's eyes belies his confident words. He takes in a long, deep breath and stands tall.

Yusaf smiles to reassure him. "Howard, your journey begins. Stretch out your hands and enter the light."

Howard does as he's instructed and walks right up to the orb. He disappears into it as though he's absorbed by the glow. *Now you see him, now you don't.*

Lissa blinks. She gasps, "Oh my God!" *It is real!*

"That looks pretty simple," says David, who looks like he has seen a ghost but quickly recomposes himself.

"Yeah, but what's on the other side?" wonders Lissa.

"So, he's gone and going back twenty years to the day?" asks Todd.

"It was for me. And for others," Yusaf declares. "The

orb is in control, as is all of Mother Nature. I am simply the facilitator."

Todd, Kate, and David stare at the orb. Watching all the different emotions morph on their faces Lissa wonders, *Are they truly believing this wild fantasy is about to come true?*

"I'll go next," says David in a commanding voice.

"Can I go with him?" Kate shoehorns close to David.

"Certainly. Just hold hands," Yusaf advises.

Kate snatches David's hand and grips tightly.

Lissa scrubs sweaty palms against her pants. Her heart drums hard against her ribs. She has never in her life experienced such a freakout. Wide-eyed and light-headed, she turns to Todd. "I think I'm going to faint."

Todd takes her hand and looks toward David and Kate. "Good luck."

"Shit! Are we nuts?" Kate shivers.

"Maybe, but what do we have to lose?" replies David. He thinks aloud, "I can't afford not to take this opportunity. No one wants a re-do more than David Stern. We need this."

Kate glances over her shoulder at Lissa and Todd. "We'll see you when we see you." She turns to her husband. "Let's go, before I change my mind."

"Okay, babe. It's go time." If David's nervous, it doesn't show.

Kate declares defiantly, "Ready or not, here we come!"

Holding hands, they step towards the orb and reach out. The Sterns disappear just as Howard did.

"Ready?" Yusaf gazes at Lissa and Todd, but she

can't look him in the eye.

"Thank you. This is an honor, Yusaf," says Todd.

"I have no doubt you will make the Deheb legacy proud." Yusaf bows.

Todd and Lissa hold hands and face the orb. They move forward, but after one step Lissa recoils. She shivers as if abruptly chilly and tears her hand from Todd's to squeeze herself with a hug. Misgivings tumble through her mind. *What will happen to our kids?* Their faces whirl about her, images of them as babies, as toddlers, as teenagers. Miles. Stella. And precious Leo. She relives having them in her womb, feeling their kicks, following their development in grainy sonograms, the fear and triumph of birthing them.

Emotions overwhelm her and she gives in to spasms of protest. "Todd, I can't. I just can't. I can't do it. What if something goes terribly wrong? What about our kids? I mean, I couldn't live with myself if I never saw them again." She bursts into tears, cradling her face in her hands.

Todd strokes her cheek damp with tears. "It's okay. I understand." Despite the words, his eyes are hard with determination. "What if I just go? This opportunity may never come again. And I have a really good feeling about this."

Panic grips her. Even if she doesn't go back, Todd's choice could impact her and the kids' future anyway. *I have no control as usual. I have no say in his decision.*

"But... what about..." Lissa reads the growing distance in her husband's expression. He is already there in that uncertain past, remaking himself. She grasps for words. The room seems to spin about her. All she can manage is a weak, "I'll see you there, well, back here—right?"

Todd takes her hand and gives her a sweet kiss. He tries to let go, but her fingers hold firm. *Isn't he going to talk about this, seek my consent?* He shakes loose and she reluctantly lets go. He steps forward, then turns back. "Wish me luck." Todd faces the light, stretches out his hand, steps forward, and disappears.

***

Yusaf and Lissa stand outside the hotel as guests, giddy with Maltese island fever, come and go. Lissa wishes she shared their excitement. On the walk back from the temple, Yusaf assured her that, in his words, "When you wake up tomorrow, everything will be as it should be."

She wants to believe him but can't stop her head from swimming with many thoughts. Guilt for having introduced the others to the orb and then chickening out. Also fear. Anxiety. Confusion. Abandonment. Loss. She clutches for hope, that all in some mysterious way, as mysterious as that orb, will turn out all right. Perhaps even better. She closes her eyes and wishes that when she opens them, her situation will be as before. Unfortunately, when she blinks open her eyes, Yusaf remains beside her, and the others are still gone.

He says, "You're not the first to change your mind."

"What happens now?" Lissa tries to take in the emptiness. "I mean, do I just keep living my life and hope things go back to normal?"

Yusaf pulls a small cloth pouch out of his pocket. "Make this tea. It will help you sleep. As I said on the walk here, when you wake up tomorrow, everything will be as it should be. I assure you. Todd will be back."

"Okay." But she wonders if she should truly trust him, having made her companions vanish. She isn't entirely confident that they'll reappear but prays they will. She intends to phone home as soon as the time of day is right, to reassure herself her babies still exist.

Yusaf gives her a patient and kind smile as if he knows what she is thinking. Lissa heads into the hotel and then glances back. She notices Yusaf peering up at the sky.

A little later, Lissa is reclining on the king-sized bed in her hotel room. An empty teacup is on the bedside table. She's still trembling and nauseous. She stretches her hand out to touch Todd's side of the bed while looking up at the ceiling. Tears well up in her tired eyes.

"Come back safe, my love," she whispers to no one, or maybe her husband—across the space-time continuum—can hear her. She stares upwards and breathes deeply, her mind still racing. But after a few minutes, she can longer keep her eyes open and falls asleep.

Chapter 4

Todd wakes with a jolt. His eyes pop wide open and he scopes out his apartment. He takes in his surroundings: the warehouse-y hipness, exposed brick, sparse furniture. His gaze latches onto the big Marantz receiver, the Pioneer CD player, the towers of CDs, the gigantic JBL speakers standing about the room like sentinels. He hadn't thought at all of his stereo gear, which fills him with nostalgia.

Sitting up, he looks at the nightstand. Before he reads the clock, he notices the key fob and—in a burst of memory—recalls his beloved red Mazda RX-7, which boasts a custom sound system, so it is more a stereo with wheels than a car.

The Toshiba digital clock reads 8:00 AM 05/05/1999.

He stares at the red LED numbers, convincing himself that he isn't dreaming. *Have I really gone back in time?* He clenches his hands, extends his fingers, clenches again. He scrubs his cheek and feels the nubby beginnings of a beard.

He closes his eyes and lets his mind reel through recent memory. The golden glow of the orb dominates everything. He sees Yusaf. He sees David and Kate walking into the orb. He sees Lissa pull away from him, her eyes overwhelmed with apprehension. He remembers surrendering into the moment and extending one arm and advancing toward the orb, into the orb.

The golden light blinded him and then...

He opens his eyes. He is here now, time having folded on itself twenty years, exactly as Yusaf promised.

Though Todd remains motionless, he can feel his consciousness spinning. His mind hasn't yet decided to accept what has happened.

Swiveling out of bed, he plants his feet on the concrete floor, smooth and cool against his soles. In the months before the trip to Malta, he'd been so doggedly tired that he had to drag himself out of bed. Now he teems with boundless energy and feels as if he could catapult himself across the room.

His attention turns to the floor-to-ceiling window, lit by morning light, and the day, this new future, beckons him forward. He launches himself upright and hustles to the window. Along the way, he catches a glimpse of himself in the mirror and halts to admire what he sees. It's the twenty-something version of his forty-year-old self. Slender. A mane of thick lustrous hair. The familiar eyes simmering from a face radiant with energy and fresh opportunities.

He takes his naked self to the window to check out the Boston skyline. He throws his arms up in a victory stance and says to no one, "Good morning, Boston. This... is... wild!" He doesn't worry that onlookers might catch a glimpse of him in the buff.

***

David wakes in his old bedroom, a converted garage. His mind is primed for what to expect so the minute he awakens, he checks his forearm. "Shit! No numbers." He scrambles in bed, the details of being in a place from twenty years ago pulling for his attention, but he's on a mission. He paws at his bedside table where *Infinite Jest* by David Foster Wallace lies open, facing downward. He grabs a notebook and pen and hurriedly jots the numbers 5, 10, 12, 20, 40, and 3. He pauses to double-check his memory. After all, the numbers have to be exact.

Certain that they are, he gives in to the moment. He looks about at the long-forgotten furnishings in the bedroom, the barely remembered posters of Pearl Jam and The Red Hot Chili Peppers. He rubs his face, slaps his thighs, and examines his body. He wonders if this is a dream. Or maybe that other life, his marriage to Kate, his son, the failed businesses, and all that heartache and debt was the dream.

His thoughts turn on themselves. No, too much history happened. He sticks his arms out as if to emphasize, *This is real. I have been given a second chance. Let's do it!*

David jumps out of bed and glances in the mirror to admire his fit-and-trim-without-trying body, the one he took for granted back in the day. "Hey there, handsome." He strikes a smirky-cool pose fit for an album cover. David scans his old room, its messy collection of clothes and sports equipment, and grins. Then he spots a Banksy print with a red canceled notice over the words: *Follow Your Dreams*. When he bought the print, he thought it was sufficiently snarky and ironic. Now with so much worldly experience under his belt and this magical chance to redo his life, he is going to do more than follow his dreams. He is going to chase them, catch them, and wring every dime of riches out of them.

He turns back to the mirror to check out his abs. They qualify as a six-pack, for sure. A huge, proud smile looks back at him. David steps into ripped jeans and though not a student, pulls on a Harvard sweatshirt. Since he lives close to Cambridge, why not?

He tears the page with the numbers from the notebook and folds it into a pocket. He ties on his high-top sneakers and bounds into the kitchen. The moment he sees his mother, he stops and gazes. A wave of poignant longing floods through him. He's gone back twenty years and so has she. Though she's in her bathrobe, her eyes puffy, her hair mess, she looks so youthful. The years to come will not be kind.

David gives her a bear hug. She is warm and firm and radiates love and goodness. He leans back to regard her face. "You look beautiful, Ma."

She eyes him suspiciously. "You angling for something?"

"No. No," he answers, patting her shoulders. "It's just that—" He interrupts himself, thinking, *I'm so, so happy*.

He hears a bark and turns his head. It's Scout, his Golden Retriever, watching from the doggie bed in the corner of the kitchen. He can't help but drop to a knee and hug his dog. Tears well in his eyes. "Hey, boy," David whispers, "I missed you so much." Out of the corner of his eye, he catches his mom watching, bewildered.

David composes himself and remembers what he has to do. He rushes out the door.

***

Twenty-year-old Kate bursts out of her bedroom in her Austin condo on the Colorado River. Looking around anxiously—it's all as she remembered—she runs into the bathroom to inspect herself in the mirror. She studies her firm boobs, flat tummy, and slender hips underneath her silk jammies—a pink cropped top and matching tap pants.

Eyes glued to her reflection, she turns her head left, then right. Runs a hand through her tangle of bed hair. Her heartbeat accelerates. *Yes!* She has gone back in time. Life has given her a gigantic do-over. "Dang, girlfriend. You look goo-ood." She turns to leave but pops back to look again, issuing a stern directive while wagging her index finger. "And I intend to keep you that way!"

She races to the other bedroom to find her roommate, Lissa, still asleep. Giddy with excitement, Kate can't wait until Lissa wakes up on her own. Kate gently nudges her friend's shoulder. Lissa groans and rolls away from Kate.

Kate starts babbling. "It worked, it worked. Ohmigod. We're back!" She nudges her again.

Lissa raises her hand from under the covers to signal *stop*. She sits up and sleepily rubs her eyes. "Ohmigod, why are you so pumped up?"

"Our redo. You, me, Todd, and David!"

"Redo?" Lissa blinks and rubs her eyes. "I have no clue what you're talking about. Before you say another word, I need coffee."

"You got it." Kate gleefully obliges and disappears toward the kitchen.

***

On his way to the minimart, David reflects on a quote by Philip Appleman that he loves: *Whatever we are, whatever we make of ourselves, is all we ever have.*

David promises himself this will be his mantra now that he has been given a second chance. His mind drifts as he surprises himself that he remembers the way to the minimart. After all, it has been twenty years. When he arrives at the minimart, he goes directly to the soda fountain to get his usual jumbo Coke that he'll pair with a Snickers bar. Before he clasps the ginormous cup, he stops and thinks, *I don't need the sugar or the calories.* And he freezes in his awareness of then and now. *Wow! What a strange reality—the wisdom that comes with age but the body of a young dude.*

He grabs a Powerball form and fills out the numbers, checking against the numbers he'd written on the note. He can feel the weight of the future prize. *Millions and millions of dollars.* The Indian clerk watches from behind the register and takes the completed form and cash from David who says, "Powerball, June 30th. Thank you."

The clerk furrows his brow. "Hmm... that's a few weeks out. Let me see how to do that."

"Never mind. Do this." David hands the clerk the note. "Put these numbers in every draw for the next six weeks. In this order."

The clerk raises his eyebrows. "That's gonna cost you."

"Not a problem." David pulls a wad of cash from his pocket and counts the money.

The clerk enters the numbers on the note, then

prints the ticket. "You must be feeling lucky."

David wants to grin but doesn't, instead replying, "Just playing a hunch, that's all."

***

Kate and Lissa are on the barstools in their condo, drinking coffee. Lissa is still trying to coax herself awake.

"You don't remember Yusaf or the orb?" Kate asks, swiveling the counter stool to face her friend.

Lissa shakes her head, giving Kate a side-eye like she has lost her marbles.

Kate's voice crescendos in frustration. "The old mystic in Malta. The one with an antique shop by the market. YOU discovered him."

Lissa's eyes widen. "What the hell are you talking about? I've never been to Malta. You're tripping me out, Kate."

"Now, I'm confused," Kate says. Her phone rings from where it lays on the counter. "I bet this is my brother. Maybe he can explain." Clumsily, she flips the phone open and puts it to her ear. "Hello?"

Lissa hears a man's voice. "Can you believe it worked? We're back!"

"Crazy, right? I'm here with Lissa."

"About that... She decided not to go. Can you put her on?"

Kate hands the phone to Lissa. "He wants to talk to you."

Lissa asks shyly, "Me?" Kate nods, but Lissa is slow to act.

64

"It's your husband," exclaims Kate, almost nonchalantly.

Lissa holds the phone in mid-air. "My husband?" *It isn't like Kate to match-make.*

Kate stares. "Todd. My brother."

I haven't even met her brother.

"Hello?" says Lissa.

"Hey, Lissa. This is Todd. I'm sure this is a bit overwhelming."

"That would be an understatement. Kate seems to think I know what's going on."

"No, you wouldn't. Of course not."

The more Todd talks, the more Lissa is confused.

Todd continues, "You didn't go back. Only we did."

"Go back from where?"

"From the future."

"The future?" Lissa feels stupid just saying this. *Am I still asleep, having a really detailed dream?*

"I know that sounds impossible, but it's the truth."

"You sure you're not playing a prank on me?" Lissa smiles slyly at Kate like she finally understands.

"Not at all. I can explain it all when I see you. Kate's flying out for my graduation in two weeks. I'm hoping you can come with her so we can meet and talk."

"I guess. Sure." Lissa shrugs, still not certain what's going on.

"You have to trust me, Lissa. I'll explain all when I see, well, meet you then. Okay if I call you tomorrow to fill you in a bit more?"

Lissa nods. "Sure. That would be helpful."

"Can you put Kate back on the phone?"

"Okay... um, bye." Lissa hands the phone back to Kate like it's a hot potato.

"Hey," says Kate.

Lissa pretends that she's not listening, but she picks up every word.

"Kate, please, refrain from talking to Lissa, or anyone for that matter, about our adventure." He emphasizes the word like it should have air quotes. "Really important to keep this... under wraps."

"Oh, so you're allowed to tell her stuff from before but I'm not?"

"I'm her husband. You have to trust me, all right?"

"Just because you say it doesn't make it true."

Although the bickering of the siblings is amusing Lissa feels shocked and affronted to hear them talking about her like this. If it is a prank, it's a very elaborate one.

"Do you want to end up in a funny farm? Even Yusaf said to watch what you say."

"Yeah, I guess you're right," Kate acquiesces. "It's not every day someone tells you they came back from the future." Kate breaks into song, "Tonight I'm gonna party like it's 1999."

"Wait. Getting a call. I bet it's David. Gotta go!" Kate fumbles with her phone. "This ridiculous flip-phone." She looks at Lissa. "Trust me. They get much easier to use with a touchscreen."

Lissa knits her brow. *What is she talking about?*

David practically shouts from the phone, "Hey, sexy mama. You should see me strutting around downtown Boston. I'm so hot, I'm on fire! Women can't keep their eyes off me."

"Well, hey there, Mr. Stern," Kate replies, amused. "Are you calling to ask me out, or are you set with the ladies of Boston?"

"Can't wait to see you at Todd's graduation."

"Me, too." Then in a flirty tone, she coos, "If you could see me now. I'm about 118 pounds, and my boobs are so perky. I'm as hot as hell!"

Lissa gapes at her friend. *WTF?*

David lets out a loud whoop. Kate pulls the phone from her ear and giggles.

"That's my girl," he says. "Hey, want to do a little sexting?"

What on earth is that? Lissa wonders. Who is this David guy and what about Matt?

"With my flip phone?"

Lissa hears raucous laughter on the other end of Kate's phone. "Damn."

Lissa decides that she has no clue what these three are talking about. Plus, Kate's brother is acting like there's something momentous about their meeting. *Todd? Her husband?* Lissa squeezes her coffee cup to steady herself. Kate is flirting with some new guy who isn't her boyfriend. Kate, David, and Todd are acting all-knowing while she is in the dark.

"Gotta run or I'll be late to econ. Love you." Kate ends the call and glows in the aftermath. She slides off her stool, dances, and shimmies, again singing the Prince song.

Lissa gasps for breath. "That was totally weird. Who's David? And what about your boyfriend?"

"He's my husband—David, that is." The words gush out of Kate's mouth. "He's going to be my husband. I mean, he's still my husband, but since we've gone back, he's not, even though he is. Matt's my boyfriend now."

"I'm so not following you."

"I know. It's confusing. Todd will explain it all later. Right now, I gotta jump in the shower." Kate turns toward the bathroom.

"So, you're telling me you can somehow see the future?" Lissa asks, massaging her temples to keep a migraine from coming on.

Kate whirls around. "Pretty much. Well, the next twenty years anyway. But don't you fret, Liss. Everything will make sense."

"Oh, that's reassuring," Lissa says, her voice laced with sarcasm.

Kate disappears into the bathroom.

Lissa remains baffled. *What the...?*

Chapter 5

The University of Massachusetts graduates and their families are gathered in the Tsongas Center in Lowell. A large banner reads, "Congratulations 1999 Graduates!" The commencement speaker—displayed on gigantic screens around the arena—waxes lyrical to resounding applause. Todd tunes out the speaker, thinking, *God, all these speeches are the same generic drivel.*

The graduating students in caps and gowns parade to the stage to retrieve their diplomas and step into their new lives. Todd walks stiffly across the stage and accepts his diploma. With his hard-earned credentials in hand, he spots Lissa and smiles. When the ceremony ends, the graduates, like countless classes before them, flip their tassels and toss their caps skyward into a cheering crowd.

The ceremony over, people flood across the arena. Todd swiftly cuts through the mob to find Lissa, his sister Kate, and his mom and dad, Elaine and Graham. Mom looks sophisticated in a black linen dress with an indigo accent scarf, and a smile lights up her face. She looks much younger than her forty-five years. Dad, a couple of years older than his wife, appears imposing and stern in his Belgian tweed suit.

"Congratulations, my darling," says Elaine, giving Todd a warm embrace and a kiss on the cheek, leaving a lipstick mark. As she wipes it off, she whispers, "I'm so proud of you."

Beaming, Todd turns to his dad, who offers his hand. "Welcome to the firm, son."

"Thanks, Dad." Todd tries for a hug, but his father insists on a clumsy handshake.

Mum turns to leave. "We'll let you catch up with your friends and see you at dinner."

Todd says, "7:00 PM at the Mandarin. Got it."

"Kate's bringing her roommate, in case you want to invite anyone," says Graham.

"Oh, I'm good," Todd replies. "Wait, can we invite David?"

"Of course. See you all later." Elaine pulls Graham away.

When his parents disappear into the crowd, Todd spots Lissa in a form-fitting blue dress, belted at the waist. She smiles at him sweetly and nervously grips a matching blue clutch purse. Todd crosses the arena floor toward her, his gown flowing.

He pans to her left and right. "I see my sister ditched you. Sorry about that. She can be impulsive at times."

"Oh, I know. She saw David and ran. I guess it makes sense."

Todd couldn't help but take in all of Lissa. "You're so beautiful."

Lissa blushes. She starts to say something but stops herself. They regard each other in awkward silence.

He laughs. "Um, want to get out of here and find a quiet spot to sit and talk?"

She nods.

He takes her hand. As they walk away, she leans into him.

***

Back at the hotel, Kate hangs onto David, who slides the door key card in and out of the lock and repeatedly gets the red light. "Damn it! The key's not working. I don't want to have to go back to the lobby."

Kate hip-checks him aside. "Here, let me try." She snatches the key card from his hand and slides it into the key slot. The light turns green. "Voila! It just took the magic touch."

"I'd like some of your magic touch."

They barge into the room, laughing and kissing. He kicks the door closed. As it slams shut, they tumble onto the king-sized bed.

Kate rolls on top of David and pushes him flat. She hooks her fingers under his shirt and undershirt and bunches them up his torso. "Ooooh... I remember that six-pack, you sexy devil." She runs her fingers down David's abs.

He sits up and it's his turn to roll on top of her. "Watch out, I'm about to have my wicked way, little lady."

They giggle and tug at each other's clothing.

An hour later, they rest, blankets, and bedsheets twisted around them. With tousled hair, Kate places her head on David's chest and sighs.

David asks, "Why the long face?"

She kisses his chest. "I'm feeling really guilty."

David wraps an arm over her shoulder. "You're feeling bad about sleeping with your husband? That's a first."

"Remember, we don't meet for eighteen months." Kate realizes how strange that sounds. "I'm in love with

Matt right now. It all feels so weird, like I'm torn between two lovers." She frowns.

"You're being way too dramatic." He eases from under her and slides off the bed. "It's no big deal." He scoops his clothes off the floor and heads to the bathroom. "Why should you feel bad?"

Kate scootches to the headboard and props pillows under her shoulders. "Cuz it feels like I'm cheating."

"Like I said, it's not cheating," he calls from the bathroom.

He emerges wearing jeans. "More like getting a taste of what's to come." He grips his crotch.

Kate hurls a pillow at him. He ducks and disappears into the bathroom again.

"Still, we shouldn't make a habit of this." She picks at the corner of a bedsheet. "I'm headed back to Texas tomorrow and need to stay on the college track."

"The typical college track, my dear, is playing the field," he says, emerging from the bathroom fully dressed, except for his shoes.

"Daaaavid, I'm serious. Don't make this any harder than it is."

He taps his wrist as if to indicate a watch and the passing of time. "Five weeks from now, I'm gonna be rich." He aims a pointed look right at her. "We're gonna be rich!"

Kate watches as he slips into one shoe, bemused by his confidence.

He pauses as he ties the other shoe. It's like he's read her mind when he says, "I'm thinking I'll head to New York and conquer the stock market."

"Ooh. Sounds like a good plan to me." A shadow

eclipses Kate's face. "But what if you conquer more than the stock market?"

David straightens and narrows his eyes. "I don't follow. You mean like conquer the world?" He raises his arms in a victory stance.

"I mean the women of New York."

David poses with a cocky grin. "They'd be so lucky." He turns his attention to her. "But it's you I want."

Kate rolls her eyes, *of course he would say that*, and swivels out of bed. Still naked, she heads to the bathroom. David slaps her behind, and she squeals in laughter.

***

Todd and Lissa settle onto a park bench near the bridge on the river walk. A light breeze casts ripples on the gentle river, speckled gold by the setting sun. Newly budding leaves on the trees glow electric green. Yellow daffodils blaze across the grass. It's as if everything is rejoicing with the advent of spring. Lissa sniffs at a lilac Todd plucks for her.

"I'm impressed you've kept an open mind and not written us off as nutjobs."

Lissa stares at the lilac blossom and slowly twirls it one way, then the other. Even before Todd and Kate sprang this bizarre story of time travel, she'd felt unmoored, drifting along uncomfortably, waiting for something to call her, to give her both direction and momentum. Then Todd came along, and it was like her internal compass quit spinning in circles to lock on a heading and her motor shifted from idle to forward. "It's weird. After you explained that to me, it suddenly seemed as if you were familiar. Like I've known you for years."

"In a way, you have known me for years." He cups her chin and lifts it so that their eyes meet.

The weird feelings simmering inside her suddenly well upward. She feels it's time to make a decision, and that the best course, the safest course, is to completely trust Todd.

"Let's do this." His words coax her closer to him. "Take each day as it comes. And starting today, Lissa James, will you be my girlfriend?"

She nudges his hand from her chin. A coy smile twists her lips. "Apparently, I become your wife, and we have a family, so it's hard to say 'no.' And I've decided to take this on a need-to-know basis. Besides, I like waking up and not knowing what the day will bring."

"Excellent plan. Speaking of, I'll be moving to Austin soon. To start a business, to watch out for my rambunctious sister, and be close to you." He gives Lissa's wrist a tender squeeze. "I see no reason to wait. Technically, I met, rather will meet you, in about two years from now at Kate's graduation. You dropped out of college."

Lissa feels herself going off-center. "Kate told me."

"It all works out." He tilts his head to again make eye contact. "That's something you regretted, but let's not worry about the past. Or should I say, the future. This time around you will complete your bachelor's in psychology and make your acting career more of a hobby. Sound good?"

That off-center feeling goes more off-center. Lissa has the impression that she's being swept away by events she can't control.

Todd shakes her arm. His voice raises to get her attention. "Are you okay?"

She averts her eyes. "I'm fine. Just overwhelmed, I guess." When he starts to speak, she puts a finger on his lips. "Right now, I just want you to get to know me... again."

He answers by sweeping her in his arms and they kiss.

***

Later that evening, Lissa follows Todd, Elaine, Graham, David, and Kate down the steps of the Chinese restaurant, having just enjoyed a feast of Mandarin cuisine.

Kate strolls beside Lissa and Todd. She says, "Mom, Dad, can you head to the car? We'll catch up. Just want to say 'night' to the boys." Graham and Elaine will be driving her and Kate to their hotel while David gives Todd a lift.

"Oh, okay, then," Elaine replies, a bit taken aback. She tosses her scarf over her shoulder.

"Thanks again for dinner, Mr. Benton," says David. "Best duck wontons ever." He exuberantly shakes Graham's hand.

Graham allows a guarded smile. "My pleasure."

Graham and Elaine turn towards the parking lot.

David tugs at Kate's hand, pulling her away from Todd and Lissa. "Great to see you, Lissa."

"You, too."

David and Kate saunter off, heads together as they whisper and chuckle.

Lissa shakes her head. "They're a match made in heaven, those two."

Todd takes her hand. "I forgot how adorable you are." Todd hugs her tightly and kisses her passionately on the lips. She pulls into him, then stops when she feels his stiffness against her belly. Her eyes pop open.

Todd leans from her and clears his throat. "Uhh," he manages, embarrassed. They're illuminated by the restaurant's marquee and visible to everyone.

Kate yells at them, her voice teasing. "Gotta go, lovebirds."

Todd and Lissa share a peck and reluctantly release each other's hands.

"See you soon," says Todd.

Lissa replies, "Take care," and steps away.

Kate grabs her friend by the arm, and they race toward the parking lot to join Todd's parents. Glancing back at Todd, Lissa sees him with a big smile. He meets up with David, who says, "Let's go, Prince Charming."

***

The day after graduation, the girls have flown back to Austin and Todd drives to his parents' place for lunch. They live in a colonial-style home in an upscale neighborhood outside Boston. It's close to the Catholic church they attend almost every Sunday.

He enters a contemporary, well-appointed kitchen, which complements the home's historical pedigree, and greets his mother. She's prepared Niçoise salads with ahi tuna and iced tea. Graham emerges from the stairway to the wine cellar with a bottle of Chardonnay.

Todd places the pitcher of iced tea on the table. "Thanks again for hosting dinner last night." He and his mom sit.

Graham uncorks the wine. "Of course. Lissa is such a lovely girl." Elaine places a hand over her glass to indicate she doesn't want any. He pours himself a healthy splash. "It's so clear that you have a special connection." Graham takes his place at the head of the table and partakes in the Chardonnay.

"I couldn't agree more." Todd takes a long sip of iced tea and clears his throat. Along the way, he'd been rehearsing his speech. What he was going to say would not only ruin the day's festive mood but could sour relations between himself and his dad for a long time to come. The key to the old man's success was his stubbornness and, to that end, he could carry a grudge for decades. Reluctantly, Todd begins, "So... Dad." Hands sweaty, he rubs his palms together, glances at his mother, then fixes a gaze on his father. "I've thought about it long and hard."

Graham cups the wine glass in his hand, his head cocked expectantly.

Todd drops the bomb. "I don't plan on joining the firm."

Graham's ruddy complexion loses all color and his eyes crinkle.

Elaine stops chewing mid-bite.

Graham takes a drink, slowly. He sets the glass on the table and smacks his lips as if this will be the last pleasant thing he'll taste in a long time. Jaw tense, he narrows his eyes. "I see. So, you graduate, and now think you know everything?"

"It's not that, Dad." Todd feels like he's been backed into a corner.

"Then what?"

"I need to strike out on my own."

"And do what?" Graham's face reddens.

"I plan to move to Austin and start a business that develops and sells health-records software." Todd's speech quickens and his tone is lighter, freer because he knows he's right about everything. "Trust me on this, Dad. It's the future."

"The future?" His father guffaws. "What are you, a psychic?"

"This venture is going to be very profitable."

"What do you know about profitable? Or business? You studied engineering. And now have a Bachelor of Science. *A bachelor's.* You're barely at first base and are dreaming of home runs."

Graham scoffs then guzzles what's left in his glass and looks at his wife. "Did you hear that, Elaine? He thinks he's too good for the firm."

Elaine's lips purse as she stares at her salad. It's as though she's praying this conversation will quickly blow over.

"I never said that, Dad. But it's best that I do my own thing. Best for all of us." Todd makes eye contact with his mom, hoping to gain an ally. She glances away in solidarity with her husband.

Graham glares with quiet fury at Todd, clearly

resenting his son's breaking loose and not wanting to hear the rest of what he has to say. Nevertheless, Todd outlines his plans.

Graham laughs mockingly. "Are you hearing your son, Elaine? Todd's abandoning the family business, discarding his engineering degree, to start a business about which he knows nothing."

"Well..." starts Elaine, used to playing the mediator between son and husband.

"I assure you, Dad, I'm not being reckless," Todd says, his hands laid flat on the table to signal his resoluteness.

His father dramatically pushes his chair back, shaking the table. The ice cubes in the pitcher rattle and tea sloshes over the rim, staining the table cover. "Your grandfather's trust wasn't meant to be squandered away!" He throws his napkin down and turns to Elaine. "See, this is why I've always said it's wrong to access funds at twenty-one. Too young and foolish to know better!"

Graham storms out. Todd and his mother share a tense look.

After a minute of silence, he says, "I'm not backing down."

Chapter 6

Lissa and Kate stroll through campus on a warm spring day, the pink dogwood trees in full bloom against a bluebird sky. A group of students play ultimate frisbee. Others "study" while soaking up rays in their shorts and UT-Austin tees. Lissa sports a sundress and Kate a swingy skirt with a light tank top. They both have the same stylish backpack they picked up at a buy-one-get-one-free sale. At the time, they'd wondered if it was dorky for them to have matching backpacks but decided, who cares?

Lissa mulls over the news Kate has just shared about David. Apparently, he's hit a huge lotto prize in New York, exactly as Kate had predicted. Lissa keeps wondering about this time-travel concept. She wants to believe. Hearing that her life doesn't exactly pan out as she expected, indulging in this outlandish fantasy seems like a safe refuge. Todd acts sincere enough so at least she's got herself a good man. With David's effortless win of a fortune, Lissa becomes more convinced they know the future.

"twenty-five million dollars after taxes. It's mindboggling," she says. Suddenly aware of the hour, she accelerates to a brisk pace so she's not late for class.

Kate quickens her steps to keep up though she couldn't care less if she's late for her class. "I know, right? Todd gets fifteen percent. That's their deal, apparently."

"I love how close they are, like brothers," says Lissa.

"For sure. Been best friends for twenty-plus years."

80

Kate flinches, then grins. "Oh, there I go again. Gotta work on that."

"I guess you can't just forget two decades of life, love, and everything in between," Lissa adds, remembering that these three have come from the future.

They stop at a fountain and Kate says, "Part of me sooo wants to drop out of college, but my dad would kill me. Then he'd have two unruly kids on his hands." She gathers her hair in one hand and sips water. "You heard he's super-mad at Todd. Not even returning his calls. But working for the family firm was a disaster for Todd. He's not a company man and has to do his own thing. I'm so happy he's coming to Austin sooner rather than later."

"I'm really excited," Lissa says, balancing on her toes.

Kate suddenly jerks upright. "Ohmigod, at some point, I'll probably be moving to New York. But hey, David and I will keep a place here, too." Her face brightens in festive optimism. She spins like a little girl in her own fairy tale world, her sassy skirt swirling with her. "And a beach pad in Malibu, a chalet in Aspen... the list goes on." Kate twirls around again, loses her balance, and stumbles.

Lissa catches her by the arm. "You're such a klutz!"

They laugh.

Kate collects herself and they proceed along the sidewalk when she whispers, "Oh, God. Don't look now. But Peter Jenkins—the Peter I told you about—is coming this way."

Lissa sees a tall young man, fashionably dressed, headed in their direction. Her eyebrows arch in distress. "Him? The one you said was my first love, the heartbreaker?"

"Yeah. The asshole who dumps you a week after he takes your virginity—that one."

Lissa gulps and resolves not to let Peter rattle her. She continues in his direction. Kate adjusts her backpack and walks closely behind.

Peter is a senior, tall and bronzed, with model good looks and a cocky swagger to match. He notices Lissa and stops in front of her, blocking her way. "Hey there, pretty lady," he says, flashing a shit-eating grin, clearly preparing for her to swoon.

Lissa is ready to lash out at him when the warm, inviting glow in his eyes evaporates her anger. She does swoon. Peter is so damn gorgeous. She feels lucky that he's chosen her.

She starts to speak and ends up stammering, "Uh... uh... uh—"

Kate jabs her in the back. Then the warnings flood into Lissa. The betrayal. The humiliation. The abandonment.

She announces, "I have a boyfriend."

That inviting look in Peter's eyes dims.

She steps around him, Kate strutting with her, raking him with a smug look and a snicker. Lissa blows out in relief. Her footfalls gather a spring. If it wasn't for Kate and Lissa's new-found appreciation of her own volition, she might have found herself as yet another notch on that bastard's bedpost.

Kate whispers breathlessly, "God, I love this time-travel stuff. It makes life so much easier to navigate. Normally, you're just blindly going through life. This way, you are both younger and wiser. You don't make mistakes the second time around."

***

David's forty-ninth-floor office has a sweeping view of the NYC skyline, including the World Trade Center towers dominating the sky. David is at his desk, and his secretary, Meredith, a conservative, fifty-something sits across from him, taking notes on a yellow legal notepad. She wears her hair in a tidy French twist. She's one of the few women who still wears suits with shoulder pads.

David points to a blank wall. "Biggest dry-erase board you can source. Put it right there."

"Yes, sir," she replies with enthusiasm.

"Here are the companies I want listed on it. Facebook, Starbucks, uhh… LinkedIn, Twitter, Alibaba, Yelp, Instagram, TikTok." Too impatient to sit still, he leaps to his feet and paces. "I'll add more as they come to me."

Meredith seems bewildered by his impulsive manner as she jots feverishly. "Hmm… Never heard of those, except Starbucks, of course." She glances at her Starbucks cup on the corner of his desk.

David suddenly stops his pacing. "Google, YouTube, that's y-o-u-t-u-b-e, Netflix, with an X, PayPal, one word. Oh, and Tesla. Send that list to Mark Sullivan. I need him to watch out for these IPOs the next decade." He thrusts his index finger upward like an exclamation point.

Meredith shakes her head, amused and confused. "Certainly. Oh, I tried Mr. Jobs again, from Apple. Still no luck."

"He's a prick. But keep trying." David clasps his hands behind his back, takes a step, then halts. "Oh, and while you're at it, chase down Jeff Bezos. He runs Amazon."

"Amazon, as in the jungle?" She quirks an eyebrow.

He chuckles. "Not quite. Huge online retailer, well, will be in a few years but right now, he's selling mostly books."

"Okay, if you say so. I'll jump right on it." Meredith caps her pen and she stands to leave, notepad in hand.

David blurts, "One more thing. Please get Mark on the phone. I want to go over stock buys for the week."

She steps for the door. "Right away."

"Thanks, Meredith."

He plunks down in his chair, energized. He picks up a Giants' blue and red football and pumps his arm like he's about to throw long. He tosses the football straight up and catches it—at once the quarterback and the wide receiver.

He snags the remote on his desk and clicks the large TV hanging from the ceiling in the corner of his office. It's a massive Sony, the largest one available, a bulky cathode ray tube model. Davis shakes his head as the TV warms up. *Look at this monstrosity. Can't wait for the flat screens. Twice the picture for half the price. C'mon, future.*

Headlines flash across the screen: 2000 World News and NASDAQ clips—Y2K averted, Bush defeats Gore, NASDAQ scrolls—eBay, Disney, Nike, Nutrisystem, Oracle, Nintendo. If you know what to expect, every one of these names is a bounty of riches.

***

Todd and Lissa sit on a blanket in Austin's Zilker Park and arrange their picnic items. He chose a spot away from Lady Bird Lake, which is a mob scene this first warm weekend of the spring. Todd lords over her in a she's-my-gal kind of way, which he is certain she enjoys. He feels like he's dating a much younger woman, one who relishes being guided by his wisdom and worldliness.

He pops open the champagne bottle with a flourish, and the cork zings upward. Without hesitation, Lissa snatches it mid-air.

Todd nods, impressed. He pours and hands a glass to her.

"Thank you." She watches the bubbles dance in her flute.

Todd fills his glass until it's almost overflowing. "To Austin! To us!"

They toast, their crystal flutes chime. He leans in for a kiss. It's a long, passionate one, as if no one is watching.

"Oh, please. Get a hotel room!" It's Kate, her usual unfiltered self. She and Matt amble close, toting a freshly baked baguette, a small cooler, and a cloth bag bulging with groceries. Matt is twenty, lanky, and blond. His long bangs are swept to the side. He sports Ray-Ban sunglasses and a navy-blue polo shirt with the collar turned up. Kate wears a light blue halter dress.

"Hi, guys," Matt says. "Todd, welcome back. I hear you're now a resident of the great state of Texas."

"I am indeed. Still settling in, but so far so good." Todd gives a thumbs up. He studies how cozy Kate is with Matt. They do make a good couple, which only means complications when David comes back into the picture.

Matt and Kate sit cross-legged on the blanket opposite Todd and Lissa. Kate begins to sort through her bag of groceries, Lissa helping. Kate nibbles on a stick of cheese.

"Kate tells me you've leased office space and hired staff. That's great." Matt offers Todd a bottle of Lone Star beer.

Todd lifts his flute of champagne. "Thanks, but I've already got a head start."

Matt pops open his bottle and takes a swig. "Not that I'm of drinking age, but when did that ever stop anyone?"

"Yes, it's all systems go." Todd empties his flute and pours a refill. "We're working 'round the clock developing software and should be ready to launch later this year. Super psyched!"

"What made you decide to go into electronic medical records?" Matt digs into a bag of chips and munches.

Todd mulls his answer. The truth is, getting in early to convert medical records to computer files is what he decided back in the future. But he couldn't say that, so he gives a vague yet truthful reply. "I predict a lot of growth in this business. It's an untapped market."

Matt nods politely. "Smart."

Kate arranges bread, cheese, prosciutto, grapes, and chocolate on a platter.

"Wow, that looks great!" Matt reaches to pinch food off the plate.

Kate playfully slaps his hand. "Wait, I'm still setting up."

"I'm so hungry," Matt says, theatrically, eyes pleading.

"And that's different from usual, because...?"

"Because now I'm ravenous."

"Gotcha." Kate rolls her eyes.

Matt pinches her butt. She squeals, he grabs her, she tries to squirm free—the blanket wrinkles, knocking over drinks—but he insists on smothering her with a bear hug.

Todd laughs. "Who needs the hotel room now?"

***

A driver stands in front of a sleek black limo at Austin's private airport. David crosses the tarmac from a Gulfstream III. This business jet is a charter. *Soon I'll have my own, a bigger one.* The driver—his ropey build reminds David of a cowboy, scraggly hair tucked under his chauffeur's cap—takes David's case and opens the limo door for him.

As the limo driver navigates through Austin's twisting highways and streets, David keeps his eyes peeled for a flower shop. He's dressed in what is now called "business casual." Basically, a sport coat over a dress shirt and chinos. To that end, now that he has money, "business casual" doesn't mean cheap and this ensemble—who knew Gucci made men's loafers?—cost him what would've been a month's salary in the old future.

While waiting for a red light, David spots Jacob's Florist. "Hey, can you pull over here? I need to pop in for something."

"Sure." The driver steers toward the curb. There's no open space so he double-parks and flips on his flashers.

Pissed-off drivers lay on their horns, and people shout obscenities. David hustles into the shop. When he enters, a wave of fragrant smells from the collage of blossoms washes over him. He doesn't have time for the clerk to make a special bouquet, so he points to one ready-made and lays a hundred-dollar bill on the counter. A moment later, he reemerges carrying a bouquet of pink roses with green and white hydrangea and pink lisianthus.

"All set?" says the driver.

"Sure am. Thanks for stopping, man."

***

Kate and Matt are in Kate's bedroom on the bed, sweaty, breathless, and in each other's arms. Their clothes lie scattered across the floor. Kate loved these afternoon romps more than anything.

The doorbell rings. They glance at each other, like, *are you expecting someone*?

Kate furrows her brow at Matt. "This one of your impromptu pizza deliveries?"

"Nope." Matt hops out of bed and steps into UT sweatpants. "I'll see who it is." He walks to the front room and opens the door.

Kate pulls the bedsheets to her neck and observes the proceedings.

David stands in the hall, flowers in hand.

Oh my God! A tidal wave of embarrassment splashes over Kate. Before she and David make eye contact, she shrinks under the covers until she can barely peek and look.

David's merry expression deflates. "Hey... you must be Matt."

"Yup. And you are?"

Kate slithers from under the covers and skulks naked to the bathroom. As she slips into a fuzzy pink robe, she listens to the two men talk.

"David Stern, Todd's longtime best friend. I'm sure Kate's told you about me. I'm like... a brother."

"Yeah, whatever," Matt answers dismissively. "Come in." A pause. "Nice flowers."

"My mother taught me never to show up empty-handed."

There's another pause, especially long and awkward. Kate studies her reflection in the bathroom mirror and frantically brushes her tangled hair. Her eyes brim with shame. Then she slows her brushing. *Why is this my problem? David isn't supposed to arrive until tomorrow. I'm not screwing things up; he is.*

She locks eyes with her reflection. This time travel presents interesting opportunities. Why not see what happens? Admiring herself, she thinks, *David wants this, he better work for it.* She sets the brush down, examines her hair, and with a shrug, decides, *this is the best I can do under the circumstances.* She cinches the robe tight and marches to the front room, shabby chic with mood lighting.

David is wearing fancy clothes and stands just inside the threshold, appearing dazed like he'd been conked on the head.

Kate gushes with false enthusiasm. "David! What are you doing here?" She leans against the couch. "Um, such a surprise to see you." She stares at him, her thoughts curdling. *It's too soon, dude. I'm not ready for you.* The moment stretches uncomfortably.

"Thought I'd stop by on my way to see Todd." David presents the flowers. "For you."

"How sweet, but you shouldn't have, not for Todd's kid sister." She emphasizes "Todd's kid sister" to play up the friend angle before taking the bouquet. "David's always watching out for me," she says with a flat tone.

"I can see that." Matt looks from David to Kate and then back to David.

His expression reeks of disappointment and indecision.

"Since you have company, I'll leave you to it."

"Yes. I'll call you later." Kate pads forward to close the door and usher him out.

David goes to leave, then spins around to give her a scheming, pointed look. "Don't do anything I wouldn't do."

Kate masks her smirk, thinking, *stop it, you devil! Both of us are playing this game.* "Bye."

Matt shuts the door and locks it. "He's an odd dude."

While Kate smells the roses, Matt looks like he smells a rat. At least the roses aren't red. The bouquet feels like pressure to move things along, but Kate can't let go of Matt. Not yet anyway. Kate feels the burden of destiny and wonders what happens if she chooses differently this time.

***

Kate strolls along 6th Street and, approaching a Starbucks, decides on coffee. But the line of college hipsters snaking out the door changes her mind. Then she spies David inside at a corner table, reading *The Wall Street Journal*. It's no coincidence that he's here.

Kate saunters past the line and plunks down on the other chair at David's table. "No latte is worth waiting in that line."

His eyes lift to give her a quick once-over. She's dressed in coed-chic: shorts, Reeboks, and a sweat top unzipped to reveal a low-cut tank. He still wears the same clothes from earlier.

She's expecting an outburst of jealousy, but he surprises her with, "Hey!" He leans in. "I just bought a nice chunk of Starbucks stock."

Kate tries to get her footing. This time-travel is going to be a spiderweb of adventures. "Why did you just show up like that? You said next week. Which would mean... not this week." She gives him the stink eye.

He folds the newspaper. "Truth be told, I couldn't wait. I wanted to surprise you. But it was you who surprised me. Matt seems really into you," he says, the light draining from his eyes.

"He is... and vice versa," she says almost apologetically. "Like I said, I'm feeling a bit torn between two lovers. I can't just switch off my feelings for Matt. I'm in love with him." And she quickly says, "Of course, I love you, too."

"I get it."

But she wonders if he does.

"I got you something." He pulls out a necklace box.

"Can you guess what this is?"

"It's jewelry." Her gaze rises from the box. "A necklace? No wait, no, you didn't. The one you gave me when Jack was born?" The thought of their son Jack unlocks a surge of warm, motherly memories.

Grinning, David opens the box. Kate's eyes pop and well up with tears as she palms the pendant. "It's bigger!"

"A full carat, VS1 quality. Only the best for you, baby."

"You've always been so thoughtful." She reaches for his hand but then hesitates. Her smile fades, and she hands the box back to David.

"What? You don't like it?" David appears crestfallen.

"I love it, but I can't take it now. What if Matt finds it? Flowers, this necklace. He'll put two and two together." Worse, and Kate suspects this is why David brought the pendant, as emotional leverage.

"Tell him it's a zirconia you bought at Macy's."

Kate considers the lie. She bursts into laughter. "The ninety-nine dollar bargain of the day!" She gazes at the pendant. The future and their son Jack are waiting. She can't help but look back at David. "I do love you, David." It's true, sort of.

"I have something else for you."

"Really?"

He reaches inside his blazer and hands her a check.

"Thought you could use some spending money while you're still here in Austin. Wish you'd move to New York sooner. It's really a great scene, Kate. Maybe transfer next semester?"

The check is for five thousand dollars. "It looks

tempting, but I like it here." She lays the check on the table. "I'm enjoying college and my friends. Besides, before you know it, I'll graduate and be free as a bird." She smiles at him.

He holds her gaze, his expression signaling his affection for her. "So..." And he pauses.

"So, what? Go ahead. You can say it." She's not sure what he intends.

"Any chance of stopping by my hotel a little later?"

Kate averts her eyes. So, it's not so much affection as it is horniness. "Um, I don't think that's such a good idea." She squeezes his hand. "Be patient. We have our whole lives ahead of us. Go out there and have some fun. Sow your oats if you know what I mean."

"Who's to say I haven't?" He shoots her a devilish look that stings a little.

***

Benton EHR Systems occupies the first floor of a small office building in a business park on the outskirts of Austin. A hands-on business leader, Todd makes the rounds to check in with his eight employees. He believes the high-tech, high-touch approach is the secret to his success.

"Rich, how's the response on the prototype testing?" asks Todd. He looks over Rich's shoulder at the screen. Rich, a balding twenty-something with hipster rectangular glasses, is a programming whiz kid.

"Aside from a few glitches, we're getting there," Rich proudly exclaims.

Todd checks the performance readout. "God, it's

slow. Can we have broadband already?"

Rich glances from the screen to Todd. "Huh?"

"Oh, nothing. Keep up the good work." Todd pats Rich's shoulder, then strides toward the boardroom to conduct interviews for the position of CFO.

One candidate is already there, sitting prim along one side of the long and shiny conference table. She's a petite Asian woman in her early thirties, with a short bob and a charcoal suit. Her hands are folded over an expensive leather portfolio on the table.

She stands to greet him. Her eyes are large and dark and catch all the light in the room in a way that pulls him in. Todd's mind revisits the rapport they shared for years last time around. His affection and respect for this woman, Ellen Chan, runs deep.

Todd practically pounces on her and gives her a warm hug. "Ellen! It's so—" With that, he suddenly realizes his error and recovers his composure.

Ellen appears completely thrown off balance and frozen, wears a meek, confused smile.

He backs away. "Forgive me. I thought you were... someone else."

"No problem," she laughs uncomfortably and then stifles it.

"Please, take a seat."

"Certainly."

Ellen smooths her suit and sits down, folding her hands on the portfolio.

Todd sorts through the files on his end of the table. "I've gone over your résumé. You're more than qualified for the job."

"Thank you, sir."

"You're a bit over-qualified actually but we will need your expertise soon, and I am one-hundred percent confident you can run my operation. We get along great."

She cocks an eyebrow.

He recovers, "I mean, I think we WILL work extremely well together."

Ellen is clearly baffled by his behavior but smiles politely. Do you have any other questions for me?"

Todd smiles at Ellen. "When can you start?"

Chapter 7

Todd and Lissa pull up to a quaint, well-presented one-story house in the Austin suburbs. They get out of his Honda Insight and stand before the house, assessing it.

"It's so charming," says Lissa.

"I thought so, too, when I saw it in the listings." Todd unlocks the front door and ushers her in with a flourish. "It might be on the small side, but it's a good starter home."

Lissa pauses in the foyer to scope out the airy and bright interior. "Wow! I like the feel of it. It has so much light. The layout is great."

"Living room, kitchen, guest room over there, master bedroom here." Todd nudges her into the hall to point out the various rooms. He leads her to the master bedroom.

She halts on the threshold to admire the expansive floor plan, the roomy walk-in closet, and the large bathroom with his and her sinks. It's not the house she's thinking about but Todd's embrace. Her heart beats faster. Her cheeks warm. "Plenty of room. Since I might stay over often, might I suggest a king-size bed?"

"You're not staying over."

His words are a cold splash of disappointment.

She doesn't move as he circles his arms around her waist. Laying his chin on her shoulder, he whispers, "You're moving in."

All the shame she just felt evaporates, replaced by

a flare of ardor. Lightheaded, she exhales and says, "You had me worried for a second."

Todd spins her around for a deep kiss. Things happen in a blur, mouths, fingers, hands, sliding, stroking, kneading. Clothing is removed in urgent tugs and flung aside. Lissa gives in to abandon and they surrender to each other's embrace, ending up on the floor. He slips off her dress, and she, in turn, peels off his pants. They fit together perfectly and don't even notice the hard, cold floor.

***

David wakes up in bed and blinks at the light streaming through the window. He takes a moment to take stock of his life in this new "past." Everything is working out even better than he could've dreamed. His lifestyle in New York City is fast and furious. He owns this luxury high-rise apartment on the forty-fourth floor in SoHo. He has a driver named Ahmed. He frequents nightclubs with designer martinis and gorgeous women. He watches his stocks go up, up, up. As he enjoys his sweeping view of the city, he thinks, *God, I love this life!*

But something nags at him, something that tarnishes the shine of his gilded existence. It is Kate. Rather, the absence of Kate. She is the one piece of his plan that so far has failed to fall into place. In the meantime, what fills the void is a collage of quick dalliances with slim women, each as forgettable as sips of yesterday's champagne.

Except for Angelika.

She stirs beside him, and he rolls over to admire

the profile of her flawless features. Even asleep, she is an exquisite example of the female kind, a stunning twenty-five-year-old Eastern European model, one he met a couple of months earlier. Angelika hooked him with her charm and the promise that the more she gave to him, the more he'd want.

His cell phone on the nightstand rings, breaking the morning's tranquility.

Angelika's eyes flutter open. She sits up and snatches her robe from a nearby chair. In one deft movement, she scoots out of bed, into her robe, and pads toward the bathroom. David looks at her empty spot on the bed and then toward the bathroom door, relishing the eddy of sensuality she's left in her wake.

The phone rings again. David answers.

"Hey, man!" Mark Sullivan shouts. When he's excited, everything that comes out of his mouth ends with an exclamation point. "Have you seen your portfolio today?"

"Not yet." David rubs his eyes. He hasn't even had coffee yet. "This good news?"

"Good news? Are you kidding? You hit the forty mil mark today! Congratulations!"

The news jolts David. He can't contain his joy, and cheers, "Woo-hoo! Forty mil, music to my ears. Thanks, Mark. Talk later." He hangs up, swings his feet to the floor, and pumps his arms to holler again.

Angelika cracks open the bathroom door. "What's going on out here? Is this some early-morning caveman ritual?"

Not bothering with a robe, David strides naked

toward the bathroom. "What's going on? Money. Lots of it."

"Oooh, this means I can go shopping." Angelika steps back to let him pass.

David turns on the shower. "Whatever you want, babe."

***

Kate settles into her new luxury condo and reflects on how this new "past" life is developing. She'd never been one to over-analyze her life, instead preferring to exist in the moment and let things happen.

What she hadn't taken into account was Matt. At first, she thought theirs was a college fling and by now she'd be ready to move on with David. But with each passing day, she falls more deeply in love with Matt. They have so much fun together; Kate can't imagine a better life.

They zip around in his vintage blue no-top Ford Bronco to all kinds of romantic adventures—hot air ballooning, ziplining, and picnics on Mt. Bonnell overlooking Lake Austin. He drives a little too fast, but Kate doesn't mind; she loves the adrenaline rush. It's so different from the staid and proper lifestyle of her parents.

Hail Mary, pray for us sinners now! she thinks with a strange mix of delight and chagrin. She knows she's a good girl, looking back with forty years of experience. She hasn't done half the bad things other girls her age often do. She squeezes in studying when she can. She figures she doesn't need stellar grades, she just needs to graduate.

That night, Kate prepares a romantic Italian dinner.

She's barefoot and wearing a miniskirt with a matching halter top. Matt's hovering about her in the kitchen. She tests a penne noodle from the boiling stock pot. "Ouch! Nope, still not ready."

"Don't overcook it. As you know, I'm an al-dente guy."

Kate rolls her eyes. "You mean, you like it raw."

"I like you raw!"

Kate bares her teeth in a mock snarl. "Grrrr."

Matt thumbs through a stack of mail at the edge of the counter. "You got a lot of bank statements here."

"I know," she answers, trying to sound as blasé as possible. "I told David to have them send me one consolidated report."

"I think he manages your money because he wants you." Matt's eyes sparkle flirtatiously.

Kate averts hers. The pasta is ready. She clicks off the burner and lifts the stock pot to pour the hot water and pasta into a colander in the sink. Steam billows about her. "I told you, he's like a brother."

"I still think he'd like to screw you." Matt wraps his arms around her waist. "But possession is nine-tenths of the law."

"Stop it, you!" Kate slaps his hands, but he doesn't let go.

"Dinner can wait?" he asks.

Kate giggles in agreement.

They start to make love standing up in the kitchen.

***

The first night Todd and Lissa move into their home, he asks her to check the mail. Lissa says no one even knows their address. In the mailbox beside the front door, she finds an envelope addressed to her.

Her eyebrows bunch in surprise and upon opening the envelope, she discovers a simple card with a note: *Will you marry me?* She recognizes the handwriting and beams at Todd.

He's watching and hands her a small black box.

Her pulse thumps as she opens it. Nestled in black velvet, a diamond solitaire ring glistens. Her heart feels as if it wants to explode. She grasps a handful of his shirt and draws him close for a tender kiss.

He pulls away, gasping. "Was that a yes?"

"Yes, yes, a million times yes!" she says, feeling herself swept away in the romantic undertow.

They settle into domestic bliss. They nest in their lovely home, Lissa doing homework and preparing gourmet meals for workaholic Todd. His company is booming under his steady hand and inspired leadership. Despite Todd's success, his father remains standoffish when he shows up at her and Kate's graduation.

Months later, Lissa and Todd are in bed reading. She's engrossed in a hardback copy of *White Oleander*. Lissa refuses to go digital because she loves the feel and aroma of paper books. She notices Todd's holding his Kindle but is staring into space.

Lissa folds her book closed, careful to slip in a bookmark. "Someone has that far-away look in his eyes. Disaster looming?"

"No, actually." He tries to sound upbeat, then sighs heavily. "Well, yes, there's always tragedy in the wings, but that's not what's on my mind. It's my dad."

Lissa sets her book on the nightstand and styles her hair in a topknot for bed. "You feel it's worse than before? I mean the first time. Ugh. I don't think I will ever get used to the past versus the new... now."

"It's not for lack of trying. I just can't win with him. But you know, I'm happier. Much happier. I love being here and getting our life and my business started now."

"Where are we, like twelve months ahead of schedule?" Lissa leans over to embrace him. "I'm proud of you and couldn't love you more, Todd Benton. Hang in there. Kill your dad with kindness, sweetheart." Lissa kisses his cheek and turns to get comfy under the fluffy duvet.

***

Kate slurps her piping hot coffee, watching the local morning news. She waits for the jolt of caffeine to kick in and absentmindedly thinks about the day ahead. She's looking forward to her yoga class and massage combo.

She's still aglow from last night's romp with Matt. Life in this new past is going to be awesome. No worries about money. No worries about the future because she knows exactly what will happen. She couldn't be anymore carefree.

A reporter stands in front of a shopping mall, saying, "The missing child was last seen at the mall. Blond-haired five-year-old A.J. Kimball was wearing blue jeans and a green sweater when he went missing from Eagle Rock Mall."

The news stuns Kate. Memories flood into her. Memories from her future. Shards of horrific images that rearrange themselves into a coherent and even more horrific whole, that of the young Kimball boy found gruesomely murdered.

She panics. *I have to act. I have to prevent this.*

She grabs her phone but stops herself from dialing. *Wait, no. What do I do? Think, Kate. Caller ID will give me away. I'll be asked how I know the details.* She hesitates, grabs her purse and car keys, and dashes out. Minutes later, Kate pulls into a gas station. She spies a payphone attached to the front wall. She jumps out of her car, dashes to the payphone, and punches the emergency digits.

"911." It's a woman dispatcher. "What is your emergency?"

Breathlessly, Kate says, "Hello, my name is, uh, Fran, anyway, that little boy missing at the mall?" *Think. What do I say?* "Five-year-old AJ? He's only like two, maybe three, streets away, to the right of the mall if you are facing the entrance. He was abducted by a plumber, I think."

"You know this man?" asks the 911 dispatcher.

"God, no! But I do know he's a pedophile." Kate spews the words, "I recall the house is off-white, the van, it's parked out front. It's grey or maybe light blue, but whatever, it's vital you get to him in, like, the next two to three hours, otherwise, AJ will be dead by tonight. Please, please hurry."

"Ma'am?" the dispatcher replies. "Ma'am, ma—"

Kate returns the phone to its cradle. She closes her eyes and holds still, uncertainty rattling through her nerves, knowing she has done the right thing but at what cost? What else has she put into play in this new future?

***

Lissa stands at her granite countertop, chopping peppers for the chicken fajitas she plans to make Todd for dinner. The small kitchen TV is on, but she's not paying attention until a reporter's voice snags her attention. "Five-year-old A.J. Kimball was found alive at this home just two streets away from where he was abducted. The suspect is in custody. Police are asking for your help in locating this woman, seen here on the surveillance tape taken from the gas station at 5th and Haverford, having called in the tip to rescue the boy."

The screen shows a black-and-white video, taken from above and to the right of a payphone. The image isn't crisp but there is no denying who the woman is.

Lissa stops mincing and gasps. "Ohmigod! That's Kate!"

Chapter 8

The windowless police station interrogation room is stark and gray with bare walls, except for a framed quote: *In three words I can sum up everything I've learned about life: it goes on.*—Robert Frost.

Todd and Kate sit side by side at a small metal table, waiting in silence. The tension is heavy, like the air has the mass of concrete. Todd's leg trembles so hard that it rattles the table.

Kate keeps her jaw clenched and, to prevent her mind from spinning in wild speculation about what could happen during this interrogation, she reads the Robert Frost quote over and over. *It's not all that profound*, she thinks, *and if you're going to decorate a wall with words, you could choose a better quote*. She wonders about the meaning of the quote in the context of this interrogation room—that no matter what happens in here—questioning about murders, kidnappings, robberies—life goes on.

Todd's jiggling leg puts her nerves further on edge, so she puts her hand on his thigh. He stops and she withdraws her hand, only to have him renew his tremors.

The anxiety weighs on Kate and she says, "I've heard these guys are always carrying, but they change the location of the pistol to keep you guessing. Where do you think he'll be carrying?"

"Who the hell knows?" says Todd, impatient with his sister's games.

"C'mon, play along."

"Oh, so we're playing find the pistol?"

Kate nods.

"Oh, I don't know." Todd shrugs. "At his waist, I imagine."

"Ankle," Kate quips. "And I'll wager twenty dollars."

Todd scoffs. "What if we can't figure it out? We certainly can't ask him."

"Then no one wins."

As if on cue, the door unlatches, and the detective enters the room. He's towering and lanky with a military buzzcut, a weathered face, and an underbite that gives him a bucktoothed appearance. A badge hangs from a lanyard alongside his striped tie.

Kate spies a holster and pistol on his belt and groans to herself. Not sure of the protocol regarding police questioning, Kate starts to stand. Todd follows her example.

The detective looks amused by their response and gestures. "Please, stay seated."

They settle back into their chairs stiffly.

"I'm Detective Manley. You are Kate Benton, and you're Todd Benton, yes?"

In unison, they answer, "Yes."

Detective Manley places a report several pages thick on the table as he takes off his coat and drapes it over the back of his chair. His shirt and pants look recently ironed. He sits and chuckles to himself before addressing Kate. "So, let me get this straight, you have a psychic ability and you've had it your entire life." His skeptical tone accuses her of being a little crazy.

"Yes," says Kate defensively, glancing at her

106

brother for moral support.

"Her 'insights'"—Todd makes air quotes—"can be helpful, but sometimes, like now, they cause confusion."

"I just wanted to help that little boy," Kate pleads, not sure what the detective will do.

"That you did. And a 'thank you' is certainly in order." Detective Manley gives a genuine smile. He straightens the report even though it doesn't require straightening.

"Thank you. Oh, you're thanking me. Huh. I'm so nervous right now." Her hands twitch uncontrollably and not knowing what to do with them, so she folds her arms against her chest, her hands in lockdown mode.

Todd regards her with a smug grin and rolls his eyes.

The detective smiles, his underbite on full display. "Yes, thank you, Miss Benton. You can relax."

They sit in awkward silence. Kate clenches and unclenches her hands to wring herself of the nervous energy.

Then abruptly, the detective announces, "You're free to go."

Kate exhales and feels her muscles go limp. "Just like that?"

"Unless you have something to add."

"We're fine." Todd reaches across the table and firmly grips the detective's hand. "Detective Manley, a pleasure."

Kate stands and, with a relieved smile, goes to shake hands with the detective when he offers a business card. She takes it.

"Give me a call if you have any more 'insights.' We can always use the help."

Kate waves the card like it's a prize. "I will. I will do just that."

"Okay, then. Talk soon." The detective rises from his chair and holds the door open.

Kate and Todd file out, Detective Manley watching.

As they leave the station, Todd tells his sister to cough up a twenty-dollar bill.

***

That evening, Lissa and Todd's place looks like a candle emporium. When Kate enters and notices the illuminated ambiance, she says, "Wow. I feel like I'm barging in on a romantic dinner."

"No, not at all. Come in, come in," says Lissa, ushering Kate toward the kitchen.

"Your place looks amazing." Kate scopes out their cozy home. "I'm so used to Todd's stark bachelor pad/man-cave look. I'm blown away."

"Well, you know, it takes a woman's touch," Lissa says daintily, kicking up her heel.

Lissa serves Todd and Kate fish tacos with fresh slaw, avocados, and a spicy salsa. As they bite into the tacos, the contents shift and drop on their plates in a messy dining experience. Her brother provides coin-style margaritas served in festive margarita glasses with fresh lime and Cointreau.

Lissa licks the salt off the rim and sips her drink. "You must be so relieved."

"You have no idea." Kate fans her mouth to stave off the jalapeno burn.

"Kate, never make that mistake again." Todd softens his tone so it doesn't sound like a scold. "We live in a digital world and everything we do can be traced."

Shove it, bro! she thinks. "Aye, aye, captain." Kate salutes Todd. "Big brother is watching. Double entendre intended."

Todd sips his margarita and stays quietly pensive until he says, "That reminds me. I've been thinking a lot about 9/11. We need to make a plan and soon."

The mention of 9/11 chills Kate's mood. Not everything in this new past is bright and cheery.

"Huh? Did you mean 7-Eleven? And are you planning to rob a convenience store?" says Lissa, playfully.

Todd and Kate exchange glances.

"Oh, nothing like that," says Kate.

"Sorry, Liss," Todd says. "You said you don't want to know what hasn't yet happened. I shouldn't have brought it up."

Lissa wears an out-of-the-loop expression, glancing back and forth between Todd and Kate, searching for answers.

Kate feels her friend's confusion and says, "Todd, this is different." She turns to Lissa. "Saudi Arabian terrorists will deliberately fly planes into the World Trade Center in New York, and the Pentagon and crash another hijacked airline, killing nearly 3,000 people."

Lissa's eyes pop, and she rests her drink on the table. She sits straight and her eyes swivel from Kate to Todd. "Jesus Christ! For real?"

"Who's to say we can stop it?" Todd's tone is of resignation. "It's not like we can hold a news conference declaring our knowledge of the future. It's not that simple. But I have some ideas on how we can keep things from getting worse."

"Should I call Detective Manley?" Kate asks. "Ask him to notify authorities?"

Todd answers, "It wouldn't hurt. But I need to coach you on what to say."

"Always looking out for me," Kate replies.

"More like saving you from yourself." Todd takes a long swig of his drink.

***

Todd sniffs that the coffee in David's office smells burnt but says nothing. They've just returned from David's private high-end fitness center still dressed in shorts and tees sweat-soaked from their workout.

Both men are so engrossed in reviewing income statements that their environment is a trivial detail. Full-length picture windows frame the Upper East Side of Central Park, providing a vista of joggers, bikers, and roller bladers in miniature zipping around the park, moms pushing strollers, vagabonds raiding trash cans, and lovers lolling in the grass over a picnic.

Todd sits opposite David at a short table. Each is riveted to his laptop.

"The numbers are staggering. You're killing it, dude," Todd says without looking up.

"*We're* killing it."

A sudden serious thought distracts Todd. He breaks focus from the income statements. "That brings me to the next topic. 9/11."

David lifts his eyes, blinking as his mind shifts gears. "That's quite the segue." He glances at a wall calendar. "Fuck, that's this September. You have a plan?"

Todd closes his laptop and crosses his arms. "I do. I'm going to warn the authorities by mail. Letters to the White House, World Trade Center, Pentagon, United, American. Someone will pay attention. Let's hope."

"But they'll probably write you off as some delusional nutjob… Or shit!" David's eyebrows arch in alarm. "What if they think you're somehow involved?"

"Anonymous letters, bud."

"Still risky."

"I know. That's a chance I have to take." Todd's voice is solemn.

"What about calling the airport and Trade Center security, day of?"

"Yes, that's on the agenda. I'm buying a burner phone."

"Tricky shit, man. Making money is easy. Saving lives, not so much. I'm glad you've taken on that duty, not me."

***

Kate dials the pay phone and hangs up. Then dials again. Hangs up again. *Oh my God, this is going to sound truly nutso. If he didn't think I was certifiable before, he'll think I am now.* She finally lets the call ring through, clears her throat, and when Detective Manley answers, she announces herself. The stark warning about 9/11 spools from her mouth, she's rehearsed it so much. Detective Manley sounds amused. He asks her to repeat what she said, and Kate guesses he's recording the call. Too late, she realizes that she could be a person of interest if they don't succeed in thwarting the disaster.

When she's finished delivering her warning, Detective Manley laughs. "Listen, I have a feeling the Trade Towers are going to be just fine. Take care." He signs off with a good-natured chuckle.

Kate holds still with the phone still to her ear, not sure if he got the message. She hangs up with a sigh.

***

Lissa carries a snack tray of fruit and cheese into Todd's home office. He wears latex gloves and jabs with purpose at the keys of a vintage Underwood typewriter.

"Why are you using that silly old thing?" Lissa asks, teasing. "Oh, I know. Typewriters are hip now."

As she sets the snack tray on the desk, she notices various envelopes addressed to the Pentagon, Federal Bureau of Investigation, American Airlines, *New York Times*. She moves to read over his shoulder at what he's written. It's a smattering of words that she recites aloud, "Osama Bin Laden, 9/11, United Airlines, Al-Qaeda is planning—"

Todd looks up, startled, and dismisses her with a curt wave.

Sheepishly, she takes the plate and leaves. Returning to the kitchen, she stews in resentment at being a bit player in her husband's new future. She keeps tabs on him, noting that when he finishes each letter, he seals it in an envelope with tape, not saliva. He uses a moist sponge to wet the stamps, again avoiding saliva, before affixing them to the corners of the envelopes. He collects them in his briefcase and heads out to his car, to a mailbox, obviously. And he did all this without once removing his latex gloves.

***

Kate squeezes her coffee mug as if it's going to fly out of her hands if she loosens her grip. She's watching CNN on Lissa's TV. In the bottom right-hand corner, the date/time stamp is September 11th, 2001, at 7:30 AM.

"So far, so good." She flicks through channels.

From the kitchen, Lissa calls out, "Hey, want some cinnamon raisin bread? Toasted with butter? Real butter, not the fake stuff."

"Oh, I can't eat," Kate mumbles.

Lissa comes in from the kitchen, munching on toast and sipping on coffee.

Kate turns to her. "This could be a tragedy of huge proportions—the worst nightmare to traumatize New York City forever and trigger a war in the Middle East. It simply can't happen."

"I know," Lissa replies in a detached tone. "You've told me. Sounds like a Hollywood movie."

"If only." Kate stares at the TV as if it were possible that her intense gaze could prevent the tragedy.

***

Todd pulls his car over in an empty side street and makes the last of the fateful calls. He's on a cheap flip phone. He finishes talking, puts the phone on the floor in front of the passenger's seat, whips out a hammer, and demolishes the phone. He gathers the crushed pieces, jumps out of his car, and drops them down a street sewer. He returns to his car, peels off his gloves, and heads home. The day's events, or rather, what is supposed to transpire, spin through his head like debris in a tornado.

Arriving home, Todd bursts through the front door, out of breath. "Done. I called in bomb scares at the airports. I called security at the World Trade Center to evacuate. Who knows if they took it seriously?"

Kate's sitting on an armchair turned to face the TV.

Its sound is off, the screen shows a commercial for laundry detergent. She says, "Well, they have to. Don't they? I mean, they have to act on threats."

"You would hope," says Todd, resigned. He leans against the wall, feeling both spent and anxious. "Now we wait."

Lissa crosses the living room to hug Todd, but he gives her a half-hearted squeeze, wanting his sister to get out of his way.

Todd asks Kate, "What time is it?"

She reads her watch. "8:40 AM. Wasn't it, like, 8:50 Eastern time when the first plane hit?"

"8:46," Todd answers bluntly. "Six minutes from now."

Kate shivers and braces herself as if an explosion is about to happen right here in the living room.

Todd stands close to grip the back of her armchair.

"So far, so good," Kate says.

"I don't know if you know this, but you've said that like six times now."

"We're a bit stressed, Liss," Todd snaps.

Lissa turns towards him, her hands on her hips, seething.

Todd keeps his eyes on the TV. "You don't—"

"Oh, my God. Stop saying I don't understand!" Lissa heads for the kitchen. Todd hears a coffee cup slam in the sink. He is vaguely aware of her muttering, but he and Kate remain glued to the TV.

David sips a cappuccino and anxiously stares out the window of his living room. Angelika had wanted to make love, but he said he wasn't in the mood and left the bedroom to fire up the espresso machine.

Angelika slinks out of the hall in her silky champagne-colored robe. "What do you see, my love? A bird, a plane, Super—"

"Oh, nothing." He cuts her off. "It's just—"

Angelika approaches him from behind and kisses his cheek. "I ordered eggs and French toast," she whispers, tickling his ear with her words.

"We have a fridge full of food," he snaps. "I could make a scramble. It's not rocket science." David's focus remains fixed on the distant New York skyline.

"Who needs the mess?" She retorts as she slides her hands underneath his robe and caresses his chest. He tenses under her fingers. "Someone could use a massage. Do you want the Angelika special?"

David's eyes and ears suddenly prick up. He explodes out of his chair and runs to the window, placing his hands against the glass as if suddenly trapped. When he peers to the far left, he drops his coffee mug and it shatters, coffee spraying all over the hardwood floors and onto his cream-colored leather couch. "No… no, NO!"

Angelika shrinks from him, surprised by his outburst. "What the hell is going on?"

"Holy shit! It wasn't supposed to happen this way!" He picks up a cordless phone and in panic, punches a number.

"Who are you calling? What's happening?" Angelika demands, confused.

David had dialed the Bentons, but he's not surprised that Kate answers. "Hello? David. So far, so good?"

"It's fucking happening!" David retreats into the bathroom and closes the door. "Tell Todd we didn't stop it."

Kate then shrieks, a cry so loud it hurts David's ear, but he doesn't acknowledge the pain. He cracks the bathroom door open and shouts to Angelika, "Turn on the TV! Please, turn on the TV!"

David hears the TV click on and he emerges into the living room. Angelika stands silent, transfixed by what is happening on the screen. Though they are thousands of miles apart, David, Angelika, Kate, and Todd watch in silent horror as the news plays footage of a plane flying into the North Tower, erupting into a ball of smoke, flame, and carnage.

David and Kate hold their phone receivers in silence as the apocalypse unfolds. They don't bother saying goodbye when they hang up. It seems pointless now.

David, stunned, turns from the TV to follow the smoke billowing over lower Manhattan.

Angelika wraps herself around him. "Why would anyone do such a thing?"

"World Trade Center, a symbol of the power of the West and capitalist society. You know, banking, free trade, liberal values, free-thinking. I mean, when you're a pillar of freedom in the Western world, you're a target. They want to watch us burn."

He pulls her close as they watch the dreadful news.

***

At the Benton house, Kate huddles with Lissa on the couch, holding onto each other as if they might fly apart into tiny pieces if they didn't. They alternate between tears and outrage as the news plays and replays the instant of the World Center impacts, their fireballs, the sickening plume of black smoke roiling skyward. The news switches to a report on the Pentagon attack and the crash of Flight 93.

Todd paces. "FUCK! All four planes. We achieved nothing! Absolutely nothing. What good is this going back crap if you can't stop shit?" He gestures wildly, filled with fury and despair. Ever mild-mannered, always controlled, his speech is seldom salted with curse words, but no one else notices. The world has changed. Forever. Again.

"This can't be happening. I mean, is this really happening?" Lissa shakes her head as she blinks to take in the enormity of the tragedy.

The news footage repeats the towers collapsing,

crumbling in on themselves in clouds of smoke and ash. Lissa whispers, "How many people were in there? I mean, it's the start of a workday—right? We could be talking thousands..." Her words trail off and she breaks into sobs, leaning against Kate who tenderly strokes her hair.

Kate grasps for a shred of hope. "I pray they at least evacuated the towers."

Even though she and Todd have been through this before, it's no easier the second time, especially because they tried to warn the world and the world didn't listen.

Chapter 9

A month later, David and Todd sidle up to the bar in a posh New York hotel lounge that's a modern take on Art Deco—speakeasy-style—all leather, cherry, and pure sheen. The dazzling scene belies David and Todd's mood. They both stare into space past the bartenders who move in bursts, yanking bottles of booze, pouring glistening liquor into a neat row of cocktail glasses, mixing, garnishing, and pushing custom drinks toward customers and waitresses. The mixology is a blur as David and Todd grapple with their roles—rather lack of roles—in the greatest tragedy to befall New York City.

Todd takes a contemplative sip from his beer. "I thought I'd covered all bases."

David drinks a Third Degree with a lemon twist. "Why didn't I think to go over to World Trade and pull a fire alarm?" He rests his forehead in his hand.

"I know, right? Coulda-woulda-shoulda. I've lost my share of sleep."

"Makes you wonder, man. Is fate simply out of our control? Can we change only our own destiny?" notes David. "I mean, maybe mere mortals can't play God."

Leaning in, Todd adds, "I know this, Kate saved that boy. His fate changed. He's alive. She will, she hopes, save Matt, too."

"Oh, that's right. Shit. His accident," says David. "They're still dating and all good?" The question sounds leading to Todd.

"It's cooling off if that's what you're asking. You two haven't talked? She plans to be here with you by year-end," Todd says like that fate is sealed.

David purses his lips, then replies, "Ah, yeah. I'm going to need to push that back."

The bartender—dressed in a neat white shirt, with suspenders and a bowtie—approaches. He has long blondish bangs that he flips out of his eyes. "Another round, or are you good?" His accent is faux-British.

David holds an empty glass aloft and nods. He then says to Todd, "I'm dating someone. It's pretty sweet."

Todd inhales sharply through his teeth. His stomach lurches. "When you say, 'pretty sweet,' do you mean it's more than a fling?"

"Shit, man, staying on track ain't that easy, especially where gorgeous girls are concerned," says David. "Or rather, one girl."

"Angelika?"

David nods.

"I get it," Todd says. "Life can be complicated. Just talk to Kate at the wedding."

The bartender sets down the drinks.

David grins like he's shrugged off their earlier concerns. He slaps Todd on the shoulder. "Your sexy best man is looking forward to it."

Todd laughs. "Well, given that the groom is a handsome devil, the best man better make him shine."

They pick up their drinks and clink glasses, the liquid shimmering under the muted Art Deco lights.

***

It's a gorgeous, crisp November day in Austin, the leaves on the trees beneath the towering Fairmont cast in lovely shades of mustard, sienna, and scarlet. On the other side of the hotel, a cluster of palm trees stands above the expansive pool lined with white pool loungers and hotel guests nursing beverages. A blanket of vapor hovers over the heated water.

On the thirty-fifth floor, a hotel ballroom is packed with attendees sitting beneath crystal chandeliers casting lovely shadows across the room. Floor-to-ceiling windows frame a view of the Austin skyline with office high rises and lofts crowding the banks of the Colorado River. Fragrant arrangements of dusty rose and pale lilies decorate tables covered in white linen.

Lissa and her father stand outside the ballroom, Lissa fiddling with her bouquet. She's adorned in an ivory satin and lace off-the-shoulder dress with long matching gloves. She wears her hair in a curly bun with loose tendrils framing her face. "Do I look okay?" she asks her father.

"Are you kidding me? I've never seen a more beautiful bride." Then he leans in as if someone might be listening. "Don't tell your mother I said that."

Lissa smiles conspiratorially at her dad and their shared secret.

He kisses her cheek. "You're still my little girl even though you've grown into a lovely young woman."

Tears blur her eyes and she glances away to hide them. She shifts weight from foot to foot, her newly-bought wedding pumps still stiff and uncomfortable.

"Are you ready?" her father asks, almost as if he is and isn't simultaneously; he could just as well have been asking himself that question.

She nods. "Yes, Daddy. Just a little nervous."

"I've got you, sweetie." And he takes her arm in his.

When Mendelssohn's "Wedding March" begins, an usher opens the ballroom door. Lissa and her father proceed forward. An audible gasp accompanies the gazes sweeping toward them. Lissa advances down the aisle on her father's arm, her steps hesitant considering the momentous occasion. Dapper in his tuxedo, he beams with pride. Some attendees reach for their tissues and mop their eyes.

Todd waits at the back of the ballroom, next to the reverend. David stands beside Todd, and Lissa's older sister, Janette. Her maid of honor looks like a very pregnant version of Lissa. Richard, bearded, thirties, Janette's husband, is a groomsman. Kate and another friend are bridesmaids. Lissa glances at Todd, whose gaze is fixed on her, a prince who has never seen such a lovely princess. With each step, Lissa becomes steadier and more at ease in her wedding pumps.

At the threshold of where Todd is standing, Lissa's father halts and raises his arm. Lissa slides free, passing herself from one man to another. Todd lovingly squeezes her wrist before taking her hand. They face one another for an instant, electric with joy, then turn as one toward the reverend.

As the officiant, he reads his sermon and projects his moving words as competently as a stage actor. He makes a seamless transition to Lissa and Todd's vows. Janette hands Lissa a piece of paper and takes her sister's bouquet at the same time as David hands a piece of paper to Todd.

Lissa goes first, her hands trembling as she reads. Her vows promise adventure and partnership, humor, humility, grace, and wonder, but mostly love. Todd's promise to honor and support, listen, understand, and love with everything he's got. David and Kate exchange knowing smiles. Todd slips a delicate band of channel diamonds set in white gold onto Lissa's finger. The ceremony closes as the officiant says, "And you may now kiss the bride."

Todd goes for the same side as Lissa and they bang noses and crack up. The crowd laughs with them. They try again, and this time the kiss is perfect. They linger as if they never want the moment to end.

Todd looks up to the watching crowd and feels content. *Everything is as it should be.* His mom beams, looking radiant in her lilac mother-of-the-groom dress. Dad denies Todd eye contact, but who cares? Todd's gaze returns to his bride.

After the final blessing, the wedding party forms a receiving line, followed by champagne. Dinner includes a formal toast with a few randy anecdotes from David about Todd. The band strikes up the newlyweds' song, "The First Time Ever I Saw Your Face." Lissa rests her cheek on Todd's chest, and he rests his head on hers as they slow dance in a tight circle. If there's a dry eye in the room, it's not obvious.

The opening numbers fade away and the band plays a medley of high-energy dance tunes, and soon people are shaking, rattling, and rolling in their wedding best, many women casting their designer heels aside and dancing in their stockings or bare feet.

Kate walks up behind David. "Hey, handsome."

David looks Kate up and down in her dusty rose T-length dress with a sheer scoop neck. Nestled in the peek-a-boo cleavage, the necklace he'd given her sparkles invitingly. "Aren't you stunning as ever?"

"Oh, you say that to all the girls. By the way, Matt's not here." Kate cocks her hip suggestively. "His great-grandma is celebrating her ninetieth."

"Thank God for Matt's granny. It's my lucky day!" David exclaims in a mocking tone. He sets his gaze fully on her and lowers his voice. "Meet at my hotel later?"

"Aren't you being a little bit forward?" Kate play-acts coquettishness.

"Okay, how about this? I'd like to request the pleasure of your company at my hotel suite. I'll be serving champagne and David tartare," he says with a continental accent.

Kate says, "It is my honor to accept your invitation." And she curtsies. "How'd you know David tartare is my favorite dish?"

"Gentleman's intuition." Snapping out of character, David says, his tone flat and serious. "No guilt trip this time?"

"No, actually. I'm ending it soon. It's time."

"Oh, no rush on my account. I have my own 'baggage' to sort out. I need some more time."

The admission surprises Kate. In fact, it hurts a little. But she hides her surprise with a teasing, "Oh, you're dating, huh?"

He mugs an innocent look. "Nothing serious. I just want to do it right. Besides, I still have a fortune to make to

125

give my future wife a lavish life."

The words "future wife" snag her attention.

Graham walks up to Kate. "May I have this dance?"

"Why, of course, Daddy," says Kate, threading her arm through his. She looks back at David, his thin smile, and the way his brow is furrowed with uncertainty.

***

Nearly a year later, in 2002, when NASA Mars Odyssey maps Mars, Tiger wins the Masters, Elon Musk founds SpaceX, and Netflix goes public, Lissa and Todd are expecting.

Kate hosts a baby shower for Lissa, even though she thinks baby showers are a little silly. Kate promised Lissa if they played stupid shower games, they would be tongue-in-cheek and make the partiers laugh. Her theme is "Over the Moon." She decorates her place accordingly with moons and stars. She serves space-rocket cupcakes and lunar cake pops.

Lissa wears a mommy tiara, and her guests *ooh* and *ahh* while passing onesies, bibs, baby carriers, breastfeeding accessories, and all things baby. Lissa and Kate get a rare moment to themselves, both sipping a mommy mocktail.

"When do you think you'll take leave from work?" asks Kate.

"Probably the minute after the contractions start. I mean, my counseling clients don't stop having needs just because I'm going to pop."

Kate remembers what it was like last time around for Lissa. She didn't have such a focus on her career in psychology. Being more of a stay-at-home mom was easier for her, but maybe she's more fulfilled this time. *Why didn't she come back with us?*

Kate looks down at Lissa's belly and rubs it. "How sick are you of people rubbing your belly?"

Lissa lifts an eyebrow.

Kate continues, "I mean, no other time in life do we go up to someone and rub their belly. Kinda creepy if you think about it."

Lissa grins. "Oh, I don't mind. I think it's sweet. People say it brings good luck."

"So how are you going to pull Todd away from his superhero role of saving the world?"

"I'm pretty sure once he sees our little one, he'll fall in love, and the world will just have to wait."

"What did you say he was doing with the climate scientists?"

"He's at the National Oceanic Atmospheric Administration in Washington studying tsunami warning systems."

"Oh. OH!" Kate exclaims, realizing what Todd's up to. "The tsunami. That's right. I hope he has better luck."

"Todd said the very same thing. I still prefer not to know the future." Lissa changes the subject. "What's going on with Matt?"

"Well, I'm letting him go. It's not easy but it's the right thing to do." Kate remembers that David used almost the same exact words about letting go of his fling.

Lissa puts her hand on Kate's shoulder.

"I'm sure it's a tough decision. I see what a loving soul Matt is."

"True. But Liss, I'm not feeling it so much. It has run its course. Besides, my future awaits with David." Kate claps her hands and bounces on her seat.

"Todd said David just bought a huge estate on the Upper East Side," Lissa adds.

The news makes Kate blush with astonishment. "He did not!"

"Oh, God. You didn't know?"

"Noooo," Kate replies. "He must want to make it a surprise."

Lissa's expression becomes circumspect as though a secret is out.

Brianne, a bouncy-blonde from Lissa's work, approaches and asks, "When do the games begin and what are we playing?"

Lissa answers, "Okay, the first one is called 'What's in the Dirty Diaper?'"

Kate scrunches her face. "Gross."

Lissa laughs. "I love it... as long as it's not the real thing."

"No, no, it's cool. We put mystery ingredients, like say, Play-Doh, in a diaper and pass it around for people to smell and guess. People write down their guess, and the people who guess right win a prize."

The partygoers go into hysterics as they sniff and pass "dirty diapers" while Kate snaps pics. She is convinced that Lissa loves every minute of being queen for a day and never wants to remove her tiara.

***

Lissa walks hand-in-hand with Todd along a sidewalk in their neighborhood, the streetlights casting a warm glow on their faces. A dog barks urgently in the distance. Cars whiz by a little too quickly for a residential street, one sports coupe with the bass rattling so loud it shakes the ground as it passes.

"I think we could use some traffic mitigation around here. The *Drive Like Your Kid Lives Here* sign is worthless," says Todd. "I mean, this stuff is getting real."

Lissa rubs her blooming belly. "God, I couldn't imagine carrying twins like my sister."

"How is she doing? The boys are what, eight months now?"

"Ten months. They are so darned cute."

Suddenly, Todd stops walking and turns to Lissa, serious. "You should go see her."

"I thought we'd drive up for their first birthday."

"No. No. Go soon—like next weekend."

"You seem concerned. What's the rush?"

Todd feigns nonchalance. "I'm just saying go see Janette and the twins sooner than later. I'll be away at a conference anyway, so spend time with your sister. Get a few mommy tips."

"Like diaper-changing practice? Do I really want to start before I have to?" She laughs.

Todd takes her by the hands and looks lovingly at her under the moonlight. "You, Lissa Benton, are going to be the best mother there is. Trust me. I know a thing or two."

Lissa knows that he's hiding something. Probably to spare her feelings. With the pregnancy, she's got enough to think about. So she laughs to humor him and offers a kiss. He then picks her up to twirl her around. She squeals with delight.

With a groan, he sets her back down. "Whoa, we got an oversize load!"

"I know. I need a t-shirt. Good thing I'm driving, not flying to Houston." She cradles her belly. "They'd charge me for excess baggage."

Todd chuckles then gets serious. "You're carrying precious cargo. Her name is Stella."

"Oh, really? I love that name."

He kisses his wife tenderly.

***

When Lissa arrives in Houston, her sister seems preoccupied, but Lissa chalks it up to motherhood exhaustion. She dreads that part of what's awaiting her but pushes it out of her mind. Janette seems relieved to have her sister's company, probably so she has an extra set of hands and a loving heart to take care of her baby boys. Janette's home is messier than usual, toys strewn across the carpet, and dirty dishes and laundry piling up. Lissa gets busy tidying up and helping Janette with meals, diaper changing, story time, bedtime. It's not lost on Lissa that she's rehearsing for her new role.

The next morning, the twin baby boys crawl around and pull themselves up to the coffee table. They're bouncing with energy, drooling as they go, and trying to put things in their mouths. Lissa keeps running interference. She coos over them. "Could they be any cuter? You are so clever, Cole. Ben, can you stand up, too?"

Cole loses his balance and lands, *kerplunk*, on his diapered bottom. He looks surprised but not distressed. The other twin claps his hands. Lissa laughs out loud and looks up at her sister to see if she's enjoying the show.

Janette has slumped into an armchair, holding a cup of tea that she has yet to enjoy. She wears baggy sweatpants and her hair is tousled. She's deep in thought, zoning out on the cuteness of her baby boys.

"Janette, you seem... distracted. Is everything OK?"

Janette closes her eyes, sighs, and changes her expression to stoic. She sets her cup on an adjacent end table. "I'm fine." No sooner does she utter the words when Lissa notices her demeanor start to crack and then like a dam bursting, the tears gush forth. "Who am I kidding? Everything's NOT at all fine," Janette sobs through her words.

The surge of pain and grief startles Lissa and she rushes to comfort Janette. "What on Earth is going on?" Lissa crouches beside the chair to face her sister, searching for answers.

"Richard's having an affair." Janette's eyes roll toward the ceiling. "Well, he had an affair."

"Oh, my God! Really?" The question sounds trite but it's all she can say.

"Yup. Sad but true." Janette lowers her head and wipes her eyes, red and wet with tears. "With none other than his dental hygienist, Erin."

Lissa lifts an eyebrow. "Erin? The mousy girl you told me about?"

Janette gropes for a box of tissues on the end

table. "So cliché, right?" She waves a tissue and scoffs, her voice muffled by the snot in her nose. "Here, let me clean your teeth and give you a happy ending."

"Oh, dear God, Janette. I'm so sorry."

"Yeah, I got an anonymous letter in the mail, and when I asked Richard about it, he was so caught red-handed, he couldn't deny it. He swears it's over but God, it's painful." She blows her nose and explains in a resolute and pragmatic tone. "Oh hell, it's probably my fault. I'm so exhausted from these two." She points to the twins. "Honestly, sex is the last thing on my mind."

"I don't even know what to say to comfort you."

Janette sniffs, then narrows her eyes as she chuckles sardonically. "Is that what you say to your clients? Some therapist you are."

Lissa hugs her sister. "It's different when it's your sister. It's hard to be objective when you love someone."

Janette rests her head on Lissa's shoulder. "I guess even big sisters need their little sisters sometimes, right?"

"Always. I'm always here for you. We'll get you through this."

They glance at the boys, who have settled into playing blocks on the living room floor. The house, which earlier brimmed with a cozy family love, now echoes with betrayal and squandered affection.

Lissa clenches her teeth, furious at the treachery and equally furious with Todd for not saying anything about it.

Chapter 10

Surrounded by piles of documents and file folders, Todd drinks more coffee than he should this late in the afternoon. He vowed to stop drinking coffee after noon, but he can't resist. The more he drinks, the faster he works, and he loves riding the productivity buzz. Focused and invigorated about the growth of his business, the steep upward trajectory is smashing all business plan projections for the year. Todd furrows his brow as he studies reports and taps away on his Dell computer, which isn't moving as quickly as his mind or his fingers. Time travel has its advantages but traveling back twenty years is like going back several centuries in the tech world. He might as well be on a typewriter.

Todd hits the keys so hard and fast that the computer freezes. Frustrated, he grouses loudly, "Piece of shit! Can I have my Mac already?"

The door flies open and Lissa storms in, shoving the door behind her with a loud bang. She marches up to Todd, arms folded over her pregnant belly. Her seething glare could burn a hole through his forehead.

Todd's smile upon seeing his wife's mood quickly vanishes. "What the—"

"What the hell is right! Me not knowing—not wanting to know the future, I should say—is one thing," she says in an accusatory tone.

Todd knows the reason for her outburst. He leans forward, anchors his elbows on the desk, rubs his forehead with both hands, then rests his head in his hands as he searches for the right words.

"Why didn't you tell me about Richard's affair?" Lissa glares at him and, not waiting for a reply, shifts her gaze away in disgust.

"I feel we mustn't interfere with people's personal lives, and as you well know, my focus is on bigger, more pressing issues," Todd explains with his palms turned up.

Lissa tightens her arms around her belly as if protecting her little one. "Seriously, Todd? To me, that would be the most important part of knowing the future— preventing heartbreak among friends and family. You have no idea how she's suffering."

Lissa lets out a whimper, then quickly regains her rage. "I could have stepped in and warned her about Erin before anything ever happened and spared her the heartache. You might be Mr. Save the World, rescuing everyone but the people we care about most," she says snidely. And in a more reflective tone. "My sister is my world."

"I know, I know. But know this, too." Todd meets her gaze. "Janette and Richard work through this."

"Oh, they do?"

"Yeah," Todd nods. He smiles, "and Erin is history."

Lissa exhales, relaxes, and slides onto the edge of his desk. "Oh, thank God." She reaches for his hand in a peace offering.

He squeezes her hand, pleased that they've made it over another back-to-the-future tiff. "And they stay together and have a baby girl, Lily, when we have Miles," Todd says. No sooner does he grin than he realizes he's slipped again.

Lissa wrinkles her brow. "Miles?"

"Our second-born child." Todd inhales sharply and apologizes with his eyes. "Sweetheart, it's a slippery slope. I'm damned if I do, damned if I don't."

Lissa purses her lips, the wheels turning in her head. She softens. "I guess you're right."

Todd stands and moves around the desk to hug his wife from behind. She lets him snuggle in.

"So we have one of each. Nice." She wiggles against him. "A perfect little family."

Todd whispers in her ear, "Three of each."

Lissa exclaims in near horror, "What?" and turns to face her husband.

He grins broadly. "Gotcha!"

***

It's late morning on a Sunday, the time when most couples are either rollicking in bed, enjoying a scrumptious homemade brunch at the breakfast bar, or sipping freshly brewed coffee and planning their Sunday fun-day. But Kate told Matt she needed some alone time, so they spent the night apart.

When Kate hears Matt's signature playful knock on the door, her stomach clenches. She cried herself to sleep and was teary-eyed while drinking her morning coffee. She dreads this talk and wishes she could just fast forward to next week.

Kate can't escape the inevitable so reluctantly slides out of bed. When she opens the door, Matt moves in for a big bear hug and she stiffly absorbs the embrace.

She wears her hair in a messy topknot, and she's in baggy sweats with a sweatshirt that's three sizes too big. Her eyes are puffy and swollen.

"Whoa! I don't like the look of this," Matt says, his face scrunched in concern. "What's wrong?"

"We need to talk." She moves to the couch and taps it to indicate he should sit.

"Um, nothing good ever started with those four words. What did I do?" he says, looking confused.

She shakes her head, her eyes brimming with tears. "Oh, you did nothing, babe. It's me."

"Whatever I did, I'm sorry."

When he reaches for her hand, Kate takes a deep, determined breath. "I promised myself I would hold it together. I'm not doing a very good job so far. Am I?" She sighs. "I love and care for you deeply, Matt. I always will. But I no longer feel... like I'm in love with you."

Matt sucks in air and appears as if gut-punched. "Ouch. The old 'I love you but I'm not *in* love with you.'" He slides his fingers through his hair. "I had the vibe that you were pulling away but hoped I was just imagining it."

Kate can't help but cry and tears creep down her cheeks. She takes his hands. "Maybe I'm a fool to walk away. We're both so young. We have our whole lives ahead of us. I want to travel, experience the world before I settle down—"

"But travel is my middle name, I'm in flight school! We can do all the adventures you want... together."

Her heart wrenches. "I'm so sorry, babe."

He wipes away her tears, which only makes her cry more. "You gotta do what you gotta do. And I don't hate

you. I love you no matter what. You'll always be my Kate."
His voice cracks and he looks down. She's never seen him
this vulnerable. Gulping to compose himself, he raises his
head and meets her eyes. He points to his heart. "There
will always be a place in here reserved just for you... if you
change your mind."

*Damn, he's making this so hard. It would be much
easier if he was an asshole about it. Am I making a mistake
that I'll regret later?* "I'm so, so sor—"

Matt stops her apology with a kiss on her forehead.
He keeps his head rested on hers. Kate folds into him, and
they hold each other and brace against the pain.

***

Todd sports a beige half-zip flannel pullover and types at
his keyboard like an inspired pianist who's composing a
sonata on the fly. He bites his lip in concentration.

Ellen enters his office without knocking. They
had agreed to meet about some budget discrepancies
she discovered. She ribs Todd for his dad pullover and
matching dad demeanor. "You're like a hip Mr. Rogers.''

Todd tugs at the pullover and laughs. "If you see me in
a bright red cardigan, shoot me. Will you?"

"Ah, c'mon. Mr. Rogers is a decent man. We could use
a few more of those."

Ellen sits opposite Todd with the heels of her stilettos
staked into the carpeting, and her laptop balanced on the
tops of her thighs. She wears slim-fitting slacks paired with
a chic blazer. Within seconds, she's rivaling Todd's typing
pace on her keyboard. Todd is so pleased to have Ellen, the
financial wizard of the operation. While he provides the

vision and the leadership for the company, she deciphers the numbers like a psychic reading tarot cards, only she's dead-on accurate. He sometimes worries she'll be recruited away, so he makes sure to keep her happy with perks and bonuses.

After they work through the budget discrepancies, Ellen notes offhandedly, "Hey, there's new accounting software I think we should implement—" she doesn't glance up.

"QuickBooks. Yes."

Ellen abruptly raises her head to look at him. "Wow! You read my mind."

"One of my many talents," Todd says, pleased with himself.

"Okay, if you're so good, what am I thinking right now?" Ellen squints at him.

He closes his eyes, pretending to be tuning into her headspace. "Todd is a cocky son of a bitch."

Ellen bursts into laughter.

He figures his guess is right on the money. Todd laughs along with her, then his mood drops. He recalls a funeral, a procession of mourners. A woman whispers to another, "Such a tragedy. Gone too soon." A floral wreath frames a photo of Ellen perched high above a Norwegian fjord. Todd glances at her, trying to hide his grief.

"Why so serious?" she teases. "What does Mr. Telepathy see?"

"I think the world of you, and always have. I mean, I always will. It's just... I get the feeling something's... up. Like, not quite right... on the home front." Todd is deadly serious.

138

Noticeably startled, Ellen freezes. "Oh, you really don't have to worry. I'm sorry if I've given you the wrong impression. I am on top of it—"

"You would never burden me with your personal life. I get that but hear me when I say, I'm here for you."

Ellen stares back at Todd. Eventually, her eyes soften behind her professional demeanor, a fissure of vulnerability in her veneer. She snaps her laptop closed and hugs it tightly against her chest. "Thank you, Todd. I'm grateful to know that." Ellen rises and turns to go. "I'll get onto the new software."

"Great," he quips, certain that he's allowed too much. He watches her stroll across the carpet.

As Ellen closes the door behind her, Todd's secretary on the intercom says, "Mr. Stern on line one."

With that announcement, his mood lifts. Todd picks up the receiver, leans back in his office chair, and props his feet up on the desk. "Hey, man."

"Just a sec, Todd. I'm talking to the movers." David shouts, "No! No! The couches don't go there. They go in the study." He says to Todd, "Let me find a quieter spot. These guys might be the best movers in the city, but it's like the frigging circus came to town."

Todd laughs. "What's up?"

"Bro, I need a huge favor."

"You can't borrow any money."

They laugh.

"Seriously, though. Kate mentioned today she plans to move here in a month." David's voice is strained.

"Yeah, Lissa said as much. Exciting, man! Oh, speaking of moving, I got the pics of your new pad. Looks insane."

"Not too shabby. So, listen, I need more time before Kate moves here. I tried to say it when we spoke, but she's not hearing me," he says with urgency.

Todd analyzes David's situation. "Oh, okay. I'll talk to her. Tell her to slow it down a bit. How long do you need?"

"You see, it's complicated. I'm seeing someone, as you know, and I... I can't end it just yet."

"Gotcha. The sex is *that* good," Todd says.

"No. Well yeah, not only that but..."

"So, are we talking three months, six months?"

"A year would be great," David says tentatively.

Oh, crap. How will I break the news to Kate? Todd slides his feet off the desk and sets them on the floor. "Have you thought this through? I mean, this could really fuck things up."

"Relax, okay?" David replies defensively. "Yes, I have. No need to lecture me."

Cradling the phone against his face with one hand, with the other, Todd massages his temple. "Do you expect Kate to just sit around and wait? You do realize she could meet someone else in the meantime."

"Yeah, well, I guess it's a risk I have to take."

Todd swallows. He doesn't appreciate David's tone. "Don't mess this up, man. Don't play with my sister's heart."

"Dude, I know, but she's the one who told me to... She needed more time herself! I thought Angelika was just a placeholder, but it's become much more."

Todd sighs. "I'll see what I can do."

"Thanks, Todd. I owe you big-time."

140

"Later, man." Seems that even in this new past, David is still owing him. Todd sets the phone down slowly, dreading the conversation with Kate. *A year. Shit.*

***

Todd leaves work early to get the talk over with. When he shows up at Kate's condo, he's still wondering why the hell he got in the middle of this big mess. Like in the old future, David was always leaning on him for help. While standing outside her door, Todd pauses and thinks, *I should make David do his own dirty work.* But he feels his sister might take the news better coming from him. He inhales deeply and raps on her door.

She flings the door open, beaming. "Perfect timing. Want to help me spring clean?" Kate's place looks dismantled with boxes and books stacked against the hallway wall.

Oh, crap. "Someone's busy. I had no idea you were actually leaving."

Kate cocks her head, inviting him in. "Well, I'm already packing. Sorting what I will and won't take to New York." She drops to the floor to wrap some fragile objects in newspaper and arranges them in boxes marked CHARITY. "I'm so excited. OMG! Lissa showed me the listing on the estate," Kate says, wide-eyed.

Oh, fuck. "David's house."

"Amazing, right? He didn't send me the link. I guess he wants to surprise me!" She claps beneath her chin in glee.

"I need to talk to you about the move," Todd says gravely.

"What about it?" Kate asks, half-listening, and more focused on carefully wrapping a cherished keepsake. "You're jealous as hell?" She laughs.

Todd sits on the floor next to her, thinking that being at her level will make him appear more empathetic, ease the blow. "I don't know how to say this, but David doesn't want you there… not anytime soon."

"What?" She drops her fragile keepsake into the box. "Are you kidding me? I just gave up this place. The clock's ticking, I gotta be out by the end of the month. We," she circles a finger to encompass him, "all of us, are already four months behind schedule! Plus, I just broke up with Matt!"

Todd wants to say *David has royally fucked this up*. He's even tempted to advise Kate to unbreak up with Matt. But he says, "I'm sorry. I don't know what to say."

Kate crosses her arms and glares. "How much more time does he need?"

Todd rubs his forehead, like a killer headache is coming on. "A year," he mumbles under his breath and braces for her response.

"Oh, for fuckssake!" Kate hops to her feet and glowers. She clenches her fists and trembles, her face a livid red. "A year? A year!" she screams. "A year to do what? To keep banging that supermodel? That's bullshit!"

Yup. Pretty much.

***

Kate gasps as she peers through the wrought-iron fence of David's new estate.

The sweeping mansion is modern with a timeless

historic feel. A quaint bridge arches over a babbling brook with a tasteful fountain and impeccable landscaping.

I can't believe this house.

Whereas before she took the David chapter of her life for granted, now she holds onto the rails of the fence and feels robbed. She'd kept her end of every arrangement she'd made with David. She is owed this new future and all its treasures.

Okay, the fact that David has curbed her for this supermodel—supermodel my ass, fancy way to say gold-digging tramp—that did sting but Kate remains clear-eyed enough to recognize the stakes of this new life. Damn straight, she's going to fight for what is due her. She's incredulous that David's doing this to her—to them. She doesn't know which tack to take with him. Pleading will seem too desperate. Appealing to his rationality might not work given he's thinking with his dick. That leaves seducing him, which she's not much in the mood to do. She settles on humor and charm. Maybe a little flirtation. Perfect. Neither heavy-handed nor whiny. No one knew how to press his buttons better than her.

When she's ready, she presses the black button on the intercom by the gate.

A woman answers, "Stern residence. May I help you?" The voice puzzles Kate as it sounds too formal and cool to be the kind of woman David would be mixed up with. Must be the housekeeper.

Kate clears her throat, "Hello. It's Kate to see David."

"Who?"

Wow. So David has never mentioned her to his

housekeeper. The bastard. She clears her throat. "Kate Benton?"

"One moment, please."

She waits, taking in the grandeur of the house, imagining herself gliding from room to room, feeling like a princess, if she can lure David away from his lover du jour. She looks down at her loose top, jeans, and flats and belatedly realizes she's underdressed for the occasion.

The gate buzzes open. Kate saunters up the walkway and climbs the steps leading to the entrance, a huge door with beveled glass inserts. The door cracks open and a middle-aged woman in a black outfit with a starched white apron opens the door. Her helmet of dishwater-blond hair looks varnished into place and she wears thick-soled oxfords. "Mr. Stern will be right with you."

Kate smiles at her. "You must be Mitza."

The woman looks perplexed, starts to speak, and instead points to the left.

Kate steps into a foyer the size of her former Austin apartment. An enormous, sparkling chandelier hangs from the vaulted ceiling. Her eyes sweep in all directions, at the bouquets of glass flowers in antique vases, at the many bronze figurines, at the exquisite oil paintings presented in gilded frames, the picture window overlooking the garden. So stunned by the opulence, all she can think is *WOW!*

The foyer leads to a wide stairway that sweeps from the next floor. David appears and begins to descend. At first seeing him, Kate can hardly contain herself. She imagines them as newlyweds, with piping music, coming into the foyer and dancing under this dazzling chandelier. Maybe even naked!

She studies him. His shirt fits close to a trim middle and his leather slippers slap the marble steps. He looks fit and glows with confidence, but even so, his gaze darts about, and avoids eye contact.

When his feet reach the floor he says, "I've got this, Mitza. Thank you."

The housekeeper excuses herself and vanishes.

"Nice to see you, Kate. Todd said you might show up," David shares with an unfamiliar formality.

"Apparently, I'm here a year too early, huh?" she asks rather pointedly. She feels awkward, as if David isn't David but a landed gentry parading around this manor. She straightens her posture, holds her head high, and tries to proceed from the foyer toward an adjacent hallway as if this place is hers. But the moment feels off like she's intruded into someone else's reality. Her toes snag the edge of a carpet runner and she nearly trips over her own feet. Before she face-plants, she catches herself. David remains somber.

"You're acting strange," says Kate. She hopes for any sign of reassurance from her once and future husband. "Hello? Earth to David!"

"Settle down," says David, not at all settled himself.

The condescending tone infuriates her. Kate balls her fists at her sides. "Settle down? That's the best you can do? I will not settle down until you tell me what the hell is going on. Here, I'll make it easy for you. Just give me a date so I can plan my move and my life and don't tell me it's in a year."

David says nothing and looks toward the picture window and to the gazebo outside, then back at Kate. She searches his face in desperation for any sign that things are still okay. He stares at her blankly.

She feels herself crumbling. "Please, God, no, don't do this... I mean, you have a chance at a re-do, and you're going to make a mess of our lives?" she shouts, then more softly, asks, "What are you thinking, David?" Tears well in her eyes and flood down her cheeks, the pain scorching her wounded heart.

Turning back to the window, he plays with the big gold watch on his wrist and finally says, "I'm truly sorry, Kate. I've changed course. I don't know what else to say... I'm headed to where I am meant to, this time around, and I—"

"Screw you and where you think you're headed! You think you have it all figured out, huh? Now that you're Mr. Big Shot, you're too good for me. Is that it? I have news for you. You're killing us and our future. You're killing Jack!" Kate is certain that the mention of their future son would knock David off his pedestal.

His face remains a stoic mask. "I've thought about that, and it pains me. Truly it does, but we have to consider the present. Where we both are, right here, right now."

The rage gushes from her. "Don't patronize me! Oh, my God, where have you gone?" She wants to grab him by the shoulders and shake the sense back into him. "Where is my husband?"

Just as he is about to speak, his eyes cut over her shoulder. Kate turns and through a door in the hallway, a woman—who else but *Angelika*—tall, beautiful by any measure, sleek and slender despite a rather protruding tummy, struts in on designer heels, shopping bags swinging from both hands. Her swollen belly is impossible to miss; her dress is form-fitting, almost as if her pregnancy is on display.

"What's going on in here?" Angelika halts, glancing first at David and then at Kate. Her eyes narrow. "Who are you?"

Kate is stunned to her core. Frozen in shock. Slowly, her nerves begin to fire, and bit by bit, the world clicks into place. "Ohhhh, I get it."

She backs away from David and races out of the house. She doesn't even remember running to the nearest busy street to hail a cab. Once in the backseat and cocooned from the outside, Kate surrenders to her anguish and howls gut-wrenching sobs. She's so turned inside out, she's unable to even catch her breath.

The driver watches her through the rearview, his dark eyes hesitant but sympathetic. Over the back of his seat, he offers a box of tissues. "I am sorry, miss," he says in a thick Jamaican accent. "Are you okay?"

She nods unconvincingly through the tears. The cab motors forward. She dries her eyes in the reflection of the side window, her thoughts a maelstrom of hurt and confusion. When they cross the Manhattan Bridge, a spasm of despair, humiliation, and anger rips through her. She rolls down the window, the humid air reeking of exhaust, yanks off her necklace—the one David gave her a year ago—and hurls the stringed jewels.

Chapter 11

Six months have passed since Kate learned about David's baby with Angelika and although she's not over it, she's trying to move on with her life. She is convinced that there is bad juju clouding David's relationship with Angelika, so their baby will not contain the soul of her baby, Jack. *David's gonna suffer for this*, she thinks. There's nothing more she needs to do.

The bank transfers keep rolling in from the Stern Trust. It's enough to mean Kate will not need to work this time around, something she is sullenly grateful for. Despite Kate's façade of resignation, the anxiety and rejection weigh on her. She wears baggy flannel PJs to hide the twenty pounds she's gained.

She's in Todd and Lissa's kitchen waiting impatiently for the stove timer. TV news drones on in the background. The timer pings. She dons oven mitts to haul steaming hot cinnamon buns from the stove. Inhaling their aroma and barely waiting for them to cool, she swaddles one in a napkin and heads to the nursery.

The nursery is white and gray with splashes of color. The wall behind the wooden cradle is stenciled with adorable jungle animals—an elephant, a giraffe, a rhino, and a tiger. Stars and a crescent moon adorn the ceiling.

Lissa sits in a rocking chair, cradling and breastfeeding Stella, her five-month-old baby girl. Stella, with rosy cheeks, a button nose, and a full head of shiny dark hair, suckles sleepily, occasionally dozing off in the middle of her breakfast.

Looking her up and down Lissa asks meaningfully, "How *are* you doing?"

"What choice do you have when someone rewrites the movie script you're starring in? You've got to play the new part, right?"

Lissa sighs. "Doesn't seem fair. I'm sorry you're going through this."

Kate nibbles at the pastry's gooey icing. "Girl, get a bun while they're hot!"

"No, thanks. I don't want to ruin my appetite for lunch."

Kate pokes back. "Your loss. You know, while I was waiting for the buns to come out of the oven, I was watching the mid-year in review. I forgot what a doozy of a year 2003 was. I mean, has been so far. Saddam Hussein is toast, the Iraq War started, and we lost the Space Shuttle Columbia."

"And Stella was born!" adds Lissa. "This is my big event of the year." With that, Lissa ends the feeding, buttons her blouse, and lifts her baby to eye level, kissing her nose.

Kate smiles. "You're doing the most important work there is—propagating the human race. I can't wait to advance my own gene pool." She sighs, then takes a bite of the pastry. "If it ever happens."

"Oh, it will," Lissa says, gazing at Stella adoringly.

"Hey, I'm thinking about getting a tattoo on my right arm." Kate points with the bun while chewing a mouthful. "Just Chinese characters."

"Really? That say what?"

"'No matter how hard the past, you can always begin again.' It's a quote by the Buddha." Kate takes another big bite.

"What if you get sick of it?"

Kate holds up a finger. *Gimme a sec.* She swallows and replies, "I won't. And I figure it's a good reminder for getting through hard times." Kate stuffs the last bit of bun in her mouth. She wipes her lips with the napkin and flattens it on her shoulder. She approaches Lissa and Stella. "Bella Stella, is it time for burpies?"

"I think so." Lissa stands and hands the baby to Kate. "Thank you, aunt extraordinaire. I love having you here."

Kate places the baby on her shoulder, "Ha! Todd would never say that. He always blames me for drinking *his* brew."

Lissa laughs in agreement. She fluffs her blouse. "I cannot wait to take a shower! It's amazing the things you look forward to when a little urchin takes over your life!" She heads out of the nursery.

Todd appears in the doorway, just back from his daily run. He's dressed in a t-shirt and workout shorts stained with sweat. "Good morning."

"Speak of the devil. It's the coffee police!" snorts Kate, while patting Stella's back.

Todd ignores her remark as he steps in to lean over and kiss the top of Stella's head. He inhales deeply. "New baby smell is so divine, isn't it? If someone figures out how to bottle and sell it, they'll make millions."

"I'll get right on that," agrees Kate.

Stella burps loudly and startles herself.

"Oh, that's my girl!" Kate exclaims.

Todd moves over to the changing table and is suddenly serious. "So, David's wedding is next month."

Kate gives him a cold stare. "Did you have to remind me?" She shifts her gaze from Todd. Resolute, she declares, "Book Mom to stay with Stella."

"Um, sure. You're going somewhere?"

"Yes, as a matter of fact, I am," Kate says proudly and with an air of mystery.

She places Stella in a baby swing. "There you go, baby girl." Kate looks up at Todd. "I'm taking a trip. Remember the book *Eat, Pray, Love*?"

Todd pauses, thinking. "Yes... but I don't think it's come out yet."

Kate shrugs. "Whatever. I'm taking a trip to India. To find myself and find a new path."

"That's great to hear." He shares a brittle smile. "Your new past isn't unfolding like we thought it would."

"So true. But no matter, we adjust." Kate pretends she's singing into a microphone and breaks into a song by Destiny's Child, "I'm a survivor. I'm not gonna give up. I'm gonna work harder..."

Todd laughs out loud as Kate waltzes out of the nursery.

***

David and Angelika's wedding goes without a hitch. The guests drink and toast on the 100th-floor rooftop patio, enjoying New York City's majestic vistas. Manhattan sparkles as the sun dips below the horizon, and the slivered moon makes its debut.

Angelika looks gorgeous in a sexy sleeveless lace wedding dress. The plunging neckline shows a hint of front and side boob—teasing yet tasteful. The dress exposes her slender, tanned back, and hugs her shapely hips and bum before flaring into a modest taffeta train. No extra post-pregnancy pounds on her.

The bride basks in the attention of her girlfriends while her six-month-old son Anton, spiffy in a pint-sized tuxedo, is paraded around by his nanny and adored by guests.

Todd and Lissa stand near David, each drinking a flute of champagne.

David holds his flute aloft. "That was an awesome speech. Not sure you needed to mention the pant-zipper story. Nice one, bro."

"Just doing my job and returning the favor of what you said at my wedding. By the way, your zipper is down." Todd stares at David's pants.

David glances down and sees that all is right with the world. "Ah, you got me!"

The two men laugh.

Lissa rolls her eyes at the guy humor, then says, "So, you haven't told us yet. Where's the honeymoon?"

A blond server, dressed in black, tops off their champagne.

"St. Bart's. We'll spend a few nights on a private yacht, and then in a rented villa on a secluded beach for several days. It was her pick."

"Oh, really?" Lissa replies. "That was my pick, too, but I was vetoed. We did a staycation because somebody said it was too extravagant. I mean, who does a staycation for a honeymoon?" Lissa skewers Todd with a pointed look of indignation.

David shakes his head. "You know your hubby. He has always been tightwad. I don't think that will ever change, Liss. Sorry."

"Unlike some people I know." Todd sips champagne. "I have more sense than money."

***

Kate has settled into life at the Sivananda Trivandrum Ashram, a retreat in the tropical foothills of Kerala, in southern India. Devotees practice yoga in the garden, performing sun salutations in the beating sun. Another group chants softly in the distance, the music of the harmonium blending with rising and falling voices. Goats and chickens roam freely on the property but steer clear of each other. Butterflies weave in and out of the marigolds and lotus flowers.

Kate crouches in loose Indian-style yoga pants and a t-shirt in a garden of pungent herbs and edible flowers. This early in the morning, she's already drenched in sweat from the humidity. But no matter, the sensation makes her feel one with nature. Everything here is so rich in color and aroma. She sees herself as slim and radiant, her skin glowing from the sunshine and a clean vegan diet.

Her forearm reveals the tattoo she promised herself. Kate trims mint leaves, inhales the fresh scent, and hands the sprigs to her spiritual counselor and yogini, Saavni, who kneels next to her. He brings a basket. Like her, he is barefoot. Saavni is dressed in a white linen tunic and pants with strands of Mala beads around his wrists. A gentle smile glows bright against his dark complexion.

"We are not human beings having a spiritual experience, we are spiritual beings having a human experience," Saavni says, sampling a mint leaf.

"I have indeed come to learn that, Saanvi. I feel so grateful to you and this community for reminding me of what matters most." She stands. "Back home, it's so easy to get caught up in the rat race, trying to keep up with the Joneses. But when all is said and done, neither the Joneses nor I get to take anything with us to the next life."

"The Joneses?" he perks an eyebrow, places the basketful of herbs on the ground, and rises to meet her eye-to-eye.

Kate laughs. "Oh, it's just an expression that means we compete with our neighbors to have all the creature comforts of life."

"Ah, yes." He cocks his head. "Because we are all on separate paths, comparing yourself to anyone else is pointless. It would be like a mountain comparing itself to an ocean—one is motionless, grand, and majestic, the other vast, deep, and in constant motion. And, as for creature comforts, they just add to the illusion that we don't suffer and die. No amount of comfort will change that fact. So, we must surrender to our mortality. And by doing that, set ourselves free."

"I'm going to miss you and this place so much. You have no idea," she says, touching her heart.

"I think I do. But remember, we are not separate. That is also an illusion."

Kate nods once. "Yes, yes, it is."

"I have watched you evolve, bloom like a lotus over these past two months. I think you're ready for your next journey."

"I think so, too. *Bahut Dhanyavaad.*"

He plucks a plumeria flower from a nearby bush and offers it to her. She curls her fingers around the petals and inhales the sweet-smelling tropical scent. Saanvi places his hands on hers.

She bows her head. "Namaste."

"Namaste."

Kate glances up at Saanvi, who wipes away her tears of joy.

***

Kate leaves the ashram feeling gorgeous from the inside out, surrounded by friends who offer farewell embraces. Children huddle around her to give flowers. She enters a taxi and waves goodbye. During the ride to the Trivandrum Airport, she reflects on what awaits her. While Kate explored a new dimension of herself, the world as she knows it carried on. She learned from infrequent phone calls that she's coming home to a niece who's now curious and crawling. A brother whose business is booming. A sister-in-law who is intent on expanding her family.

Todd filled her in on David's lucrative deals and financial success but also the negative developments on the domestic front. David doesn't approve of Angelika's carte blanche approach to her lifestyle. She frequents Chanel and Givenchy and treats herself to regular ninety-minute in-home massages while the nanny watches her son.

Having had a personal shift in India, she thinks, *David's drama is not my problem*, and she feels relieved. Before this trip, she would've secretly cheered his misery. Now, she sloughs it off. Despite the painful shame that he inflicted on her—it was almost as if David enjoyed rubbing her nose in the humiliation—she looks back on the episode as a necessary step in the process of discovering herself.

She knows that for one person, the world stopped while she was on her quest. Matt patiently tended a torch while she went to find herself, not knowing if there would be a place for him when she returned. He said it so beautifully in his letters to India. At the time she'd broken up with Matt, she would've told him to get on with his life. Actually, he had. Just as she had done. Now their lives were converging again, only a little further along. When she sees Matt in his pilot's uniform at the airport, she runs and throws herself in his arms and kisses him like it's the first time.

A month later, Matt and Kate have dinner at UCHI Japanese Restaurant. They hold hands at a corner table after a dinner of Asian fusion delights and sake. A waiter delivers coconut and mango sorbet to share.

Kate finishes telling him more about life at the ashram. "I'm sorry. I think I went on too long. It was just so incredible and have so many stories!"

"I'm so relieved." Matt exaggerates a *whew!* "I thought you were going to tell me you fell in love with your guru."

"Oh, please. That's so damned cliché. My spiritual teacher was amazing and thankfully not one of *those*

156

gurus."

"Haven't you heard, when you love something, set it free. If it comes back to you, it's meant to be."

Kate smiles. "I have heard that, yes. I used to think it was a trite way of rationalizing a breakup. Now I realize the wisdom to it." She dips her spoon into the sorbet and slowly relishes the icy sweetness. "I learned a lot about myself while away. I was able to distinguish between the things that really matter and the BS."

"Uh-oh. Hope I'm not in the BS column."

Kate waves the spoon. "Are you kidding me? I so love having you back in my life."

Matt holds her gaze and gets serious. "Marry me, Kate."

She drops her spoon, missing the sorbet dish and in trying to recover the spoon, she topples her empty sake glass. "Oh my God." She scrambles to stop the glass before it rolls off the table. "What?" The glass saved, she looks at Matt. "I mean, yes, of course!"

They laugh and hold hands.

"Yes, yes, yes!" Kate cozies up to him.

Matt cups her cheek, and they passionately kiss.

***

The morning sun radiates through the skylights in the Sterns' expansive master bedroom. Skylights are an expensive luxury in Manhattan's high-rise market; it means you have the big bucks to splurge on top-floor real estate, which to David, is precisely the point. From the closet, where he slips on his slacks, David says, "I love

157

waking up to natural light. It's the best alarm clock there is."

Swaddled in alpaca designer blankets and 1,000-thread-count cotton bedsheets, Angelika lifts her sleep mask and squints against the cascade of sunlight. "It's too damned bright in here. My mask doesn't even begin to do the trick. I'm going to order some blackout shades." With that, she rolls over and puts a pillow over her face.

David walks to her side of the bed, fiddling with his tie. "You know you have a son who wakes up at 5:30, right?" Asking the question upsets him and, frustrated, he undoes his tie with a jerk.

Angelika groans, "That's Mitza's job. She gets Anton up and fed. No big deal."

Redoing his tie, David says, "Actually, it is a big deal. You barely take care of your own child. It's shocking and frankly borders on neglect."

With her perfectly manicured nails, Angelika flips him the bird and she sits up in bed, twisting her hair into a messy bun.

David moves closer to savor her expected reaction. "You know what's also shocking? Your credit card statement. Do you realize you spent $36,000 last month?"

Angelika throws him a defiant look.

David continues, "Just an FYI, I put a ceiling on it. Your new spending limit is $20,000."

Angelika swivels out of bed, jumps to her feet, and snarls. "Go to hell!" You've got more money than you know what to do with and now you set some arbitrary spending cap just to piss me off. Everyone I know has nannies 24/7,

158

and they spend whatever they like." She furiously pulls on a kimono-style silk robe and yanks it closed.

"Hey, maybe if I see you acting more like a mother, oh, and a wife, I might change my mind." David turns for the door.

Angelika, complexion flashing red with rage, picks up a vase of fresh flowers from her bedside table and hurls it at David. He artfully dodges it. The vase hits the wall and smashes into pieces, the flowers fly, and water stains the carpet.

Staring at the bouquet carnage and the scarred drywall, David says, "Make that $15,000."

Angelika lunges towards him. He doesn't resist and lets her shove him out of the room. "Get out. Go! I fucking hate you!" She slams the door in his face.

David stands in the hallway, chagrinned by the way everything between them has gone sideways. He says to the door, "Now it's $10,000."

Angelika's scream pierces the door and reverberates throughout the apartment.

Chapter 12

It's early evening and the Benton corporate headquarters is quiet, except for Todd furiously clicking away at his keyboard, adding the finishing touches to a project proposal due to a client tomorrow. Todd arches his neck and cracks his knuckles over his head, realizing that his back is sore from crouching over his keyboard for hours. It's a bit of a rush job, but he's pleased with how it came out. He'll have Ellen review it before sending it out.

With that thought, Todd has a sudden realization. A memory from the future hits him with a grim hospital scene, an unconscious and sedated Ellen with thick bandages on her wrists from a suicide attempt. She usually succeeds at everything, but thank God, she failed that time.

Shaken by the memory, he hurries into her office. If he is to stop the tragedy, he must act now.

Ellen looks gaunt, hunched over her keyboard while her hands aren't moving. She stares blankly at her computer. It's so unlike her to not be razor-focused and moving at a mile a minute. Not today. She clearly has something weighing on her mind.

He knocks on the door jamb to get her attention.

"Oh, Todd," Ellen says, caught off-guard, blinking hard a couple of times.

"I just sent you the proposal," he says, though to pass along that reminder is not why he's here. Continuing the pretense, he asks, "Would you have time to look at it tonight?"

"No problem." She straightens her slumped posture. Her words sound positive, but her lackluster tone is unconvincing.

"Is everything okay?"

Ellen acts surprised by the question. "Yes, of course."

Todd decides at that moment to cut to the chase since he knows how her life will soon play out and not for the better. He stands directly in front of her desk. "I worry about you."

She looks at him, her eyes misty.

"Ellen," he says to prompt a response.

Neither utter a word for what seems like a minute.

Todd rubs his hands together as though he's searching for just the right words. "I have this gut feeling things are rough on the home front—"

Ellen interrupts, her voice sanguine. "You know marriage. Who called it a tomb of love?" She pushes out a half-laugh and a sad smile.

"Like I said," Todd continues, "I really feel you're facing a challenge. It might be good to talk to somebody."

She sighs. "It's not *that* extreme. I'll be fine." She crosses her arms over her chest and tightly hugs herself. She stares at him with a blank expression, then drops her gaze to the computer screen and pretends to focus on her work.

Todd thinks, *Ellen really needs help. This is no time to be delicate*, and pulls a chair from another workstation to roll it beside her desk. He rotates her chair—her reaction is passive as they sit face-to-face.

He means business. "When I say you have trouble

on the home front, I'm talking about domestic abuse. But not physical, emotional. I know that emotional abuse is just as bad. You're putting up with that abuse for the sake of your marriage, but you have to consider that your well-being is more important."

Ellen drops her mask of overachieving perfection. She gazes at Todd, vulnerable, raw. "You're right... you're absolutely right." She appears as if she's trying to find equilibrium.

Todd realizes he has been holding his breath and releases it. "Lissa has an associate you should meet with. Talk through your troubles."

Ellen stays quiet.

Todd forces the issue. "Promise me you will."

Ellen nods, tears now escaping from her eyes. "I will. I promise." She plucks a tissue from a box on her desk. She looks up at Todd. "And thank you."

***

David plays with his son on the floor, who giggles every time his dad makes up a silly voice for each of the animal finger puppets. "Again," says Anton. "Again." And he erupts in a belly-laugh and slaps the floor like his dad is the funniest person on Earth. David doesn't know who's enjoying it more—him or his little buddy in stitches.

A butler enters with the phone, almost apologetically. "Sir, Todd Benton calling. Do you want me to tell...?"

David rises from the floor. "I'd better take it."

On cue, Mitza sweeps into the room and scoops up

Anton for his bath.

He reaches for David. "Dada! Dada!"

"See you after your bath, buddy." David takes the phone and heads to the kitchen to raid the fridge. "Bro! How're things in the Benton-verse?" He peruses the shelves for a snack.

"Just shuffling papers, pretending to work while the little lady cooks baby number two," Todd says, laughing.

"Dude—the pretend non-workaholic. You're not fooling anyone." David pulls out slices of cheese and salami and places them on the counter. Then he pours himself a bourbon, neat.

"Life's good. Who are we to complain—right?" Todd replies. "Hey, do you have suggestions on where to stay when I fly up next month? I want to try somewhere new. Maybe something boutique-y."

David arranges the cheese and salami into bite-sized stacks and wolfs them down. "How about something David-y, like my place? I'm sort of bach-ing right now," he says, trying not to sound like he's chewing a mouthful of food.

"Angelika's away?"

"Yep. She's away, all right." David laughs sardonically. "As in, she packed up and left." He picks up his glass of bourbon and heads to the couch, sipping as he goes. He loves the first burning sip that sends a wave of tranquility through his body.

"Wow. That's a shock."

David sees no need to sugar-coat the obvious. "Yeah. It's pretty much a screw-up."

The conversation goes quiet. David stares at his glass and considers downing it with one swallow.

Todd finally says, "I guess you can fill me in when I see you. Just shows you—life isn't easily navigated, even when you get a second chance."

"Damn straight. I sometimes wonder if what I'm doing is better than the first time around. The stress is no different. I really blew it with Kate. I think about that all the time now. I'll have to make it up to her somehow. There's got to be a way we can return to our scheduled program." He jokes, but he's not really joking.

Todd pauses and sighs. "David, man, Kate's moved on."

"Huh?" He sets his drink on the coffee table.

"She's engaged."

The news makes David's inner compass start to spin. He thinks, *Wow*, then repeats it when he says, "I mean, wow, good for her. Matt's the lucky fella, I take it?"

"No, she fell for the mailman."

"What?" David's inner compass spins faster.

Todd replies, "Of course, it's Matt. They actually seem really happy. Listen," Todd puts an edge to his tone, "I warned you that this could happen. But did you listen?"

David stares blankly at a Warhol painting of neon-colored donuts he bought at a Christie's auction. He fell in love with it, but at this moment, he thinks it's the gaudiest thing ever. It reminds him of how he "fell in love" with Angelika, who turned out to be the worst choice ever. It makes him realize that you can't trust falling for things and people. *Damn it! Shouldn't I have learned this lesson already with my knowing-the-future advantage?*

He considers this new future, which has become a labyrinth of unexpected turns and unwelcome surprises. "Anything else?"

"Nah, good buddy. Thought you should know. See you soon. Take care, man." Todd signs off.

David hangs up and retrieves his glass of bourbon. He finishes the drink in one gulp, leans his head against the back of the couch in surrender, and sighs. *Leave it to me to fuck things up.*

***

Kate is with Matt, Todd, and Lissa enjoying an elegant dinner at the Driskill Grill Restaurant in Austin. They're each nibbling on a Nova Scotia lobster galette from the chef's tasting menu.

Kate can't wait to share her news with Lissa and Todd but she's waiting to see if they notice her off-white beaded bridal dress. She realizes she might have to give them another clue.

In the meantime, Matthew takes up the slack in the conversation, explaining proudly as he does so, "I fly modified Boeing 757-200s. DHL has had a fleet of these for two years. I love flying them. Just love my job." Matt takes Kate's hand and smiles at her as if to say, I love you, too.

Todd says, "Good for you, Matt. Too many people make the mistake of not choosing a vocation that makes them happy. As you say, you gotta love what you do or what's the point?" Todd rubs his fingertips to pantomime money. "When you're just working for the Benjamins, it can make you pretty miserable."

"I loved being a social worker until life got in the way. But I love this even more." Lissa caresses her blooming belly. Todd leans in for a smooch. Lissa returns his kiss and then studies Kate's appearance. "That's a lovely dress. The beading's so intricate."

"I'm glad you noticed. It's new." She glances at Matt, then turns back to Todd and Lissa. "And it comes with this." Kate reaches into her purse, pulls out a short veil, and drapes it on her head. She glows underneath her veil.

Todd and Lissa exchange surprised glances.

"Wait. You two got married already?" asks Lissa.

"Hit the courthouse this afternoon." Matt beams with pride as Kate snuggles up to him.

Todd gives Matt a high-five. To Kate, he says, "Didn't you feel like having a big ceremony and all that?" He mouths "this time" so only she can see.

Kate winces at the memory of her wedding to David. *Did he have to bring that up?*

"Weddings are overrated," she responds, keeping her tone mild with some effort.

Lissa offers a toast. "To a lifetime of happiness!"

"And great sex!" Kate chimes in.

Todd raises a hand. "TMI."

Everyone around the table laughs and clinks their glasses.

"Even though we did the drive-through wedding thing, we're planning a celebration back home to keep Mom and Dad happy," says Kate.

"You're smart," Todd replies. "I told Lissa, as she planned ours, 'Just wait and see. After ten years more than a third of the wedding guests won't even know you.'"

"I know, right? Like Dave—ah, what was I saying?" Kate says.

Todd jumps in. "Never mind. I agree with you. Waste of money."

They all shift and avert their eyes during the awkward pause.

Kate breaks the silence. "Oh, we have photos. Some are serious. Others are totally goofy." From her purse, she quickly pulls out a stack of photos taken at the courthouse. "Check out this one where he's posing with my veil."

"Oh, you make a lovely bride, Matt," says Lissa, giggling.

***

David, Todd, and sharply dressed board members of the Stern Corporation wrap up their meeting. Everyone is downright giddy over the company smashing quarterly earnings projections. The other eight attendees leave the conference room comparing notes about upcoming European travel plans.

David and Todd return to sit at the long, shiny table with its box of donuts and pyramid of uneaten half-sandwiches.

David's shirt tugs at the buttons around his mid-section, which is thickening from stress-eating. The donuts taunted him throughout the meeting. So far, he has resisted their siren song, but he feels himself weakening. "Did I tell you who I had dinner with last week?"

"A hot date?" guesses Todd, smiling.

"Ha! Hardly. Jeff Bezos."

"Even better than a hot date! Seems like a solid guy," Todd says, sipping from his Styrofoam cup of black coffee.

David munches a half-sandwich as he talks. "He's a little full of himself, but that goes with the territory. Oh, you'll love this. I suggested he look into electronic books. I told him, 'I'm just throwing a bit of kindle on the Amazon fire. Something to think about.'"

"Whoa! Nice."

"I could see the cogs turning!" David grabs another half-sandwich.

"My cogs have been turning, too. We've got major events coming up. First one, the Houston Super Bowl shooting. Remember the lone gunman who killed ninety-two people?" Todd says.

David jots down, *Super Bowl Feb—Patriots $* on a legal pad. "Oh yeah. Wasn't he a Colts fan pissed about their semi-final Patriots' loss?"

"A little more than that. Disgruntled fans don't go on a murder spree."

"For sure the guy went cuckoo. I like a good game as much as the next guy, but some people take their sports way too seriously," says David, finishing his lunch by surrendering to a glazed donut.

"'Bad Call Made Him Make a Bad Call' was the headline. Anyway, we've taken measures, Kate and I, to bring attention to that."

"Way to go," David says, half-interested in Todd's good works. "How's Kate?" he asks, looking slightly pained but trying to cover it up.

"Married. She and Matt went to the courthouse last week."

David struggles to conceal his disappointment. "It's ironic. I was at the divorce 'court' last week too." He shakes his head. "Gotta watch out for those beautiful vampires. Angelika is out for blood despite the fact she walked out on me and little Anton."

"Hey, quick question. What did you just jot down?" Todd asks provocatively.

David taps the legal pad and flashes Todd a sheepish grin. "Oh, this. Just reminding myself to, you know, place a bet."

Todd reads the note and shakes his head, not bothering to hide his disgust. "Seriously, man? I was just about to talk about the Asian tsunami that killed 340,000 people, but I'm guessing you're not that interested." Todd sorts papers and files into his briefcase and stands to leave.

David tamps down a flash of guilt by thinking about how much Todd's altruism has benefited from his financial input. He has given his friend way more than fifteen percent, after all.

"You're right. I'm a jerk. You're a much better person than me, even the second time around. Sit and fill me in," says David, patting the table.

Todd snaps closed the latches on his briefcase. "To each their own. I still love you, bro." He checks his watch. "Actually, I've got a plane to catch."

David stands up from the table and grabs another donut. "I'll walk you out."

Todd looks at him, askance. "Sure you need that

second donut? Remember last time?"

Todd gestures to a protruding belly. "Ah, Christ! You're right!"

With a flick of his wrist, David expertly frisbees the donut in the trash can.

Chapter 13

The newlyweds settle into their new loft apartment.

"I just love these built-in bookshelves behind the spiral staircase. It feels like we live in a bookstore." Kate sits on a short stool as she shelves books from boxes.

Matt kisses the top of her head and scans a box. "Hemingway, F. Scott Fitzgerald, and Steinbeck—huh? I mean, they're classics, but why hold onto those relics? You'll never read them again."

Kate peers up at Matt. "I can't let go of my American Lit books with my highlights and comments in the margins. That was my favorite class in college. They're treasures, you minimalist, you." She leans to grasp *The Lovely Bones* by Alice Sebold and *Middlesex* by Jeffrey Eugenides and offers them to Matt. "Here. These two are contemporary. At least I read," Kate retorts, enjoying ribbing her husband.

"I read," Matt says defensively.

"Car and plane mags don't count."

"Touché!" Matt heads back to the kitchen to unpack appliances.

Kate's phone rings. Caller ID says it's Detective Manley. She fights off the sudden somber mood and for Matt's sake, adopts a cheery tone. "Hello? Oh, yes. Hi. Happy New Year to you. Um, just a sec." She covers the mouthpiece. "I need to take this in the other room."

Matt shrugs and continues to unpack.

Kate ducks into the guest bedroom and plops onto the California king bed topped with a fluffy duvet. A pressure builds, the stakes are high, and if all goes well, she'll avert a disaster. She lets out a sigh and fumbles in her jeans pocket to pull out a note. She's lying next to a decorative pillow that says Live, Laugh, Love. "Thanks for calling me back, Detective."

Detective Manley clears his throat. "I want to start by saying I'm sorry about 9/11. I'll be frank. I didn't take you seriously, and I apologize."

"Thank you for saying so. This one's a doozy. Not like 9/11, but it's almost in your backyard."

"Go on," says the detective.

"Houston Super Bowl in February. My visions show me a disgruntled Colts fan on a revenge mission. He will be heavily armed. He has a rifle with a bump stock."

He inhales abruptly. "Revenge for what?"

"All kinds of stuff. He's deeply in debt and borrowed big time to lay heavy bets on the Colts." Kate closes her eyes, thinking hard, trying to remember more details. "Basically, he's been a loser all his life and wants others to feel his pain."

"Like a mass shooting will make things better."

Kate reads from the note. "He'll shoot from his hotel window, the second or third floor. I remember he was—" *Oh, ugh!* She grimaces, recalling the horrific images from television. "I mean, I see him firing at fans leaving the stadium as they head to their cars. Ninety-two people die with many more injured."

"That's insane."

"That he is. Well, he'll claim he's incensed about the loss in the playoff game. It only makes sense in his twisted mind."

"But they don't play the Patriots for two more weeks," says Detective Manley.

"Oh, okay. Well, the Colts lose, and there will be a lot of contention."

"Aha," Manley allows, his voice distant. "Just curious… How do these visions come to you?"

"Dreams. Mostly," Kate says, hoping he doesn't delve too much because she doesn't have a well-developed cover story.

"I imagine it doesn't make for good sleeping," says Detective Manley.

"You're right, it doesn't." She prays he's asking out of curiosity instead of back to questioning her credibility.

"You've given me a lot of homework."

"I really hope you can stop him."

"I'm on it. As soon as we end this call, I'm calling the police chief in Houston. I truly appreciate this tip, or whatever you call it."

Kate exhales, relieved he's taking her seriously. "Only too happy to help."

"Take care, young lady."

"You, too."

Kate hangs up the phone and lays in bed, remaining still as she stares vacantly at the ceiling. For now, the weight of saving lives lifts from her. But fear lingers. *What about next time? What if this charade about dreams unravels?* With a start, she sits up and dismisses those misgivings. *Next time, but what about now?* This is her time to revel in this new life with Matt. She scrunches up the note, tosses it in the trash, and skips out to Matt, giving him a peck on the cheek.

"What was your top-secret call about?" Matt looks slightly hurt that he was left out.

"Just girl stuff with Lissa. Nothing a guy would care about." Kate proceeds to hug her husband. She feels genuinely happy about her life and her future. Then a small thought sneaks in as if to whisper, *David*. And she swats away the thought. *Who?*

***

Todd looks pained at his desk, glancing between a screen and a spreadsheet. He's holding his head as though it might explode if he were to remove his hands.

Ellen pops into Todd's office, holding something behind her back. "Got a minute?"

"For you, always. I welcome the interruption. I'm finding some bothersome discrepancies in this expense report."

"Why are you working on that? It can be handled by your trusted CFO."

"I wanted to lighten your load. You've got enough on your plate."

"About that…" She presents him with a Bonsai tree. "This is for you." She beams.

He holds up the plant to check it out. "What did I do to deserve this?"

"Thanks to you, I lightened my load." Ellen bounces on her toes, light and sparkly, like her old self. "I left him!"

Todd's face lights up. "Oh, Ellen, I'm so proud of you. It takes courage to walk away."

"My therapist, Dr. Cowan, helped me see the forest

174

174

for the trees. But you made all the difference. You cared enough to help me help myself."

"I'm so relieved to hear this. Tough situations often escalate. You could have ended up in a very dark place. Like a point of no return," Todd says and shudders at the thought of the previous outcome.

"Yes, indeed. Your sixth sense was spot on. People say that guys don't have well-developed intuition, but you're different." Ellen turns to go and then twists around to face him. A tear escapes from her eye. "I can't thank you enough."

***

David is doing intervals on his treadmill, in a full-on sprint while watching, but not really watching, CNN. Sprinting provides a much-needed catharsis from the alimony nonsense his wife is putting him through. This effort on the treadmill is a metaphor for this ongoing legal endurance contest, and David feels he's running out of steam and patience. What's her game? To punish him? Why? She fights like she's got nothing to lose, because no matter the breaks, it's his money that she's spending.

His phone rings. His divorce attorney on Caller ID. David slaps the treadmill controls to slow his pace to a jog. "Hey Raoul, what's the latest?" asks David, breathing hard.

"Sounds like I caught you in the middle of your workout. Should I call back?"

"No, I'd like to know what she said." David slows to a walk. "Well, I do and I don't."

"Not good news, I'm afraid. She rejected it."

David turns off the treadmill and steps off to mop his face with a towel. *Why is Angelika doing this?* He slumps onto a bench. "I don't know what to say. This is what, the seventh offer?" David pops up and paces back and forth. He halts in front of the water cooler. "I want this done. Now. Go back and ask them what it will cost to settle."

"You won't like it one bit," says Raoul.

"I know I won't like it. What else is new? But I also want to get on with my life."

"I hear you. I'll make the call."

David hangs up and plops down on the bench again. He stares into space and sighs. He winds up like a pitcher and hurls his flip phone against the wall. Then, as if time shifts into slow motion, he watches the phone shatter and the pieces ricochet every which way, littering his home fitness center. *Why is everything turning to shit?*

***

Kate and Matt enjoy a lovely brunch at home, blueberry pancakes topped with whipped cream, Canadian bacon, and mimosas. Technically, her drink is just seltzer water and OJ, but she pretends it's a mimosa. Then the first wave of nausea strikes, and she instantly regrets their lavish meal, wishing she had opted instead for dry toast. Urgently, she pushes from the table and hurries to the bathroom. Along the way, she doesn't understand why it's called morning sickness when it can strike at any time. She wants to rename it all-day sickness.

She makes it to the bathroom in the nick of time. After her first bout of vomiting, Kate settles next to the toilet in her PJs, her face washed out, her hair tousled, waiting for the next wave of nausea. *I can't wait to be done with this.*

Matt stands outside the bathroom, talking to the closed door. "Sure you don't want me in there, babe?"

"No way. I look like a vomiting zombie. Plus, what would you do? Hold my head while I hurl? Oh, crap. Oh no." She pulls herself over the toilet bowl, purges, and heaves, gasping. Bracing against the sink counter, she rises to moisten a washcloth under the faucet, then wipes her face. The cool moistness brings a moment of relief, but the queasiness returns. Defeated, she slumps to the floor, leaning on the bathtub for support.

Matt chuckles outside.

"Seriously? You find this entertaining?" Kate shoots back. "Why is it some people laugh at the misery of others, like in this case, when they want to puke? We should Google that," says Kate, staving off another wave of nausea.

"We should do what?"

"I mean..." Kate searches her memory. "Yahoo. Ugh. Never mind."

"Babe, sorry if I appear insensitive. I just find you so cute and funny. Even now."

She suppresses a gag from the bile pushing up her throat. "There's nothing cute or funny about morning sickness. This didn't happen last time."

"What was that?" Matt says. "Last time?"

Shit! Kate once again put her foot in her mouth. She scrambles for a reply. "I said I think that was the last time."

If this baby is making me ill, is it going to be my Jack? A fresh wave of misery strikes. *What if it's not? What if I never see him again?*

***

To celebrate Super Bowl Sunday, heavily pregnant Lissa is baking her special strudel. She takes a break to play blocks with Stella, who's sixteen months old and obsessed with stacking things. Lissa sits on the floor and adjusts her body to find a comfortable position. She chuckles, imagining wearing a t-shirt that says *Oversize Load*. She's due in March and is already way bigger than she was with Stella at eight months.

The kitchen door opens. Todd rushes in, bringing with him the scent of the outdoors. "Man, I needed that. Something smells good."

Stella squeals and runs to her daddy to show him her blocks. He reaches down and picks up Stella and her handful of blocks. She shrieks in delight.

Lissa smiles. "I'm baking strudel. The Lichsteins are popping in during the Super Bowl. Remember?"

"Oh, that's right. Any calls?" Todd asks, sounding anxious.

"Afraid not," Lissa replies, anticipating his disappointment.

Todd sets Stella in the middle of her collection of blocks. "The waiting game kills me. It really does."

Lissa pushes herself up from a seated position and goes to hug him. "You've done all you can with letters and calls. Kate spoke to the detective. Still, being realistic,

178

nothing changed with 9/11."

"I know, fate versus destiny." He forces a smile but even he knows it looks fake. "I did this—came back to make change—for the better. It's so much harder and more stressful than I ever thought."

***

Kate scours the TV news for any reporting on the Houston shooting. Thankfully, she's home alone, so doesn't have to explain anything to Matt. Nerves tight with worry, she clicks from channel to channel. *C'mon! C'mon!* Then bingo! A muscular, bald policeman is being interviewed in front of the Houston Comfort Inn.

He wears a tactical vest labeled SWAT and scans the parking lot, looking jumpy as he explains, "There was an arsenal in his hotel room. A cache of guns, bump stocks, AR-15s, and suitcases of ammunition. He could've taken out... oh, I don't even want to speculate." The cop's voice quakes. "There would've been carnage."

The news features a mugshot of a pasty man with an extreme buzz cut and an American flag t-shirt bulging at the belly. Kate glowers at his image, thinking, *Got you, you son of a bitch.*

The news cuts to a family of four, huddled together, with the mother as the spokesperson. The words gush from her mouth as her kids and husband nod frantically. "We had just checked in and were headed for our room when a SWAT team appeared in the hallway. They motioned that we drop our bags and run to the stairwell. We had no idea what was happening. I mean, I figured it was some kind of

179

bomb or terrorist plot. I shudder to think we were on the same floor as that maniac!"

Kate clicks from channel to channel, all of them reporting the attempted mass shooting. She jumps up and down in gleeful twirls, saying, "Yes! Yes! Yes! Todd, we did it!" She grabs the phone to share the wonderful news.

***

The Bentons' neighbors, Morina and Zander, arrive with their toddler son, Oliver. The pregame telecast blares in the background, featuring three overly coiffed sports commentators frantically trying to upstage one another with manic predictions and prognostications. Todd hands Zander a beer and tries to pretend he's not as tense as he feels.

Oliver runs over to Stella, who's holding a stuffed tiger. He looks like he's trying to figure out how to steal the tiger, but Stella has a firm grasp on it and shoots the boy a threatening look.

"I'm so looking forward to this game," says Zander, taking a long drag from his beer.

"Z put $100 on the Panthers," says Morina. "Fingers crossed."

"Oooh! Patriots win. Sorry, I mean, they'll probably win," says Lissa.

"Yeah, I'm with Lissa. I'm all-in with the Patriots." Todd wonders if he shouldn't flaunt his time-travel advantage. He goes to check the ribs in the oven and returns to the living room. "Not quite there, but just wait, they're finger-licking good."

A cellphone buzzes in Lissa's apron pocket. Lissa and Todd tense up and exchange glances.

She answers. "Hello. Oh, we just donated. But thank you." To Todd, she whispers. "I'm with you. I want this over already."

Todd's cellphone chimes. They glance at each other again.

He retrieves the phone from the carrier on his belt and reads the caller ID. He hustles for the kitchen. Lissa follows.

He says, "Hello?" and pauses for several seconds, just listening. His eyes are fixed on the floor. He blurts out, "Kate, that's great, like unbelievably good news." Todd fist pumps and Lissa guesses why.

"Well done, sis. I can't thank you enough." Todd hangs up. "They got him!" He embraces Lissa, her pregnancy girth coming between them.

Lissa squirms to get breathing room. "Thank God. But if you squeeze me any tighter, I might just give birth right here."

Todd pulls away. "Sorry, sweetheart. I'm just so, so happy."

Morina passes the kitchen door with a bellowing Oliver in tow. She nods at Lissa, who strokes Todd's hair and turns away. The two moms herd their restless toddlers and the tiger into the backyard.

Todd returns to the living room and hurdles gleefully over the couch like he's competing in the Olympics. He plops next to Zander and scoops his beer, finally able to relax.

Zander is bewildered by his jubilant host. "What's

all the excitement?"

"Excited for the game! Just wait for the killer halftime show. It's Janet Jackson and Justin Timberlake." Todd wants to say, *just wait until Janet Jackson's wardrobe malfunction.* He chuckles to himself. At some point, the network will report the aborted shooting but not until later to avoid spoiling the game.

"Let's go, Panthers!" shouts Zander, raising his beer.

Todd bites his tongue, gives his friend a consolation pat, and settles in to watch the game. He thinks, *It feels so good to save lives. To change fate for the better.*

Chapter 14

A thunderstorm offers an impressive light show through David's office windows. Lightning bolts fracture the night sky in dramatic flashes and illuminate the Manhattan skyline.

David admires his newest artistic acquisition, a contemporary painting that portrays a black skull scarred with bold colors, scary eyes, and gnashing teeth. David paces eagerly, pitching his stress ball from one hand to the other as he chats with Todd on speakerphone.

Todd says, "I got the email. Image still downloading. Can we get wireless already? Okay, got it. Wow! That's a bold piece. Looks street-art-inspired."

"It's Neo-Expressionism," David corrects. "This, my friend, is *Untitled* 1982 by Jean-Michel Basquiat. I—I should say we—paid $4.5 million."

"Ho-ly shit. Hate to say you might have been taken."

David snorts. "I'm not worried. It will sell for $110 million in 2017. I remembered reading about the Basquiat story back in '17, as clear as day. I've been on this piece for a while."

"I should never have doubted you, man. Think of all the good we can do."

"Yeah, yeah, yeah," David replies, not bothering to hide his cynicism.

Todd sighs deeply.

"You do good. I do me. Gotta go. See you next

week." David abruptly hangs up. He moves in to inspect the piece. He smiles and crosses his arms, pleased with his acquisition and the profits it will bring him.

***

In front of a modern four-story glass office building with the logo Benton EHR Systems, a ribbon-cutting ceremony is underway. A crowd of 120 people waits on the grass out front. Todd offers a few words about how his success is attributable to so many in attendance. He thanks a few key people and calls them over to stand beside him along the ribbon. He shares his vision for the company's future, then announces, "Ready?" and with a huge pair of scissors, cuts the ribbon to a hearty round of applause.

Curiously, as he walks from the ribbon, the crowd doesn't move, as if they're expecting something else. Ellen races over, followed by a colleague holding what looks like a giant canvas wrapped in gold and white paper. Ellen exclaims, "One moment, everybody! There's more. We'd like to honor the most amazing founder and CEO, who leads with vision, passion, and boldness." The colleague steps forward as Ellen says, "Todd, we want to present you with this as a token of our appreciation." Everyone cheers as Ellen hands him the gift.

Todd blushes. "Oh, you didn't need to do this." He carefully tears the paper to reveal an oil painting within a gilded frame, a group portrait of him and his family. Lissa smiles lovingly at her husband as he tips the portrait in her direction.

Todd stares admiringly at the painting, speechless,

trying to control his emotions. He doesn't want to break down in front of such a large audience of peers, friends, colleagues, and community members. "I don't know what to say. I'm humbled by your gift. This is absolutely stunning. I will hang it with gratitude. Thank you."

Another employee takes the painting away, and Todd kisses Ellen on both cheeks.

This is the cue for everyone to mix and mingle.

Todd gazes about for his family. Along the edge of the lawn by the honeysuckle, his daughter Stella, in a pink pinafore dress and pigtails with ribbons, plays peekaboo with Graham, Todd's father. Close by, Kate and Matt hold hands, she sporting a swollen belly and looking uncomfortable. He might not have noticed the first time around, but the wisdom of years has taught Todd to be extra-sympathetic to pregnant women.

Todd says, "Really glad you made it, Dad. Means so much."

Graham stops playing for a minute. "Personally, ribbon cuttings are a bit of a grandstand," he says dismissively. When he makes eye contact with Stella, his face lights up. "I see you!" Graham chases Stella, who squeals as she runs away to weave in and out of the milling crowd.

Todd grits his teeth and watches his father go. *Would it kill him to say he's proud of me just once?* He attempts to mollify himself with the thought, *Oh, who gives a crap?* But if he is honest with himself, he admits that he still seeks his dad's approval.

The crowd trickles into the building's reception area where a buffet lunch, tables, and chairs are set up.

Todd sees his mom at the dessert and coffee station and strolls over.

Elaine points to a stack of cups. "Want a coffee, darling?"

Todd treats himself to a white chocolate mini torte. "That would be great."

"We're so proud of you. Of course, your father won't admit it. Despite my trying every which way to get him to accept that you've done great on your own, he will not." She shakes her head disapprovingly as she fills a cup from the coffee urn.

"I bet if I had chosen to work with him, we'd have had even bigger issues. I can't win." Todd sighs. Even in his happiest moments, the fights with his father still dog him. And worse, what Todd knows about the future means that he has to patch things up between them before it's too late.

"In my book, you're a winner." Elaine, beaming with pride, caresses Todd's cheek.

"You're the best, Mom." The need to issue a warning nags him. "Oh, I wanted to ask you," Todd says, raising his index finger as if the thought had just occurred to him. "Has Dad had his heart checked lately?"

Elaine furrows her brow. "No, not that I'm aware of. Why do you ask?

"Well, you mentioned he doesn't exercise and seems stressed lately. I'm just saying, maybe you should book him a checkup."

Elaine chuffs and grins. "You know he's never been keen on going to the doctor."

Todd drapes a hand on his mother's shoulder,

"Mom," and looks intently into her eyes, "book him a physical as soon as you return home. Have them schedule an angiogram. Promise me you'll do that."

Elaine smiles, warmed by her son's genuine concern. "Alright, I will. I promise I will."

***

When David rings the doorbell, the chime goes on forever. It's so Angelika. He stands in the elevator foyer outside her penthouse apartment, holding Anton, his eighteen-month-old son.

This delay is her usual theater. Not only did he schedule this visit, but the doorman in the lobby also alerted her of his arrival. In the ten minutes between then and now, she had plenty of time to get ready. *Christ, Angelika could give lessons in haughty disdain to Marie Antoinette.*

Anton fusses and squirms, so David tries his routine of goofy faces and silly noises, which usually works to mollify the toddler. Not today. David wonders if the hand-offs are harder because Anton is getting older.

Footfalls approach the door from the other side. The deadbolt clicks and the nanny swings the door open. "Hola, Mr. David."

"Hola! I'm so sorry to give you a cranky boy." David bounces Anton on his hip. "I've tried all my tricks. Nothing's working."

"Oh, no problem. We'll fix it." The nanny smiles. "Won't we, nino?"

David attempts to hand Anton over, but the boy

clutches for him and cries.

The sobs tear into David. If it were up to him, he'd keep Anton, but the court's custody order decided otherwise. David pries Anton's little fingers loose. "Love you, buddy," he says.

Angelika skulks to the door and leans against the door frame with her arms crossed over her yoga tank. She wears loose pajama-like bottoms and props one foot on the opposite knee to assume a tree pose that radiates contempt. Her hair is styled in a messy updo, and she wears freshly applied pink lipstick. Her eyes peer through David like he isn't there even as she says, "We need to talk."

These four words usually herald bad news, but the fact that she even wants to talk takes David by surprise. It's been that relentlessly toxic between them.

Angelika sighs, then softens. Her gaze settles on him. "Look. I want to make peace..."

"I'm all ears," David says, relieved.

"I'd like to take Anton to Prague. For like, a few months, maybe six, so he can be around my family."

David processes what she's said. "Six months. That's a long time. Sorry, I'm just not comfortable with that."

Angelika doesn't budge or change her facial expression. She's clearly just waiting for him to say yes.

"Don't do this, Angelika. Do you really want to make it more contentious between us? It's not good for Anton." David realizes he's pleading but, at that moment, he has the horrific image of Angelika's tongue scrolling out of her mouth like a tentacle and coiling itself around his son. David shifts his footing, sensing that the building is swaying. The thought of Anton taken from him feels like the world is about to collapse beneath his feet.

Angelika's eyes harden, becoming reptilian cold. "My legal team has already drafted documents in anticipation of you being you." The toxicity in her voice is pure venom. "You can't win this."

"I don't want to 'win.' And I don't want to fight anymore." David whispers. "I suppose I can visit," he allows, resigned. Angelika has him cornered. The foyer shrinks around him and it's as if he's being squeezed so oppressively that the hurt makes tears flood into his eyes.

Her eyes study his, and she smiles for the first time during their exchange. She taps the nanny on the shoulder, who pivots with Anton and disappears around the door.

She drops her leg and stands flat-footed, half hidden by the door. "I know you could've made this difficult. So, thank you." And just like that, she closes the door. The deadbolt clicks.

David stares at the door, wondering how he could be so successful professionally but such a pushover when dealing with Angelika. He shuffles toward the elevator, his esteem in shambles. *What did I just agree to?* He's heard about countless mothers turning their children against their fathers in divorce; the kids became so brainwashed they were completely estranged from their dads.

He sets his jaw and straightens his back. *I won't let that happen.*

***

Kate, heavily pregnant and on the verge of tears, stands at the front door of their apartment. Matt is dressed in weekend warrior wear—a sporty t-shirt, shorts, and high-top athletic shoes. He's fired up for the day's adventure. "I get it. You're a little emotional right now. It's probably just your hormones talking."

She wants to scream at him, the way she did in the future when she heard that he was dead. The heartache rings in her head so all she can sense is the grief.

"No, it's not. Please don't go. Not today," she begs, rubbing and gazing down at her belly. "This may be hard to hear but with a little one on the way, you have to think about someone other than yourself. You have to curb your adrenaline-junkie activities and put our family first."

Looking away, he says, "It's the time I feel the most alive—when I'm soaring among the clouds, then push out of the airplane and drop. Everything is quiet except for the whoosh of the wind." He looks back at her. "Besides the odds of dying from a skydive are next to nothing, that's a fact. The most dangerous part of my day will be the car ride to and from the drop zone. Hell, even walking across the street can be fatal. I could get hit by a bus tomorrow. Just saying."

Kate knows this but also knows that destiny is not on his side. She covers her face and bursts into a sob. "Just trust me on this. Not today!"

Matt keeps glancing down the hall, his focus on his destination. "Honey, this is really something you don't have to worry about."

Kate steels herself. "It is when I know something will go horribly wrong this time." She puts her hand on his chest to stop him. She feels his heart beating. "Matt, I know for certain something bad is going to happen if you go." She pauses and tries to convince him with a terrified stare. "You'll die."

"Oh, c'mon." He throws his hands up. "Now you're being ridiculous. Why would you say that?"

"Because I know," she says calmly. She reveals the truth about this skydiving excursion, sharing details that astonish him. She feels she has no choice.

***

Later that day, Matt, grounded by Kate and her dire prognostications, throws his head back and downs a double shot of tequila. Truth is, the alcohol doesn't help. No matter how much he drinks, his world remains askew. It wasn't just how Kate relayed, with terrifying precision, the details of his death from a parachuting accident, but her claim that she had come from the future.

He was incredulous at first, convinced she had conjured the whole thing just to assuage her unreasonable fear of losing him. *Pregnancy does weird things to a woman's brain.* Kate had pointed out all the world events she and her brother, Todd, predicted. This included sports games they put bets on and had an uncanny knack for winning. His heart had started beating faster than it did when he was about to go bungee jumping.

Once she started on about the number of disasters she and Todd had mitigated, or even averted, he realized she was telling the goddamn truth. This created a rift in his worldview that was wider than the Grand Canyon. He'd always been pragmatic about everything.

If it is possible that Kate folded time through a supernatural portal, then what else of this world is an illusion?

He slams the shot glass on the counter and pours himself another double before heading to the bathroom. Kate reclines on their king-sized bed with a book lying on her chest. When Matt enters, she sets her book aside.

"Okay, so, I have more questions. After I 'died,' did you remarry and have more kids? And were you happy?" asks Matt, slurring his words.

"Yes. No. Well, oh, God. Can we not talk about this anymore? Honestly, all that matters is the here and now."

She holds out her hand. Matt interlaces his fingers with hers and sits next to her. Kate wraps her arms around him to cradle him and offer an emotional refuge. Matt touches her swollen belly.

She grasps his hand and leans into him. "I love you so, so much, Matt. I don't want you anywhere but here with us."

***

Lissa wakes with a jolt, panicked, and looks around, fully awake, nerves sizzling in alarm. She pushes herself up onto her elbows for a better view. His side of the bed is empty. The panic intensifies. "Todd! Todd?" She jumps out of bed, throws on her robe, and heads out of the room, tying her robe as she scurries downstairs. She rushes into the kitchen. "Todd? Todd!"

He's at the kitchen table, dressed for the day,

and eating breakfast with the kids. Nothing is out of the ordinary. She exhales in relief.

Todd looks up from his paper. "Good morning, Mommy." He takes a moment to read her expression and perks an eyebrow. "Bad dream again?"

"Yes. I wish it would stop. It makes me dread sleeping." She takes in the serene calmness, inhales the aroma of freshly brewed coffee, and crosses the kitchen to hug her babies and shower them with morning kisses.

Miles squirms in his highchair, and Stella giggles.

"Just tell yourself, 'It's all okay.'" Todd folds his newspaper and gathers plates from the table. He carries them to the sink.

"You say that, but every time I wake up in such a panic. It's silly, I know."

"Hey, thanks for getting up at the crack of 8:00," he says, teasing while scrubbing a pan under the sink faucet.

"I was up half the night with this little fella. I'm afraid he's officially a bad sleeper." Lissa pours herself a giant mug of java and takes a sip, closing her eyes to savor the first taste of black coffee. "What would I do without coffee?"

Todd looks at Lissa and tilts his head. "Hold onto your hat, Liss. In about eighteen months, you'll be the mother of three!"

Lissa shoots him a sideways glance of disapproval.

"Better get used to it," Todd says, clearly delighted by his growing family.

"Please tell me I get some childcare help." Lissa's distracted by the thought of having such a large brood and accidentally pours too much creamer into her coffee. *Oh well*. She stirs until the brew is a light brown.

Todd arranges the dishes in the drying rack and grabs his to-go mug. "Oh, you figured it out last time. Gotta go. I'm already late for a meeting I'm running." He gives Lissa and the kiddos drive-by kisses and dashes out.

Lissa is irritated by his comment. *You figured it out last time. Easy for him to say as he waltzes off to work*. She pictures herself passing through the kitchen on the way to work as Todd toils with the kids. She misses talking to adults. Even listening to people whine about their problems all day is better than endless housework. *If I had gone back, I would've done this part differently. But how?*

When the phone rings, Lissa considers letting the call go to voicemail—it's just one more thing vying for her frayed attention—but something tells her it's important.

"Hello?"

"It's showtime!" proclaims Matt.

"Oh my gosh. Now?"

"You betcha. I'm at the hospital."

Giddy from the great news, Lissa turns to Stella. "Aunt Kate is having her baby!"

***

David meets with his associates and a team of architects in the boardroom. The blinds are drawn and the only light in the dim room comes from the slide projector beaming images onto a screen. They review plans for phase two of a Manhattan waterside luxury housing-retail project. Architectural renderings cover the table.

Stacy Kimball is the lone woman at the table. She's

in her mid-thirties, has a thick mane of dark hair, and wears a stylish dress, a dark color that blends with the room's murk.

One of the architects clicks a remote and advances through the slides while others narrate design details.

"I like it!" says David.

"You won't like the numbers, David. This plan puts us twenty-two percent over budget," says an associate.

Stacy pipes up, making eye contact with each of the attendees as she speaks, as though being center stage comes naturally to her. "The market for sustainable design and construction continues to grow. I haven't run a project in the last three years that doesn't take into consideration our responsibility for the environmental footprint. Many aspects of our lives, whether construction or consumption, are going green." She says this with a commanding confidence and sits poised, prepared for any pushback.

David doesn't hesitate to respond. "I agree with Stacy. It's the future. The solar panels and LED lights stay. Great job. I really like your forward-thinking approach."

"Oh, I'm pleased we're on the same page."

David glances at the meeting agenda. Every item has been checked off. All eyes at the table are fixed on him. "I guess that's it. Please incorporate Ms. Kimball's recommendations and get back to me. Any questions?"

There are no questions.

He stands. The overhead fluorescent lights flicker on. "Thank you for a great meeting. See you next month."

Stacy is the first to gather her files, stands, and, aware that the men are giving her the once over—again, nods to the group. "Gentlemen." Hermés briefcase in hand, she glides out of the boardroom.

David smiles after her, impressed. Actually, more than impressed. He shakes hands with a few associates as they leave. Others clean up meeting notes and presentation materials.

David leaves the boardroom and walks over to Meredith's desk, leans forward, balancing on his fingertips, and says, "Get me Stacy Kimball's number. Her cellular, that is."

Meredith's eyes widen slightly, but she remains composed as she searches for Stacy's number on her computer. "Certainly, sir."

***

Kate rests in her hospital bed, a little pale, with dark circles under her eyes. She's the good kind of exhausted, after having run a life-changing marathon. After seventeen hours of labor, it was touch and go for a moment, but she managed to avoid a C-section. When the nurse placed him in her arms, saying he was a normal, healthy baby, she said, "Oh, thank God," and cradled him like she would never let him go.

Her baby boy, like a slumbering angel, is next to her swaddled in a hospital bassinet. On the far side of the room, Oprah drones from the TV anchored just below the ceiling.

Todd enters the room. He holds a plush teddy bear. "Congratulations, Mommy!"

Kate fumbles for the remote and clicks off the TV. Beaming with joy, she doesn't know where to begin as she relates what happened. "Lissa was amazing. She cut the umbilical cord, 'cuz Matt just about fainted. You know what wimps you men are." She laughs.

Todd chuckles. "Where is Matt?"

"He's grabbing a bite with his parents. I honestly think he needed a little break from baby land. I mean, don't get me wrong, he is over the moon about having a son." She pulls the bassinet close and with a tender reach, lifts her baby out as though he were breakable, fragile. She places him on her chest and breathes in the new baby scent and smiles. "Do you think he looks like me or Matt?"

Todd laughs. "It's hard to tell in the alien phase."

Kate frowns. "My baby's not an alien." She smiles. "He's an angel."

"Oh, Mom and Dad send their love. They look forward to meeting your little man at Christmas."

"Want to hear something wild? I was just watching Oprah. I think she went back too! I swear she did the Yusaf sign." She demonstrates the hand gesture near her heart. "She did the very same thing."

Todd's amused. "Either that or she was just scratching herself."

"I know what I saw. Besides, it would make sense. Oprah has conquered the world!"

Clearly wanting to change the topic, Todd said, "Hey, did you pick a name?"

"Jack. My son's name is Jack. And don't tell me it's weird."

"Oh, I think it's great. Only this time, he's a towhead like Matt."

Kate suddenly flashes back to David beside her, and

their dark-haired son, Jack. Their threesome felt sacred, like nothing could ever break their bond. She remembers how afraid David was to hold his son the first time. How his eyes were filled with tears of joy.

Gazing at her newborn, the towhead, Kate trembles. Those memories claw at her. She feels like she's betrayed the other Jack, who now will no longer exist. The treachery becomes so painful that she suddenly breaks into sobs. In panic, she offers the baby to Todd, who takes him. She crumples against her pillows and weeps. Tears stream down her cheeks and she doesn't try to stop them.

Todd lowers the baby into the bassinet and goes to his sister. He reaches for her hand, his expression one of confusion. "I'm sorry if I upset you."

With both hands, Kate takes his and holds on for dear life to prevent her from being dragged into an abyss of despair, drawing strength from her brother. "It just hit me. Your babies all turned out the same, the exact same, right? But I'll never get Jack back. That Jack. It's like he died. Worse, like he never existed." She blots her tears with a corner of the bedsheet. "I've missed him every single day. I thought having a baby would take that pain away. It's not like I don't love this precious little guy. I do." Her gaze cuts to the bassinet and her eyes well up again. "But he's a different baby, like you said." Kate sobs again, convulsively.

Todd stares at her, helpless.

Minutes pass before she can speak. "I prayed he'd be exactly how he was before." Kate chokes.

Todd senses his sister's pain and moves to sit by her bed, taking her hand.

"I can only imagine how hard it is for you. I won't even try to soften the loss you feel. But Kate, please know this. You are where you're meant to be right here, right now." Todd slaps his thighs. "Trust me, you're not alone. I've dwelled on this during many sleepless nights." He stands and goes over to scoop up the newborn. He offers the baby to Kate, who wraps him in her arms. "Look into those eyes. That's the soul of your son. It's Jack."

Kate's tears subside as her little one peers up at her, wide-eyed and vulnerable. He's pure potential. The sparkle returns to her eyes. She leans down and kisses her baby's soft forehead. *Hello again, my sweet boy.*

Chapter 15

Todd insisted that David take a book of quotes, *Begin it Now* by Susan Hayward, on the flight to the Czech Republic. David promised he would. Despite David's insistence that he wanted to experience an old-fashioned Christmas in the old country—never mind that David's ancestors hailed from Scotland—Todd knew that his good friend's reason for the trip was that he desperately missed his son. Angelika's promise to take Anton for six months turned into nine months, twelve, longer.

His ex-wife's disruption to his plans makes David think that much in his life is out of balance, like he needs to do more than make money. A quote from the book by Robert Byrne runs through his mind as he strolls through old town Prague. "The purpose of life is a life of purpose." *Am I living a life of purpose?*

With a light dusting in the old town square and illuminated gothic spires piercing the night sky, he feels as if he's inside a snow globe. "Carol of the Bells" plays as David threads through shoppers bundled up against the frigid air. He tunes out the faces until he sees a little boy who looks exactly like his son Jack at age two. He does a doubletake and watches the boy until he's out of sight.

David's memory shows him Kate and Jack in upstate New York on a winter get-away. Kate lies back in the fluffy snow and makes a snow angel. Little Jack watches and then falls back and mimics her—a tiny snow angel. Then Kate hops up and reaches down for a handful of snow. She packs the snow into a little ball and lobs it at her boy. When it grazes his head, he giggles. He makes his own snowball, throws it, and Kate positions herself so it hits her smack in the face. Jack thinks it's the most hilarious thing ever.

David, with a far-off look in his eyes, no longer sees Prague, no longer sees that debt-ridden future that he'd escaped. Instead, he sees sweet memories, now vanishing like wisps of smoke. He wishes he were back in New York with Jack, his beloved little boy. And Kate. He tightens his scarf, then continues down the street, lost in remembering. Lost in regret.

***

The Bentons are hosting Christmas dinner for their family and closest friends. Their home is festively decorated with fresh garland draped around the windows and a bow of holly strung across the fireplace mantel. In the hearth, a fire crackles and wafts a smoky pine scent throughout the house. The towering Christmas tree is decorated with glistening antique balls and tiny white lights. A Boho-chic angel watches over the tree. Dean Martin softly croons "Let it Snow" from unseen speakers.

Kate sits on the couch with baby Jack on her lap. She watches as Stella serves plastic food onto fancy plates to imaginary guests. Miles toddles around with his toy Dyson in the hallway with Graham. Lissa plops down on the couch with Kate, handing her a glass of water and coos over Jack.

Kate glares at the water and frowns. "Hey! Where's my eggnog?"

"It's spiked," says Lissa. "With vodka."

"Just how I like it." Kate grins.

Lissa shakes her head no. "Just kidding."

"Aw, c'mon. It's Christmas." Kate pouts.

"Soon, Kate. Soon. After you're done breastfeeding. In the meantime, we don't want a tipsy baby." Lissa kisses Jack's pudgy cheek.

A gust of cold air from the foyer announces Matt's arrival. He bursts in with a box of wine. "Ho, Ho, Ho! Merry Christmas!" He does his best Santa Claus impression.

"Speaking of tipsy..." Kate mutters under her breath.

Matt rests the box on the counter between the front room and the kitchen. After snagging a can of beer from the refrigerator, he chugs it as he saunters on his way to the den.

Lissa tracks Matt's passage, leans toward Kate, and whispers, "Should I be worried?

"I'm at my wit's end." Kate gives Jack a protective hug. "He says it's to numb his brain."

"About what?"

"You know," answers Kate conspiratorially.

"He still hasn't accepted it?" Lissa presses.

"The more he thinks about it, that I know the future, the deeper he falls into the hole."

"He needs therapy. Should I talk to him?"

"I've asked him to talk to you, Liss. But he says therapy is for losers."

Lissa sighs. "I'll get Todd to talk to him."

"Please do." Kate hands baby Jack to Lissa. "I'm going to run interference." She heads to the kitchen where the busy elves, Todd and Elaine, prep dinner. A medley of Christmas-dish aromas hangs in the air. Todd meticulously carves up the ham, each slice perfectly proportioned, fanning out on a silver platter. Graham hovers over the platter and steaming pots, looking like a hawk ready to pounce.

Elaine peeks into the oven. "We're ready in ten. I just need to mash the potatoes." When she sees Kate, she says, "Will you supervise your father? He thinks this is a sampling kitchen."

"Dad, Mom says, 'keep your hands out of the cooking!'" admonishes Kate.

Ignoring the directive, Graham spoons a mouthful of creamed corn. Kate tries to grab the spoon from him. "He's too quick on the uptake for me!" she says, laughing.

"Gra-ham," Elaine scolds, drawing out his name, like he's been a naughty boy, "you can wait like everyone else."

"You're the boss!" But Graham's not done. He moves on to his next unsuspecting victim, his son. He leans over Todd and pinches a slice of ham.

Kate shakes her head at her father's shenanigans.

"I owe you a big thank you, son," Graham says to Todd.

Todd stops carving. "Why's that?" It dawns on him. "Oh, right, the angiogram. Glad you got it checked and are getting treatment." Todd smiles, glancing to meet his father's gaze. "Nice to know we'll have you around a bit longer."

"You know doctors. They like to exaggerate. Especially if it pads the hospital bill. Said I could have dropped dead any minute. Ha! Ridiculous, if you ask me. While I'm as fit as two horses." Graham flexes both arms as he scoffs. He nabs a green bean and leaves the kitchen.

Todd plunges the knife into the juicy ham and slices. He mumbles, "If he only knew."

Kate nods gravely in agreement, just as Matt returns to the living room, speaking too loudly to Lissa about how much he loves Christmas. It's all the liquid holiday cheer inside him talking.

Todd, Elaine, Lissa, and Graham simultaneously turn their attention to Kate. She gestures, *I got this*, and with a smile, goes over to Matt, takes his hand and they head outside for a chat. He's pretty good about sobering up and switching to water when his wife asks him to.

*****

David emerges from the elevator with eager anticipation, walking briskly into the lobby of the Four Seasons Hotel in Prague, sparkling with traditional holiday decorations. The giant Christmas tree is adorned with hand-strung cranberries and hand-crafted ornaments, sparkling white lights, and a radiant star at the top. Miniature Christmas scenes of villages with gingerbread houses, horse-drawn carriages, sleighs, and skating ponds are displayed throughout the lobby. Hotel guests stop to admire the scenes before checking in at the front desk or heading to their rooms. From the back of the lobby, elegantly dressed carolers sing acapella Christmas songs in Czech.

David sees a strikingly handsome European man with salt and pepper hair, a neat beard, an ascot, and a gray wool coat worn open over a gray suit pushing a stroller across the lobby. A striped woolen scarf drapes from his shoulders. David thinks it odd that a man his age is pushing a stroller until he notices that the baby is Anton.

Anton!

Spotting Anton, David hurries over with a big grin. "Anton. Daddy's so happy to see you, little fella!" Without thinking, he drops to a knee and reaches for his son, who's bundled for the winter cold.

"Ahem," interrupts the man. "I beg your pardon."

David looks up at him, insulted by the tone. *Beg pardon? This is my son.*

The man smirks imperiously. "You must be David." He says this like David is a street bum who wandered into the hotel, uninvited. "I'm Henri. So nice to meet you. Again." His English is cultured, precise, and dripping with condescension.

David now recognizes the man from the brief time they'd met in New York. "Oh, hi, Henri. Yes, nice to see you." David gestures toward Anton. "Would you mind? I've been looking forward to holding him." The idea of asking another man permission to hold his own son burns David, but he swallows his pride.

Henri nods for David to proceed. At first, Anton seems happy to be in David's arms but after a short moment of admiring the carolers, he begins to squirm. He looks back at Henri. "*Tata. Zpivat!*"

"*Ano zpivat,*" replies Henri.

"You're his uncle, I take it?" David says, impressed with his deductive powers.

"Oh, no. I'm Anton's stepfather."

David inhales sharply and masks his shock. *What the hell?*

"Angelika didn't tell you? We married last month," Henri says matter-of-factly.

David scrambles to maintain his equilibrium. "Oh, she failed to mention that. Not that we talk much."

"We dated before she met you. I guess you could say we've come full circle." Henri smiles while David glares at him, retracing the trajectory of that love affair.

Mutual animosity sparks between them. The two men avert their eyes toward the carolers and endure an awkward pause.

Henri breaks the silence by announcing, "Well, I'll leave you to it," says Henri, fiddling with his ascot that doesn't need adjusting.

David smiles wanly, thinking, *Only a pretentious heel like this douche would wear an ascot. What chafes more is that this freeloading bastard is living like a prince thanks to my alimony money to Angelika.*

David sets Anton back in the stroller and takes command of the handles. Henri folds the scarf over his ascot, buttons his coat, and dons leather gloves. David wheels the stroller from Henri and announces over his shoulder, "See you in three days."

Henri leans to make eye contact with the boy. "Very well. Bye, Anton!"

Anton waves. "*Ahoj, Tata.*"

"*Ahoj.*" Henri waves then pivots smartly to walk briskly towards the revolving doors while David and Anton head to the elevator. David stops at the concierge desk, leans forward, and whispers as if he doesn't want anyone to overhear. "Would you please tell me what Tata means?"

The friendly clerk beams. "Of course. It means daddy."

David, quietly furious, clenches his jaw. *Just fucking great.*

Anton tosses in the stroller as he looks from side to side. "Tata?"

***

The day after Christmas, Todd nurses a slight hangover. He promised himself he wouldn't drink too much spiked eggnog like he does every year. But the rich, creamy goodness just goes down so easily. How can he resist? It's a vice, he knows but he consoles himself with his favorite quote from Abraham Lincoln, that a man without vices has few virtues.

Todd is at his desk, glued to the television, and is startled when Lissa places a fresh cup of coffee in front of him. He didn't even notice her enter the room. She stands behind him to watch the news.

A young black reporter with dreadlocks and a clipped British accent says, "Aceh in Indonesia is the region most devastated by the Indian Ocean earthquake with the epicenter off the west coast of Sumatra. The casualty toll is expected to be well over 200,000. A state of emergency has been declared in Sri Lanka, Indonesia, and the Maldives."

Lissa crosses her arms. "I thought you said the toll would be over 340,000!"

"Last time, yes. The estimates were over 300,000.

Today, they're saying it's 200,000. I'm guessing it will land with around 230 to 250,000 lives lost. But our warning towers have likely saved 80 to 90,000 lives. That's a good-sized town for that part of the world. We can raise the alarm, but people don't have to listen. I've done my best so I can't complain."

"You did good." She wraps her arms around Todd as they continue to watch the news coverage. He takes her hand and kisses it.

***

Over the next two years are the Kashmir earthquake, the London bombings, and the North Korean nuclear test; the YouTube and Wikileaks launches; and Obama's fortuitous bid for the Presidency.

Kate hosts an elaborate Kentucky Derby Party at her new estate in early May. It sits on a half-acre parcel with majestic trees, trimmed hedges, and stone walkways. An impressive fountain sits in the middle of the circular drive. She bought the 8,000-square-foot Georgian-style home after the full renovation and interior decorating. She bought it turnkey and was happy to pay the premium. After all, she's made a lot of money through David and Todd's investing partnership as well as her own betting and stocks.

Kate takes pride in showing off her new home and loves to throw parties. Her two favorite things about Derby Day are: it's an excuse to wear elegant hats— the more colorful and exotic the better—and she loves betting, especially now with her competitive advantage.

Kate organized a betting pool with thousands of dollars at stake. This year, she put substantial money on Street Sense. She wanted to lay a truly heavy bet but that would draw too much attention beyond the fact of her knack for consistently picking the winners.

Wearing an elegant dark blue feather fascinator with mesh and linen obscuring one eye, Kate is going for festive yet mysterious. Trying to be a gracious hostess, she makes sure the guests have everything they need. Meanwhile, three-year-old Jack drives around in a mini-Ferrari—replete with his imitation of souped-up car noises—delighting the partygoers as Matt chases after him, whiskey in hand.

Kate's friends mix and mingle, sipping on refreshing mint juleps with fresh mint from her herb garden. Amid arrangements of colorful spring blooms, caterers serve bourbon-glazed ham, grilled crostini with asparagus, watermelon tomato salad, and Derby pie.

The festooned guests are clearly enjoying themselves because Kate must ding her glass several times before anyone notices. "The Derby is about to begin."

Everyone quiets and fixes their attention on the big-screen TV. Kate uses the remote to increase the volume of the broadcast.

And the horses are off! The guests shout at the big-screen TV, each rooting for their pick. The thoroughbreds pound over the muddy track. Street Sense muscles to the lead. They all cheer as the horse gallops across the finish line.

"I won!" shouts Kate, jumping up and down,

holding onto her hat.

A guest wearing a whimsical orange hat standing next to Kate says with a laugh, "You always win, Kate. Always. How do you do it?"

Kate shrugs and raises both palms to the ceiling. "Just lucky I guess."

***

Todd returns from his trip to New Orleans just in time to go with Lissa to her OB/GYN appointment. They sit in the waiting room as women in all stages of pregnancy file in and out of the office. Some expectant mothers sport cute baby bumps, while others look decidedly uncomfortable and ready to pop. The first-time mothers are easy to spot—filled with anticipatory anxiety. Lissa wants to reassure them that it will all be okay.

As they wait to be called forward, Todd fills Lissa in on his trip to New Orleans. "Mayor Nagin and I walked along the 17th Street levee. He explained that their levees had been undergoing a feasibility study for seven years and were told by the Levee Board it could take up to twenty years to upgrade. I said, 'What if a Category four or five hits? Your levees aren't providing a solid flood-protection system.'"

"What did the mayor say?"

"He acknowledged it would be disastrous and that he'd bring it before the board."

"Sounds like he kicked that can down the road."

"I hope he's good for his word. And that they do something before the flood."

"I sure as hell hope so, too." Todd shakes his head, remembering the last go-around.

"Lissa Benton?" says a Latina nurse's assistant in pink scrubs.

Lissa and Todd hop to their feet.

"Come on back. Dr. Ling is ready for you."

The nurse's assistant ushers them to the ultrasound room and records Lissa's vitals. "Please undress from the waist down. You can keep your shirt on."

Lissa quickly slides off her pants, sits on the exam table, wrinkling the paper coverlet, and draws a sheet over herself.

Dr. Ling knocks and enters. "Hi, Lissa and Todd. Ready to peek at your little one?" She snaps latex gloves over her hands.

Lissa nods. She knows the drill and lays back on the exam table and lifts her shirt.

"Okay, this is going to be a little cold on your belly," Dr. Ling says as she squirts gel onto Lissa's abdomen.

Todd holds Lissa's hand as he watches the gel get rubbed on her rotund bare belly.

The doctor slides the ultrasound wand across Lissa's slimy skin, her eyes fixed on the monitor. The threesome is quiet, trying to interpret the light and dark shadows.

After a few minutes, the doctor says, "Everything looks good." She looks relieved as if she's had to deliver bad news one too many times.

Todd and Lissa exchange a smile. He squeezes her hand.

"Do you want to know the gender or do you want

211

it to be a surprise?" asks Dr. Ling, assuming she's the only one with the secret info.

"His name is Leo," Todd says.

Dr. Ling glances from Todd to Lissa and back to Todd again. "Ah. Good guess."

"To be fair, I had a fifty percent chance of getting it right."

Lissa obscures her grin with her hand. *Liar, pants on fire.*

Chapter 16

Todd helps Lissa out of the minivan in the driveway. She's bedraggled but happy. She wasn't ready to come home; she could've used a few more days in the hospital recovering with around-the-clock care and ready-made meals.

Elaine holds her grandchildren's hands; together, they are the greeting committee. Stella and Miles's lives are about to change forever with a new sibling added to the mix. Todd proudly shows them baby Leo asleep in the car seat.

"I present your brother and grandson, Leo," says Todd.

Elaine coos. "He's precious." She reaches out to have her first snuggle with her third grandchild. Todd carefully transfers the little bundle to her. "Don't drop him," he jokes. "That was nine months of hard labor."

"Tell me about it," says Lissa, gazing down at their creation.

Elaine cradles Leo in her arms and breathes in his scent. "He looks just like Granddad. Don't you think so, Miles?"

Miles glances at his baby brother and then at his grandma with a puzzled look. "He's weird-looking. You think Granddad looks weird?"

Everyone laughs.

"Out of the mouths of babes," says Elaine, smiling.

That night, when they're alone, Lissa breastfeeds

Leo while Todd watches Hurricane Katrina footage—the flooding, the desperation, the wreckage, the carnage. He sighs, as if he has resigned to fate. "There's only so much one man can do."

"Don't be so hard on yourself." Lissa gazes down at their baby, her eyes filled with wonder, "Look what one man helped me make."

With the arrival of little Leo in 2008, the world keeps turning: Cyclone Nargis, the Sichuan earthquake, Mumbai terrorist attacks, Boris Yeltsin's funeral, and the Dalai Lama receiving the Congressional Gold Medal. Life marches on.

***

Todd steers his golf cart on the green, thinking, *What a perfect day for eighteen holes.* Not a cloud in the sky, and a light breeze blows that he could blame for any shortcomings in his golf game. He and Matt stop their cart at the seventeenth hole. They hop out to grab their clubs and assess the next shot.

"It's birdie time," says Todd, loving his time on the green. This is a new interest this time around. He finally gets why so many people find golf relaxing.

But Matt seems more interested in finishing his Smirnoff than this splendid day under such a perfectly blue sky. He says nothing as Todd sets up and hits the ball perfectly. "Yes. Yes, get in there!" Todd pumps a fist and proudly walks back to the cart to slip his club into the bag.

Matt tosses the empty can into the back of the cart with a pile of others. He selects his club and tees up.

He studies the fairway and then Todd watches his focus go from the ball to the fairway, ball, fairway, ball. He positions and repositions his golf club, his cleats, club, cleats. Then he squints into the sun. And still, he doesn't swing. Instead, he says, "So, Kate told me she had just one child last time."

Todd looks surprised but responds in earnest. "Uh, yes. She never got pregnant after Jack. He was her only child. Although back then, of course, he looked just like David."

Matt's head snaps toward Todd, mouth agape in surprise. "Oh, really? Oh, really! I see. She never wants to talk about it. You just told me much more than she ever did."

"Christ!" Todd shakes his head. "Forget I said anything. I assumed you knew the whole story. Sorry, man. Really."

"It's fine. All cool." Matt shrugs. He turns back to take his shot, whacks the ball, and misses… badly. "Damn it!" Disgusted with himself, he shoves his club back into his golf bag and fishes another Smirnoff from the cooler. He slumps into the seat on the passenger side and slugs back a gulp, not even looking like he enjoys the taste or the buzz. He stares straight ahead, brooding.

"You could take it as a compliment," Todd offers. "Like she chose you this time around." It was only a partial lie.

A sullen look comes over Matt's face. "Aren't you and David best mates?" When Todd doesn't answer he adds, "Were you and I even friends last time?"

Not really, no. Todd doesn't know what to say. At this point, Matt wasn't even alive anymore. No matter which way he swings it, Matt's situation is partly his fault. He, David, and Kate are complicit in rearranging Matt's life and fate.

"One of the benefits of Kate's decision—" Todd begins.

Matt interrupts. "What gave you the fucking right?!"

Todd slides into the driver's seat and in silence, steers the golf cart to the eighteenth hole.

***

While at the office, David's mind drifts back to his weekend in the Hamptons. It was a much-needed break from work pressure and his struggles with Anton, who, at almost six years old, prefers Angelika, his mommy. This rejection saddens David, but he keeps trying to think of ways to win his son over.

What keeps him on an even keel is that he and Stacy still bask in the flirty-fun phase of their relationship. Last weekend they invited friends to his East Hampton estate where Stacy got to show off her talents as a hostess—running around making sure everyone's drinks were topped up and offering delicious homemade pasta and sauces, all family recipes she learned from her Sicilian grandmother.

The reverie over, David checks his investment portfolio on the computer. His phone rings. He smiles when he answers. "Michael Burry. I was just looking at the fund. You must have read my mind. Is it payday?"

"Yeah, man." Burry gloats, "Those who bailed are reeling."

David laughs and snags a mini basketball from where it rests on his desk. Gleefully, he says, "Trust me on this, Hollywood will make a movie about what just happened. *The Big Short*. Celebrate next week. Lunch on me. Take care, Burry."

David hangs up and immediately hails Meredith on the intercom. "Call Mark," he says. "Tell him Scion Capital is liquidating."

When Meredith answers, "Yes, sir," David can hear the excitement in her voice.

David pops up and hurls the basketball toward a hoop in the corner of his office. *Swish!* He throws his arms up in victory and grins. "I still have it!" he proclaims to no one. When his phone rings, he sees Mark is on the line.

"Sully, are you sitting down? The Scion credit default swaps you tried to talk me out of? We're getting a 489 percent return."

A triumphant shout erupts from the phone.

***

Kate hosts Lissa for a lunch of chicken salad with grapes and walnuts in her bright and airy kitchen. A fresh bouquet of elegant flowers on the kitchen table fills the room with the sweet scent of gardenias. The nanny, Telma, watches the kids in the living room while baby Leo sleeps.

"See those flowers from Matt?" says Kate.

"Yes, they're gorgeous. How sweet of him," replies Lissa as she squeezes a lemon into her iced tea and stirs.

Kate shoots Lissa a cynical glare.

"What? You don't like them?" asks Lissa, taking a sip of her tea.

"No, it's not that. They're forgive-me flowers. A few days ago, Matt fell down the stairs."

"Oh, no! Is he okay?"

"Yes, thank God."

Lissa thinks for a moment. Kate waits for her to realize something's up. "If he fell down the stairs, why did he give you flowers?"

"To apologize for his drinking."

"Matt was so drunk he couldn't manage the stairs?"

Kate nods. "He hit his head. I ran over to help him up and he was completely incoherent. Ugh." Kate shakes her head in dismay.

"Did he get a concussion?"

"No, he was just *that* drunk. I got him into bed and checked to make sure he was breathing all night. But I was so shaken by what happened that I went downstairs and cried my eyes out."

Lissa touches Kate's shoulder. "It's tough. I know. He needs help."

Kate feels like she might cry again, but then shakes it off. "I keep telling him. But it's like he's doing this to hurt me on purpose." She sighs. "Last week he said to me, 'Didn't see this coming, did you?' but he wouldn't remember, so I haven't talked to him about it sober."

"Let me know if I can help in any way. I hate to see you like this. You don't deserve this."

Kate pats Lissa's hand. "Thanks, Liss."

Lissa's expression abruptly brightens. "Guess what? Newsflash! I decided to audition for a play next month."

"You had the acting bug last time around."

"What a mistake that was," Lissa says in a monotone,

"or would have been, to dump my degree."

"That's why they say, 'young and foolish.' I have news, too. We're about to start in vitro."

"Oh, yay!" Lissa claps her hands.

Telma comes in with a UPS package and hands it to Kate. "For you, Mrs. Armistead."

"Thank you, Telma." Kate rips open the package and pulls out a giant pink fleece thingy. "It's here!"

Lissa gives the garment a skeptical once-over. "What in the world is that?"

"It's a Snuggie!" Kate holds it up.

Lissa frowns. "It looks like a glorified sleeping bag. Please tell me you don't wear that horrid thing."

"'Fraid so. I just invested in the company that makes these. It'll be worth $500 million in a few years."

Lissa's eyes widen. "Holy cow! David isn't the only one with the share market smarts."

"I learned the hard way not to wait for him."

"Does he still put money in one of your bank accounts?"

"Ah, yeah. At least he's good for something." Kate says with disdain.

"Put it on. Let's see how truly tacky it is," says Lissa.

Kate tries on the Snuggie and models it like a runway supermodel with a stern look, dramatic strides, and sharp turns while the fabric flops about her limbs.

She and Lissa crack up.

"I'll get you one for your birthday," teases Kate.

"Oh, God. Please don't," says Lissa, laughing.

***

Todd and Stella race their bicycles up the driveway to the garage, their faces flushed and happy.

"I won!" proclaims Stella. "That means I get ice cream."

They hop off their bikes. Todd pushes his blue mountain bike and Stella her pink cruiser with tassels. He opens the garage door with a remote and sees Miles in a Disney Princess Belle dress painting at an easel. Todd's face feels hot as he and Stella park their bikes inside. He gives his kickstand an extra-hard thwack with his foot. "Where'd you get that princess dress, Miles?"

"From Mom," he answers.

"Whatcha paintin'?" asks Stella, not at all surprised to see her brother dressed as a princess.

"You, me, Mommy and Daddy, and baby Leo." Miles doesn't look up from his easel.

Stella runs over to see it. "Ooh. Good job, but you made my hair curly. It should be straight."

"It's prettier with curls."

Stella shrugs, "Whatever," and runs into the house, her tennies lighting up with every step.

Todd paces in the garage, agitated, thoughts churning. Ever since Miles has started dressing like a precious little girl—even Stella doesn't wear such getups— he and Todd have drifted apart. He gives Miles a little man-punch on his princess arm. "You missed a great bike ride, bud. We went all the way to the park."

"Oh," says Miles, half-listening.

The bland reply stings. Todd can't help but see all his hopes and plans for Miles—sports, father-son outings—whisked away like dust and there is nothing he can do to stop it. Todd gets international awards for saving entire communities from disaster and yet he can't salvage this floundering relationship with his son. For the moment, he gives up trying to connect with Miles and heads into the kitchen.

Lissa is at the stove, stirring veggie chili she made for dinner while Leo swings in his baby rocker. "Oh, hi!" She holds an inviting smile, but he's in no mood for affection.

"I had a nice lunch with Kate today."

Todd remains stiff and leans against the island as though it is propping up all 165 pounds of him. In a whisper-yell, he says, "You're encouraging this. Painting is one thing, but wearing a princess dress? We've talked about this, Liss. Last time, we were very clear on directing Miles toward team sports."

She stops stirring and peers up at him. "This is who he is, Todd. We must embrace and love our children for who they are. If we're not their champions, who will be?"

"You're going too far. He's gonna get bullied at school."

The stove timer pings. Lissa dons an oven mitt. "Getting my degree 'this time around' taught me a few things." She pulls cornbread from the oven.

Under his breath, Todd says, "Sometimes I wish you hadn't."

Lissa drops the pan on the bench with a clang and glares back at her husband. "Last time I couldn't be an actress. This time I can't be a counselor who cares about her own children's psychological wellbeing. Are you going to have another go-'round and turn me into a fucking finger puppet?"

Todd can't believe his ears. *Women escalate everything so quickly. I was trying to discuss my son's delusions, but she's gotta make it all about her.* What he can't tell her is that Miles is his only hope for all the father-son things he wants to do. It's never going to work with Leo. In fact, it won't be long before the cat's out of the bag.

Poor Leo will never be able to throw a fishing line, steer a boat, or ride a scooter. Because of the pain he'll be in he can't endure sitting for a movie or a baseball game. Shit! He won't even be able to speak clearly.

Todd knows he should placate his wife, but this is too important to get sidetracked. "Miles will go camping with me. He'll learn how to light fires and tie knots. I'll show him. We'll go away with the guys from soccer. We'll talk about the space program, third-world countries and the economy."

"So?" Baby Leo is howling, and Todd does his best to ignore him.

"So, he can't do all that in a goddamn dress!"

Lissa picks up Leo, puts him over one shoulder, and taps his back rhythmically. "You're doing it again," she says, clucking her tongue. "You're talking like the future is set in stone."

"Lissa, this path he's on. I didn't let it go this far last time. I joined him up to a soccer team. Harsh as it sounds, I made him put on the shorts and socks. He got over it."

"Did he? Doesn't sound to me like you would have even known how much damage you were doing. Certainly more than a few snot-nosed bullies."

Stella enters the room, dolly in hand. "Mm-mm!

Something smells yummy!" Her bubbly comments defuse the tension.

"It's cornbread sweetie, go wash up." Lissa steps to the door and shouts into the garage, "Miles, dinner is ready."

Todd clenches his teeth. Miles enters the kitchen and twirls in his costume.

Lissa gives him an embracing smile. "Come here, you lovely princess."

Todd's mouth opens. He stares at this strange, new, stubborn version of his wife, hands upraised. It's like he's nothing but a picture on the wall watching the scene unfold. "Miles is not a fucking princess. He's my son. You have no idea what you're doing to him."

Lissa glares at Todd, her eyes shooting daggers.

Miles grabs onto Lissa and sobs. "Do I have to give up my dress?"

She caresses his head. "No, sweetie, you don't."

Todd slams the door of his office and locks himself in, dismayed at how he became the villain in his own household.

***

David paces the sidelines, watching Anton play with his AYSO soccer team. His little boy is fast and has good feet, as evidenced by his goal, the team's only one so far. David tries not to look at Angelika and Henri, who seem extra lovey-dovey today, perhaps for his benefit. Yet, the few times he glances at them, Angelika seems more focused on David than either on Henri or their son's game.

David winces as the same feelings of rejection and jealousy he had upon seeing Kate and Matt together surface. *"Sow your oats,"* she had said. *I only did what you told me to do, Kate.*

The whistle blows, signaling the end of the game. 1–0. After the teams line up and high-five their opponents, the little soccer players skitter all over the field and join their respective families.

David approaches his son and holds his hand up for a high-five. "Hey, buddy. Awesome goal!"

Anton barely looks at him. "Uh-huh."

David stands alone, feeling stupid for expecting more from Anton, and watches his son make a beeline for Angelika and Henri, who high-five him. A shadow of sadness overtakes him. Once again, bitter thoughts worm through his memories. He sees himself with Kate as Jack scores a touchdown. Afterward, they high-five and savor a moment of pride. David sighs. There is a yawning pit in his belly.

Oh, Jack, what have we done?

***

As Kate walks toward her home, basketball in hand. Jack races ahead on his scooter. She notices a police car parked outside her home. Two police officers stand by the squad car, one with mirrored glasses and slicked-back hair and the other chubby and bald.

Jack stops by the police officers and gazes up at them, wide-eyed. "Hi, Mr. Policeman."

The cops acknowledge him with simultaneous nods.

The presence of the police startles Kate and she hurries to catch up with Jack. The cops act like they've been expecting her, and it is the officer with mirrored glasses who speaks. "Mrs. Kate Armistead?" When he takes off his sunglasses and studies her with eyes heavy with foreboding, her pulse quickens. She drops the basketball, and it bounces on the driveway, the percussive sound trailing off.

Kate struggles to maintain a sense of calm. "Is there a problem?" The words no sooner leave her mouth than she realizes there is a problem.

The chubby officer notes the neighbors sizing up the drama. "Ma'am, it would be better if we went inside."

Kate feels an undertow pulling at her legs, dragging her to a bad place she doesn't want to go. She manages to ask, "Is something wrong?"

Neither officer answers and she wonders why they're stalling.

She follows Jack as he scooters up the driveway to the front door. The cops turn toward the whoosh of a rapidly approaching car. It's Todd's Lexus swerving into the driveway. It jolts to a halt, tires chirping. Todd jumps out.

"What's going on?" Kate asks. Her concern turns to panic.

"I'm her brother. I've got this," Todd says to the officers. He goes to Kate and with a distinct look of dread takes hold of her shoulders.

"We'll leave you to it, sir." The police sound relieved at having been spared this unpleasant task. They return to their patrol car and drive off.

Kate feels the blood rush from her face. She stares

at Todd, waiting for him to explain.

Todd's nostrils flare as he searches for the right words. "Matt… went skydiving today."

Kate screams, "No! He said he was going to work. He's at work!"

Todd casts his eyes downward and shakes his head as if to say, *It's bad. Real bad.*

"No, no, no!" She sobs and covers her ears. "Please, no. It can't be true. Oh, my God!" She collapses on the step and buries her head in her hands.

She senses Jack running toward her. His kind words break through her sorrow. "Mommy, Mommy, don't cry. It's okay." He strokes her hair like she has done to him.

Kate trembles and she wrings her hands. "He promised me," she repeats. The onslaught of shock and sorrow sends her mind reeling.

Todd sits beside her. He scoops both Kate and Jack in his arms and draws them together as if his embrace can stop the pain, as if he can shelter her from a widow's fate and Jack from a fatherless future.

Kate stares at the ground. Last time it was so hard to make ends meet, but at least she and David had each other. Their Jack was a really vibrant personality, one of the popular guy's guys. It's like he had to prove he was better than his father at just about everything, something she knew chafed at David.

Even if she thinks blond Jack is the same person deep down, she knows the profound impact the absence of his father will have on him. He will not be the same.

Chapter 17

After the funeral, Kate and Jack return home with her parents. Kate had written and rehearsed a eulogy and barely made it through the reading before leaning into her dad and sobbing. He had agreed to stand next to her as she delivered it. She had written some humorous anecdotes, which gave the attendees some much-needed comic relief but had only made her sadder in the telling.

The guilt weighs on her and she keeps thinking, *If only he hadn't gone skydiving that day. If only I had known and stopped him. He'd still be here to tuck little Jack into bed with his favorite stuffed panda.*

Dad carries a flower bouquet. It's so large, his face is obscured. He sets it down on the kitchen table. Mom steps around him, looking preoccupied, and rearranges the blossoms to appear busy.

Kate pulls Jack up to the kitchen island. His innocent face brightens her outlook. "It's you and me now, little man. We're going to make Daddy proud," she says, grateful that she must be strong for him. Otherwise, she might totally fall apart.

Jack points skyward. "Dada up in heaven!" He waves to the sky and looks up as if expecting to see his dad. Kate kisses him.

Mom reaches for Jack. "Let's take you for a bath, sweetie."

"No bath," he whines and kicks his feet in protest.

"Oops! I shouldn't have said the B-word," says Elaine.

Kate hugs Jack. "The secret to bath-time is running boat races. Just prepare to go to battle and get drenched in the process." She laughs and the levity refreshes her. At this moment, her little boy is her saving grace.

Mom scoops him up and heads upstairs. Dad remains downstairs, a calming presence.

Kate walks over to the flowers, inhales their scent, and takes the card. It reads, *Thinking of you always, love David.*

Her first reaction is surprise, which sours into resentment. She rips up the card and tosses it into the trash can.

Dad says, "I think you could use a good soak in the tub yourself, love."

"Thanks, Dad. Have I told you how much I love you and Mom? I seriously don't know where I'd be without you both. Scratch that. I know exactly where I'd be—lost." She feels so vulnerable. The tears start to flow.

"You're stronger than you know, my Kate." Graham stands over her to kiss her forehead.

She weeps and leans into her dad for a comforting embrace. Her mind wanders over all the recent problems with Matt.

Ever since she told him about the Deheb Orb, Matt had been lost. There is a demon in the recesses of her mind trying to tell her something. The words are too horrible to hear so she squeezes her eyes shut, trying to block them from surfacing. Having been warned about his fate in Kate's first life, Matt was extra-careful about safety. He had told her as much.

He had said it himself, *"The chances of someone*

dying from skydiving are almost nothing."

      She has to know the truth. Pulling away from her dad, she does a quick search online. Her heart sinks as the number comes up in bold on Google: 0.0007%.

***

Todd and David are enjoying gin and tonics at David's home bar while his staff sets up the dinner table.

      "Kate always says, 'Like tea, we don't know how strong we are 'til we're in hot water.' I'm proud of her and her ability to prevail." Todd takes a sip of his drink.

      David shifts uncomfortably and his face drops. "Bro. I've never said it, but I'm really sorry I didn't follow through with Kate like I should've. I live with the guilt of not doing right by her. Now I get what it means to have found a soul mate."

      "Well, yeah, you messed up. But hell, we all fuck up even when we get a do-over. Trust me, I'm nowhere near Mr. Perfect the second time around either. The good news is Kate is getting out from under this awful tragedy." Todd is about to take a drink when he stops in sudden thought. "Oh, did I tell you? We bought a new house, thanks to the latest Stern windfall. So, thanks to you." They clink glasses.

      "You deserve it. I mean, you're on a higher mission that is seriously admirable—saving lives and improving our planet—as opposed to your best friend who's a selfish son of a bitch."

      "Don't be so hard on yourself," Todd says. "You're a good guy, too. You're not on a save-the-world mission this time around. But you are helping many people prosper.

That's huge, man."

"To a great business partnership!"

They clink their glasses again. David empties his drink and holds up his glass.

A staff member scurries over. "Another? Or are you switching to wine?"

"Another cocktail, please."

Stacy strolls in wearing a sleek black suit, looking business chic. She totes a designer briefcase. "Todd Benton?"

"That would be me." He moves to stand.

"Oh, please, no need to get up. I've heard all about you. Lovely to meet at last!" She sets her briefcase on a table.

"Likewise. I hear congratulations are in order."

She beams and extends an arm to display a shimmering solo diamond set in platinum. "Yes, I do believe I 'tamed the shrew,'" she says, laughing.

"That's the nicest thing anyone has ever said about me!" David replies.

Todd laughs and David smirks. A server hurries over and offers a tray with a Cosmo to Stacy.

She salutes David with the glass. "Thank you, my love."

Todd smiles, noticing how sweet they are together. Yet he can't dismiss David's indecision. One moment he's pining for Kate, the next he's latched onto Stacy.

***

With an armful of laundry, Lissa strolls into her master bathroom and discovers Miles on a chair in front of the mirror. He's wearing her silk robe and applying blush on his cheeks.

Both are equally startled, only he drops the blush, and it smashes on the floor, a rosy, pink scattering of glass shards strewn across the marble tile floor.

Oh, dear. Her seven-year-old looks like a clown with his overly rosy cheeks and red lipstick outside the lines of his lips.

"Oh, no! Mommy, I didn't mean it!" he says, panicked.

"It's OK, Miles. I'll clean it up." Lissa grabs a towel and wipes up the mess. She feels guilty for projecting any disapproval.

Frantically, he tries to put the makeup away.

"Miles, look at me."

He tries, but he's clearly too ashamed to make eye contact.

She clasps his little shoulders. "It's really OK."

Miles sheds a tiny tear as he stands before his mom with a droopy posture, still not convinced he's not in trouble.

"You're not in trouble. You can use my stuff any time."

Miles's face lights up. "Really? Any time?"

"Well, maybe not right before bedtime." She envisages all the russet and pink-smeared pillowcases. She's going to have to show her son how to use make-up remover before her daughter. "And maybe not..." She trails off. Lissa foresees lots of drama in the future with

Todd's recriminations heaped on her. On the one hand, she wants to nurture Miles and on the other, she can't take her marriage with Todd for granted. He is a good father who only wants the best for his family. It's a tightrope that she's forced to walk. "We don't need Daddy or Grammy walking in like I just did. How about you ask me in the future and when it works, we will make a plan?"

Miles nods so enthusiastically, he looks like a bobblehead. "Mommy, do you like my lipstick?" he asks a little shyly. Miles pulls free and turns to admire himself in the mirror.

Lissa stands behind him and hugs his shoulders. "It's very pretty."

"Mommy, what if I wish I was a girl?"

"Miles, you can be whoever you feel you are. I sometimes wish I were something else, too." She loves her child, no matter what. Whatever Todd thinks, she is in control of her own behavior.

***

Kate and Lissa stroll through the bustling shopping mall, the sweet scent of waffle cones wafting in the air. They had lured their kids away from the ocean-themed kiddie play area with the promise of ice cream. Unlike last time, Kate does not indulge in one for herself. Shopping bags weigh their arms as the kids lick their ice cream cones, half of which they're wearing on their faces.

Kate notices that Leo's chops are particularly covered. There's chocolate and jimmies on her nephew's shirt as well. She remembers him last time around and feels saddened he has to prevail—yet again—through his physical challenges. *But here we are. In the now, right?*

"You okay?" Lissa prompts.

"God, I so needed this." Kate heaves and exhales. "It's nice to have a normal day after all the crazies. I know they say that grief is a process, but they failed to mention it's a fucking boomerang. You think you're past the worst of it, and WHAMMO! It comes back and hits you like a ton of bricks."

"Oh, Kate, I know. I was taught that you just have to let it come—don't fight the grief. Feel whatever you need to feel, even if that's fine."

Sometimes Kate is glad that her best friend is a counselor. She really is a great listener.

"A little retail therapy helps!" Kate joyously holds up her bags.

It was about this time, in her first life, that Kate was grieving the death of her father. She and Lissa came on this very shopping trip. She reflects on the different style of clothes she's been able to buy this time around. Not only are there more designer labels, but they are four sizes smaller.

***

In his home, Graham reclines in his favorite leather chair, watching excitable news anchors banter.

Todd approaches him, weary from his red-eye flight and carrying cups of tea. He hands Dad his tea and sits in an adjacent chair. The weight of doom hangs over them, yet they pretend to watch TV. "Mom put milk and honey in it the way you like." They sit in a silence that grows deeper and gloomier with each passing moment.

It didn't happen like this last time. There was no time to prepare. And his sister wasn't already grieving. Todd notices that his tea has cooled and decides he has stalled long enough. "When should we tell Kate?"

Dad holds his cup of tea with both hands. "Not too soon. She's been through so much with Matt's death." He sips.

Mom hesitates at the doorway, heads for her recliner, and cries softly. Dad places his cup on the end table and her cup rattles against the saucer as she sets it next to his.

Graham extends his hand to take hers. He squeezes her fingers, a loving, tender gesture. "I've had a pretty good run, love. I could have dropped dead before now, you know. We all have to go some time."

"This is so unfair." Her eyes moisten and her chin trembles, but she stops herself from crying. "I just want us to grow old together. Was that too much to ask?"

Todd has no answer and his heart aches at the sight of his stricken mother. "Mom, let's focus on getting the best treatment possible." Todd's gaze shifts to his father. "I promise I'll fight for you, Dad."

***

The lights are low in Kate's bedroom as she and Jack snuggle, reading the bedtime story *Goodnight, Gorilla*, for the third time. The book is so worn, the pages have smudges and tears, but her boy never tires of it. Recently, he asked his mom if he could have a gorilla for a pet. "He could live in my room."

"Maybe a puppy would be better," suggests Kate. "How about if we just visit the gorilla at the zoo?"

The puppy idea pleases Jack so much, he forgets about having a gorilla as a roommate.

Some days Kate feels the gaping hole of the threesome turned twosome. Other days, she feels like their sweet twosome is all she needs to be happy in the world.

Halfway through the third reading, Kate realizes Jack is fast asleep. She watches him slumber for a few minutes, which is one of her favorite pastimes. It's like having a resident angel. Of course, there are times during the day when he is so far from angelic that she wants to pull her hair out. But she likes the fact that he's pure boy—a happy ball of kinetic energy.

Not like Miles, who appears to be dragging Todd and Lissa down an unfamiliar road. Kate is sure that Todd put a stop to his son's gender experimentation last time around. She wonders why he hasn't done it this time. Miles wasn't the happiest teenager, upon reflection. Sure, he played the ball games and did the trips with his dad, but Kate recalls her nephew becoming like a statue boy frozen in time. Waiting to be discovered in a different world.

Kate places the book on the bedside table and gently rolls Jack into a comfortable position, putting the blankie in his arms. "Goodnight, sweet boy."

She leans back in bed and smiles as she looks over at the statue of Mother Mary standing next to a Buddha on her bedside table. *Things are different this time around, but we are all going to be all right.*

***

David is in his walk-in closet, dressing smartly for dinner. He slips into his dark gray slacks, slate-blue dress shirt, and loafers with no socks. He grabs a tie and slings it around his neck, awaiting tying. As he dresses, his thoughts drift to Kate and her unthinkable loss. He tries not to let her perceived pain eat away at his own joy— right now his life is pretty damn good—but he's not always successful.

When his phone pings, he glances down to see an auto-reminder: *Tuesday 4:00 PM. Therapy with Dr. Cowan. Already*? He sighs and enters the bathroom to spray cologne. The TV in his bedroom catches his eye. With a remote, he turns up the volume to watch Charlie Rose interview Howard Buffet about his book, *Fragile: The Human Condition*.

Charlie shows the book and some of the photo inserts. The camera freezes on a photo of a filthy child in rags, sifting through a trash heap for food. There's something about the vivid green in the child's eyes that cries out, that shows the world of need in one glance.

"This book documents life stories in sixty-five countries," explains Charlie. "It is about personal accounts, some successful, some heartbreaking. *Fragile* portrays the challenges of life for four billion people. It is their perseverance and determination that allow for hope, but it is a hope that can only be realized through action."

"But that action must be applied with wisdom and humanity," Howard Buffet says, "I make the point that technology can't fix everything. Loneliness. Frustration.

Despair. These stories are about real people with real suffering,"

David quickly ties and straightens his tie, nodding approvingly. *Good on you, Howard.*

***

Lissa walks into the living room with twenty-month-old Leo. Kate has stopped by for a visit. Lissa plunks down next to her on the couch. Her new home is a two-story, contemporary style with vaulted ceilings and windows facing a park. Despite this abundance, her life feels that it is lacking, like she's been saddled with an enormous load for an arduous journey uphill and that she's only at the base of the mountain.

"How's my darling little nephew?" asks Kate, leaning over to caress Leo's cheeks. "I'm sorry about his prognosis."

Where to begin? thinks Lissa. "It's hard to take it in. They say he will walk but never be able to really run, kick a soccer ball, shoot hoops..." *Life seems so unfair.* She bursts into tears, startling Leo, then quickly gathers herself. "We'll figure it out as we go, I guess."

"You did last time. You will again." Kate covers her mouth.

The sorrow drains from Lissa, replaced by something like fury. She stares at Kate in disbelief. "Last time? No way would Todd..."

Her husband enters the room. Her eyes slit and, through gritted teeth, she manages to say, "Tell me this did not happen last time."

Todd keeps his cool. "Let me explain..."

237

Cradling Leo, she glares at her husband in disgust. "You always say you're doing things right—doing it better this time around. You're saving the whole fucking world. Did you forget to save your family along the way? Why on God's earth did you let me give birth to a baby with cerebral palsy!" With Leo in her arms, she rises from the couch and moves towards Todd. Kate tries to take Leo, but Lissa pulls away. Tears wet her eyes as her face darkens. "Why?" she screams.

Todd motions that she sit back down. "Liss, please calm down."

"Don't patronize me," she shoots back.

He waves his hands. "I thought with the extra bedrest and scans you would carry him longer, which you did, and he wouldn't be born breech, which he wasn't this time. That he would be okay."

"Why did you not tell me?"

Todd softens his voice to maintain control of the situation. "Because I didn't think this would happen. I… we… took every precaution. But life has other plans. I can honestly tell you that despite his limitations, we love him as dearly, as we did last time. Leo is our son, and he is meant to be here regardless."

Lissa moves away, clutching her baby boy. She glowers at Todd. "Did you stop to think about the pain this would cause? Every. Single. Day. To think that my son will never live a normal life and will struggle mightily will break my heart, one tiny piece at a time. Didn't you notice that last time around?" She pauses, her eyes squinting in rage. "You know Todd, you're not God!" She storms out of the room.

Later that evening, Lissa, in a robe with wet hair, leans over Leo's crib and caresses his tiny chest, warm through his pajamas. His ribcage expands with each breath. She loves him with every part of her being. The rancor from earlier is gone, replaced by a tranquil bliss.

Todd quietly pads in with stockinged feet and stands behind her. "Forgive me, Mommy," he whispers.

Lissa eases as he wraps his arms around her. Lissa pivots to rest her head on his chest and sighs. Todd kisses the top of her head.

She gazes at their sleeping baby boy, whose lips quiver as he breathes. "He's pretty perfect. Isn't he?" she whispers.

Chapter 18

Todd and Elaine share a table in front of the Otis Hotel's ballroom in Austin. A *2009 Benton Foundation Honor Roll* banner displays across the stage, marking the black-tie International Conservation Gala. Light from the opulent chandeliers sparkles on the crystal glasses arrayed in neat rows throughout the ballroom. At each table, fuchsia and white orchids float in bowls of water.

Elaine kisses Todd on the cheek.

He gives her a hug. "Thanks, Mom. I'm glad you're here."

"Are you kidding me? I wouldn't miss it for the world. I'm just sorry Dad couldn't make it. These social events take too much out of him," she says, her forehead creased with concern.

"I know. I'm also worried about him. It must be hard on you."

Touching Todd's shoulder, Mom says, "Don't worry about us, dear. You have enough on your mind."

Todd glances up at Kate and Lissa sitting across the table, whispering as they pretend not to be checking out David and his date.

Kate leans close to Lissa and says, "Did you see Mr. Bigshot over there with his wide-hipped date?"

Lissa brings a hand up to hide her laugh.

Todd frowns and admonishes, "Actually, it's his fiancée, Stacy. She's really quite lovely, Kate. I think you'd like her."

240

"I doubt it," Kate scoffs and gulps from her cabernet sauvignon.

The emcee, a balding man with a closely trimmed beard and a beaming smile, says, "Alright, everyone, if you could all take your seats, it's time to start the festivities. Without further ado, I'd like to introduce our guest of honor, the reason we are here, Mr. Todd Benton."

The audience applauds as Todd, face flushed, steps up to the podium, tension coursing through his body. Even after years of leading his company, public speaking still gives him the jitters. He pulls note cards from inside his tuxedo jacket, shuffles them onto the lectern, clears his throat, adjusts the gooseneck mic, again clears his throat. "Thank you for joining us. Tonight, we honor those in our community who share our same, simple goal—to improve the lives of those in need, here and abroad."

The audience applauds.

Todd waits for the clapping to fade before returning to his notes. "The work we do at the Benton Foundation would not be possible without the generous support of our donors, in particular, my dearest friend, David Stern, and the Stern Corporation who, over the past ten years, have provided us extraordinary financial support, allowing us to do the work we do." Todd pauses and leans forward into the mic. "David, come on up here!"

All eyes turn to David, who's at a front table adjacent to where Lissa and Kate sit. He looks dashing in his tuxedo and Stacy is radiant with pride.

She makes a show of kissing David on the cheek. He then runs up to join Todd, careful not to spill the glass of wine he's carrying, the epitome of ease and confidence.

Todd is envious of David's ability to step into the limelight with such poise.

David takes in the room with a commanding look. "So, here's the deal, Todd wants me up here to showcase the Stern Corporation, but I'm actually here for a different reason—to talk about Todd Benton."

The audience applauds again, accompanied by a few whistles.

David gestures with his glass of wine. "Mr. Benton is the most selfless, generous man I've ever known, and trust me, I know a lot of wonderful people. As the rest of us go about our days, he is singlehandedly changing the world. His concerns are the world's. He's a real superhero but without the cape and spandex. At least in public. Who knows, he could be Batman!"

The crowd roars with laughter. While David continues to sing Todd's praises, Todd's face warms with embarrassment, and he wishes he could melt into the floor and disappear.

David notices and wings an arm around Todd and does so without spilling a drop of wine. "You see, folks, he's not doing any of this for the praise. He's a behind-the-scenes benevolent force." David gives his friend a loving, brotherly smile. "I'd like to propose a toast to the greatest guy in the world, who gives us all hope that the world is becoming a better place." He holds his glass high. Lissa raises her glass, Kate reluctantly does so. Others tap spoons against their glasses and the ping of crystal fills the ballroom, followed by cheers and hearty applause.

When Todd and David step down from the podium, Todd appears ready to throttle his best friend. "Duuude, what the hell was that?"

"I thought they should know," David replies offhandedly. "I mean, I wanted them to get who you are on a visceral level."

Todd shakes his head in mock umbrage. "Oh man, you've got it coming. Just you wait!"

David turns and anchors both hands on Todd's shoulders. He holds his friend's gaze. "You deserve it. I mean that. You really do."

Todd finally accepts the praise. "Thanks, man."

Dozens of guests mob Todd, who is tired but thankful for this night, wishing his dad would delight in his success but suspecting he never will.

***

Kate strolls over to the hors d'oeuvre station. David walks up beside her with a swagger. She stiffens and acts like she's very focused on the smoked trout blinis with crème fraiche and doesn't notice him.

"Hey. Don't I know you from somewhere?" David offers.

"Maybe." She nonchalantly lifts one shoulder, while filling her plate.

"Kate, you look as gorgeous as ever," he says, not bothering to disguise the flirtatious tone.

Kate rolls her eyes. "You're really packing a lot in this time around, aren't you? Which reminds me..." She smirks at him. "I'll bet one of those lil' blue pills is kicking in right about now?"

"Ha! Yes, I am. And why not? I have a lot of stock in

Pfizer after all. Hell, I'm my own best customer."

"Yup. You're all about the money, honey." She looks as if she has more to say but steps away in disgust.

David chuckles self-consciously like he's trying not to feel the backhand of a rebuff, and he shakes it off.

***

Lissa and Kate enjoy a picnic in a park next to the monkey bars and swings where the kids play. They brought PBJs for the little ones and Greek food for themselves. They've polished off the hummus and Greek salad and have left the honey-sweetened baklava for dessert.

Leo, with braces on his legs, struggles in a wobbly gait to catch up with Stella, Jack, and Miles. He falls but gets right back up and chases after the others. His face is strained, but he's smiling.

Kate calls out, "You're such a trooper, Leo!" and she pops a dolmade in her mouth.

Lissa becomes solemn. "Last week he said, 'No like these legs, Mamma. I want new ones.' It broke my heart. Actually, my heart breaks a little every day."

"You'll plan a surgery in a few years. It will help a lot."

"Yes, Todd told me. Good to know. The last surgery was so hard on him, yet we saw little results." Lissa sips an iced tea mixed with lemonade.

"Trust me," Kate insists, "The next surgery you do is laser tech, and it will make a big difference."

Lissa is relieved to hear this.

"Speaking of which, I'm scheduled next week for

my lumpectomy. Then hormone therapy. It'll be much easier to deal with than last time."

"You had chemo and a double mastectomy before, right?" Lissa asks, horrified.

"I've avoided that ordeal this time. Thank God for checkups... and golden orbs!" Kate laughs aloud at her inside joke.

Lissa still wishes she knew more about the time travel experience, the Deheb Orb, and its keeper, Yusaf. And she still wonders why she chose not to go back.

Nearby, a young couple has more of an elaborate setup than Lissa and Kate's—a fancy picnic basket with champagne. The woman's head rests in the man's lap, and she's looking up at the clouds, wistfully and teary. They're cranking "Man in The Mirror" and singing along.

"They've been playing Michael Jackson songs since we got here. What's the deal? I mean, I like him well enough, but how about some other tunes?" Lissa starts to laugh then stops. "Unless." She checks her phone. "Oh no! He died today."

Kate perks up. "What? Michael Jackson? How?"

"Drug overdose," Lissa reads from her phone. "Propofol. They say his doc administered surgery anesthesia so he could sleep. Really effed up. That's... so, so sad."

"The list grows." Kate leans in. "Next, Whitney Houston and then Prince."

"No way! I don't believe you. I mean, I do, it's just—"

"Hard to believe, I know. Should I tell you about George Michael?"

Lissa closes her eyes and holds up both hands. "Stop! This is way too much. Wow. Just shows you, life is precious."

"Indeed, it is. Speaking of which, here's hoping the last round of in vitro worked." Kate peers up at the sky. "Please, God, if you're up there? I promise I'll be good."

Lissa shares a guarded smile. "God doesn't work like Santa Claus."

***

Lissa stands upstage wearing a sexy dress and red lipstick with her hair in an up-do. Two actors are stage left, waiting for their cues. The Third Coast Repertory Theater Company is rehearsing *Marie Antionette.*

"Oh, we're always in fights," says Lissa as Marie Antoinette, conveying exasperation but not overacting. She feels in her element here, not as a mother, but as a queen; not serving others, but rather others serving her.

"Same old?" asks the actress playing Lamballe.

The director interrupts, "That's great. And just cheat out a little as you come stage left when you say your line." The theater lights have been dimmed, the red chairs empty, except for Steven's, the director, sitting in the fifth row. He's a thirty-something man who's mastered an insouciant scruffy look yet projects a charming voice that carries across the theater. He wears glasses with thick, blocky frames, the kind that convey cool geek.

As Lamballe comes downstage Lissa begins her lines. "I do like to disport myself. I'm sorry, even buffeted by the outcries of peasants—I'm a queen. I cannot simply forfeit my luxuries—" says Lissa with royal elegance and entitlement.

"No, it'd be calamitous," replies the actress playing Lamballe too eagerly.

"Ann, you stepped on her line a bit," Steven abruptly corrects. "Watch your timing." Then adoringly, he says to Lissa, "You were born to play a queen!"

"Why, thank you." Lissa, face flushed, curtseys.

They share a sweet laugh.

She draws in a sharp breath when she notices the other actors exchanging knowing glances.

***

A few weeks later, on opening night, Todd, Stella, and Miles join the audience in a standing ovation for Lissa and the cast's stellar performance.

Stella sidles up to Todd and says with a huge smile, "Wasn't Mommy so great?"

He nods emphatically. "Yes. Yes, she was."

The cast stands hand-in-hand at the front of the stage, sharing an effervescent smile with one another and the audience, then bowing in sync.

Todd can't remember the last time Lissa looked so joyful. Until now, he had forgotten about this side of Lissa. He thought she had changed into a more serious, subdued person. But now he knows otherwise, and the uneasiness of witnessing her blossom this way puts him on edge. If he and the kids hadn't brought a celebratory bouquet for her, he would have made an excuse to head home after the show and told Lissa the kids were too tired to meet her backstage. He doesn't want to trespass onto her enchanted world of happiness where rejection will sting him more intensely.

When the curtains close and the theater begins to empty, Todd says to Stella and Miles, "Let's go find Mommy." The threesome wanders backstage with the bouquet of red roses for Lissa. They mill around while the cast talks animatedly about opening night, reviewing their performances and mistakes, laughing all the while. Todd and the kids wait at the threshold of a corridor.

"Where is she?" his daughter asks, peering up at Todd.

"I'm not sure," he says, caressing her head. "Maybe changing out of her costume."

An actor overhears their conversation and says, "Lissa's still in her dressing room. Go on back." He gestures toward a door down the corridor.

Todd approaches the door, which is ajar. He pushes it open and finds Lissa and Steven in front of the makeup mirror haloed by a circle of bright lights. They're in giddy conversation. Lissa still wears her full costume, including her pouffe wig, and Steven is leaning over her. Todd catches her eye in the mirror. Caught off-guard, she swivels in her chair and smiles uncomfortably, projecting a less confident Marie Antoinette despite being in her regal attire.

Miles and Stella crowd against Todd and he senses that they have interrupted something, like a dramatic coaching session, but it feels more intimate. It's as if Lissa as Marie Antoinette belongs to this man and not to their family. The thought burns like bile. The back of Todd's throat tightens and his teeth clench.

"Mommy, your hair looks so puffy!" Miles holds up the bouquet.

"Oh, do I still have this thing on? Silly me," Lissa says, removing her towering wig to reveal her real hair flattened under a net. She sets Marie's pouffe over its plastic stand on the vanity. "Are those for me?"

Miles nods and hands her the bouquet.

"Thank you, sweetheart!" She sniffs the flowers. "They're so lovely."

"You were so good, Mom!" Stella beams with pride.

"Thank you, Stella."

Todd goes to give Lissa a kiss, but she turns toward Steven. "This is my husband, Todd."

Steven extends his hand.

Todd shakes his hand and tries not to glare. "Nice to meet you."

"Your wife is quite a talent," says Steven, his attention fixed on Lissa.

Todd smiles at her. "Yes, she is. Full of surprises!" When he leans in for a kiss, she stiffens slightly and half-heartedly meets his lips.

***

Todd slumps at his desk, puzzling over a spreadsheet. Kate storms in without knocking and slams the door behind her, startling him.

He can't read her expression. "Geez. Everything okay?"

Kate hustles toward his desk, smiling. "More than

okay. Fantastic! Can you guess what just happened?"

"You won the lottery."

"Better than that."

"Better than winning the lottery? You fell in love?"

She rolls her eyes. "That's your best guess?" She pulls out a positive pregnancy test and waves it in the air. I tried to get hold of Lissa but she's rehearsing. I had to show someone. You were the next best thing!"

"You did it. Well done!" Todd says, beaming.

"I'm beyond excited." She glances skyward. "Thank you, Matt. We're having a baby! But since you're in heaven you probably already knew that." She turns to Todd.

Todd sends her off. "See ya!" His eyes rest on a photo of Kate, Jack, and the late Matt. Todd wonders what the near future will bring.

***

Lissa's eyes blink open and she sits up in bed in a panic. Todd's side of the bed is already made. She glances around to see his briefcase on a large stool in the spacious walk-in closet. Lissa breathes a sigh of relief and slips out of bed. *Why do I keep having this recurring nightmare?*

From downstairs, Stella and Miles are going at it in the living room and Lissa hurries to run interference.

When Stella sees her mother, she cries out, "Mommy, Miles was playing with my American Girl doll, so I took it away."

Lissa points a finger. "Stella, you can share your dolly with Miles."

Stella shakes her head. "Boys shouldn't play with dolls!"

250

Todd dashes in to see what the fuss is about, carrying Leo and a set of leg braces. "Calm down, Stella. You'll wake up the whole neighborhood. Miles, leave her dolls alone!"

Lissa glares at Todd. "Um, I was handling this."

"Yeah, well, Liss, Miles needs to learn how to play with boy toys."

Miles wails, "Why can't I have my own dolls?" and stomps upstairs. They hear his bedroom door slam.

Todd sighs, lowers Leo to the ground, and begins to put on his leg braces. Leo squirms and resists. "These help you walk better. Come on, buddy."

"I don't want..." Leo starts to cry.

Todd grips Leo. "Stop it, Leo. We're putting these on!"

Lissa moves in to rescue her son. "It's okay. We can put them on later."

Todd doesn't budge or make way for Lissa's intervention. He forces the brace on Leo's left leg while his son sobs. Todd yells over the crying, "He wears the braces. It's for his own good. End of story."

"Oh, right, how could I forget? The world according to Todd." Lissa cradles her son and wipes his tears.

Todd stares at her, his eyes smoldering with anger and hurt. Lissa turns her back on him and removes Leo's braces. She hears his feet scuff across the carpet as he leaves the front room.

Later that day, Todd is nearly late to a meeting he's hosting for several scientists from the National Earthquake Hazards Reduction Program (NEHRP). He's rattled from his tough morning and tries his best to focus on a large map of

Haiti at the center of discussion.

"You've got all our geologists, including Mr. Prepetit, warning an event is inevitable. We're all on the same page. The Haitian government is spending all its money on four-wheelers for senior officials. Given its corrupt political agenda, we must find alternative ways to prepare emergency supplies for when a quake hits."

Todd is smothered by the irony and his own hypocrisy. Here he is planning to contain earthquakes and he can't even manage damage-control with his own wife and family.

***

Lissa and Steven sit on the edge of the stage in the John Henry Faulk Theater. Lissa swings her legs like an excited teen. She never feels so alive as when she's on a stage; every part of her awakens from sleepwalking through life. In the act of pouring herself into a role, anything feels possible.

Steven sips coffee from his tin cup, held by a wire tin man as the handle. "Want some?"

"Sure! It smells divine." She takes his cup and sips from it, leaving red lipstick on the rim. Her eyes pop wide open. "Yuck! It tastes like battery acid." She hands it back to him.

"That's how I like it—strong—like my women."

Lissa laughs. "Plenty of those types in the theater world. How is it you're still single?"

Steven says nothing but holds her gaze. It's obvious he doesn't intend to answer but she doesn't care. All that matters is the attention he brings to her.

He puts down his cup and picks up a script. "I've finished the last rewrites for my work." His voice grows giddy. "And the company agreed to produce it. We're putting it on its feet next month."

"That's fantastic. You did it!" Lissa says, touching his leg.

"Can you believe it? And I have the perfect role for you!"

She considers what he said. "Really?"

"Take a look. It's almost like it was written for you." He hands her the script. As she reads, he tenderly brushes a lock of hair from her face. She smiles up at him, her cheeks warming with color.

***

David, Stacy, and Anton are seated in the fifth row at the Gershwin Theater, watching *Wicked* starring Idina Menzel and Kristin Bell. For most people, the tickets are impossible to get, but David scored three with his connections. Stacy is sandwiched between David and Anton. During Elphaba's rousing, "Defying Gravity," David's phone vibrates. He sneaks it from his pocket and sees that the screen has lit up with a text from Todd. *Tohuku Japan earthquake. Mother Nature's kicking my ass!* David does a mental eye roll and slides the phone back into his pocket.

Stacy nudges David and points. Anton is glued to Minecraft on his iPhone. David shrugs. *Whaddya want me to do?*

Stacy taps Anton on the arm and motions for him

to hand over his phone. He flips her off. She stares at him, stunned, as he turns back to his game. She turns that stare to David, who repeats his previous gesture. *The kid is an asshole. What can I say?*

***

Reclining in her hospital bed under harsh florescent lights, Kate holds her sweet baby girl, Abby, whose rosy face is smooshed from the traumatic journey down the birth canal. Monitors flash and beep incessantly, nurses scurrying in and out, but Kate tunes them out. Her best friend sits on the edge of the bed, and together, they shed tears of joy. Abby's tiny hand is wrapped around her mother's finger. Her eyes are scrunched shut.

"She's the most beautiful baby ever," Lissa says, tenderly touching Abby's head.
"Look at those golden wisps of angel hair!"

Kate strokes the baby's face. "She's pretty perfect, I must say. Look at that little pouty mouth. She's gonna be a heartbreaker! We'll just have to keep the boys away from her."

Lissa grabs her iPhone. "Come on, we gotta Instagram this miracle girl!"

"Oh my God, no." Kate grimaces. "I look like a star in a horror flick called *Momzilla*."

"You do not. You look like a gorgeous mama."

"Alright, but if it doesn't turn out, promise me you won't post it."

Lissa crosses her heart. "Promise!"

They capture silly and serious poses until Kate is happy with one.

Later, Lissa posts the photos on Instagram. Within minutes, Kate notices they get over 300 likes, one of which is from David.

Chapter 19

As Todd drives to his parents' place from the airport, a John Lennon quote runs through his mind: "Love is a promise, love is a souvenir, once given never forgotten, never let it disappear. *Never let it disappear.*" Lennon's words are particularly poignant now.

His mom had called to tell him and Kate to come to her home right away to say goodbye to their dad. With a heavy heart, Todd thinks about what an intense couple of years it has been—the Haitian earthquake, the Japan earthquake and tsunami, tornadoes, and the Egyptian Revolution, and now his dad lay dying at home. Todd isn't ready to say goodbye. But when will he ever be?

Todd pulls up into his parents' driveway and slides out of his rental car. He steels himself against the pain of seeing his dad, his once-powerful dad, his once all-knowing dad, now fragile and weak. He rings the doorbell, listens for the chime, and sees his mom peek out the window adjacent to the front door. She smiles when she sees him, but it's not her usual vibrant smile. When she opens the door to let him in, she appears drawn and weary.

"Now dear, I want to prepare you. Kate was shocked and very tearful when she first saw Dad yesterday. She's out with the kids at the park right now." Elaine lays a hand on Todd's shoulder. "But make no mistake, he's still every bit your dad and he's got his wits about him. I don't know if that's a good or bad thing. I might prefer to be out of it during my final days."

She takes Todd by the hand and leads him toward

the master bedroom. Mom stops before they go in. "I keep imagining what life's going to be like without him. It just seems unthinkable."

Todd squeezes his mother's hand. "We'll be here for you as much as you need us."

"Thanks, dear." She pushes the bedroom door open.

The lights are low and the room smells stale but hygienic, as if his mom has been cleaning to beat death at its game. The head of the bed is slightly elevated, and Graham is surrounded by lots of pillows. His eyes are closed, his skin waxy, and his breathing labored under an oxygen mask.

"Graham, honey, Todd is here," Elaine says in a soothing voice. "I'll leave you two alone." She quietly closes the door behind her.

Dad's eyes flutter open and with a slight smile, he says, "It looks worse than it is. Really."

Todd settles next to his dad on the king-sized bed. Up close, Graham looks gaunt, pale, and fragile. When he takes his father's hand, Todd's eyes well up.

"I have something to tell you, Dad." Todd breathes deeply as he prepares to tell his father about their travel back in time.

When Todd finishes his story, Graham pulls the oxygen mask away. A blush of color brings vitality to his face. "I'll be damned. That's one heck of a story." He sputters, coughs, and with clumsy movements, replaces the mask over his mouth and nose. He takes a raspy breath.

Watching his father deteriorate like this torments Todd, and he struggles to hold it together. "I wanted to have a relationship with you like the one we have now. We didn't have that before and you were gone before I could change it. This time, at least we got three more years together." Todd can't stop the torrent of emotion. His face contorts, and tears stream down his cheeks. "I love you, Dad. You have no idea."

Graham squeezes Todd's hand with a feeble grip. His bones feel like twigs. "I think I do. I love you, son. Thank you for giving me a second chance."

Todd squeezes Graham's hand and lays his head to share the pillow, wondering if he's listening to his father's last breaths.

***

Huge bouquets of white lilies decorate the funeral home chapel. The scent of polished floors and oak wafts through the chapel. Graham's service is underway with his brother delivering the eulogy. He relates poignant and funny stories, helping mourners laugh through their tears. Near Graham's casket, a photo of him in better days is adorned with flowers.

David and Stacy are seated a few rows from the front, holding hands. David recalls a time when his son from the other life, a young Jack, and Graham fished off a jetty and ate peanut butter and jelly sandwiches. David wipes tears with a tissue Stacy gave him. He didn't come prepared. As the service concludes with the pianist playing Leonard Cohen's "Hallelujah," Kate and Todd receive condolences from guests. David and Stacy walk up to Kate, who props a squirmy Abby on her hip.

Kate's eyes shine with tears. "Hi, Stacy."

"My sincerest condolences," Stacy says, head cocked, eyes filled with empathy.

"Thank you."

Abby coos and reaches for Stacy.

"Oh, I guess someone wants to say 'hi,'" Kate says with surprise.

Stacy takes Abby in her arms. "Well, hello, sweet girl." She is mesmerized by Abby, who makes her laugh and points to a statue of an angel. She walks her over to give Abby a close-up.

David's eyes still feel moist and his face sags with grief. "Your dad was the greatest."

"Yes, he was. Though I'm not sure how close you two were this time around."

David averts his gaze. *She's right.*

"All good. Been meaning to tell you something, David..."

He braces for an insult.

She says, "I forgive you," with no drama in her voice. "I should've known that making you wait would have consequences."

He blinks as his mind processes this. "Oh, wow. I didn't expect that. I appreciate it, Kate."

They share a moment, not saying anything.

Stacy and Abby rejoin them. "Your sweet girl loves that angel. She asked if we could take the statue home. I said that she had to stay here to look over all the sad people."

Kate scoops up Abby and kisses the top of her head. She says to Stacy, "You will make a great mom."

"Thank you. If I ever get to be one," Stacy replies, exasperated. "We're trying... about to start in vitro."

Kate hugs Abby. "That's what I did to get this little one."

"Really?"

"It's so worth it, even though it's a pain in the ass, literally. But you get used to the shots." Kate pats her rear.

"Especially if I play doctor!" says David with a chuckle that lightens the mood.

They exchange laughter.

***

Kate, Jack, and baby Abby eat noodles for dinner. Abby is in hysterics, but Kate and Jack can't figure out why. Then Kate notices most of Abby's noodles on the floor. She'd been secretly dropping her noodles for the dog, Wilbur, who quickly lapped up the evidence.

Abby drops the last of her noodles as she sings to the tune of "London Bridge," "Noodles is falling down, falling down, falling down. Noodles is falling down. My fair lady."

"Okay, silly, these aren't playthings. They're your dinner." Kate takes a spoonful of noodles and serves it to Abby, who locks her lips. "I've never known anyone, kid or otherwise, who didn't like noodles. C'mon, sweet girl, you need to eat."

Abby shakes her head.

Kate's phone rings. "Hey, Stacy. Great timing. I needed a break from Romper Room." She looks at the mess on the table and sighs. "What's the latest?"

"No one told me fertility treatments would be a

full-time job," complains Stacy.

Kate gets up and moves away from the kids. "I know. It seems a lot. But you have to keep your eyes on the prize. In vitro can take a while, even years."

"That's what I'm afraid of."

"Then again, you could be pregnant next week!"

"I feel crazy, and it's more than just the hormones."

"The desire to have a child is all-encompassing. I get it. Baby fever takes hold and doesn't let go."

"After three rounds of trying in vitro, adoption seems like a better option. I tried to talk to David, but he doesn't want to hear it."

Abby drops another noodle on the floor for the dog.

Kate shouts, "Abby! Stop it!" Then to Stacy with a calmer tone, "Are you sure you want kids? Right now, my little angel is anything but!"

Stacy laughs. "I have such a bad case of mommy fever even naughty behavior sounds adorable."

"So you're done with in vitro?"

"I've got another scheduled. Ugh, I hate thinking how I'll feel after the procedure."

"Be positive," says Kate. "That might be the one that does the trick."

"Thanks," Stacy answers, sounding resigned. "I don't know how I'd get through this without you."

"Hang in there. Take care, Stace." Kate hangs up and moves back towards the kids. Thinking back on the phone call, she smiles and shakes her head. "Life is so strange. Who'd have thought?" She ponders how friendly she is with David's wife, of all people. Jack looks up at her, confused.

***

Lissa and Steven sit at a table in the corner at Starbucks, tucked away from prying eyes. A line of restless coffee addicts snakes through the store. The baristas move manically at the espresso machine, cranking out lattes, cappuccinos, and other specialty drinks.

"Can't believe I'm outta here tomorrow," says Steven, sipping his triple espresso with no frills. His eyes sparkle as he gazes at Lissa.

"You have an opportunity of a lifetime. I mean, it doesn't get better than directing and starring in a Broadway show." She holds up her café mocha for a toast.

Steven toasts. "I'm really going to miss you."

"I'm going to miss you more."

"I wish you could come with me."

She pauses and her motherly responsibilities flit through her mind. She feels trapped. "In another life, I'm afraid. In another life."

They hold each other's gaze for what seems like forever. Steven reaches across the table and takes her hand. They entwine with ease. Lissa looks away as tears slide down her cheeks.

***

The years 2011 and 2012 whiz by: Putin is elected, Bin Laden is killed in a surprise attack, and Facebook has its initial public offering at $104 billion. Todd often contemplates the present as much as he does the future while wading through this "redo." He marvels at how much

262

stays the same and often wonders if things are just meant to be.

Todd walks up to Miles, the puppeteer of his sister's dollhouse, where he has created a Barbie-verse, with drama and conflict and lots of outfit changes and stupid hairstyles.

"C'mon, Miles, we're going to Stella's game," says Todd, gazing down at the world of pink. He has tried every trick he knows to steer Miles away from a feminine trajectory, but this time nothing works. It's like Lissa's sympathy for it has made Miles immune to Todd's gentle steering.

It's not that he wants a macho son, it's just that he wants one with a normal boyhood—roughhousing, climbing trees, and taking part in ballgames. With the onset of puberty, Todd has no idea how to navigate those shoals. To make matters worse, Lissa doesn't seem to mind that their boy is more feminine than Stella.

Without turning away from the dollhouse, Miles says, "I don't want to go. It's boring."

"Miles, you need to learn from your sister how to compete in sports and be a team player." Todd grabs Miles's hand and yanks, but Miles resists, clutching his sister's Barbie. He starts to cry.

Lissa runs in. "What's happening in here?"

"Daddy says I have to go to the game," Miles fusses then pleads, "but I wanna stay home." He waves the Barbie like a wand.

"You don't have to go," says Lissa.

Todd glares at his wife, but she doesn't react.

Stella, now twelve, runs into the room wearing a

baseball uniform. "Let's go! I gotta warm up."

Leo, now seven, sits in the hallway, waiting to leave.

Lissa and Todd whisper-fight while heading out to the driveway, one accusing the other of undermining their parental authority.

Todd picks up a cooler and tote bag full of snacks and continues to the van. He slides the door open and loads the car. "I'm just saying he should want to come to the game and not stay cooped up at home, doing whatever it is he does."

Lissa grabs his shoulder to turn him towards her. "You know what? You're no different from your father. You're making Miles feel the way you did. History is repeating itself."

Todd starts to defend himself. His face feels hot, and a nauseating dread suffuses his soul. *This can't be happening. This is not what's supposed to happen!*

Stella jumps into the car. "C'mon, Dad. I can't be late like last time!"

Last time, he repeats to himself bitterly, *last time Miles did as he was told. He wasn't playing with Barbies. He wasn't "bored" at the game. We shared a Coke and threw fries at someone's dog to stop it from barking.*

Todd helps Leo into the van and slides the door shut with a bang. Lissa waves to Leo and Stella as the van pulls out, but in the rear vision mirror, he sees her hands on her hips. *When did she become such a bitch?*

***

Kate and Lissa jog side-by-side on a trail in the city park. They're running at a nice clip, weaving in and out of walkers, meanderers, and fellow runners. Despite the brisk pace, they manage a lively back-and-forth without losing their breath.

Lissa is worked up, telling Kate about Todd's being incorrigible. "The world according to Todd," she says.

"Yep. He's a bit of a know-it-all."

"So, did I complain about him the same way last time?" Lissa asks breathlessly.

"No, he gets under your skin more this time. I think that's because he's a know-it-all who actually knows it all!"

Lissa laughs. "Gee, thanks. You're a big help. Seriously though, were we, like, really happy last time? Great marriage, right?"

"Hello! You renewed your vows on your tenth anniversary."

Both women stop. A group of hardcore runners gallop by.

"Shit. Fuck. I did it again. Sorry, Liss," Kate places her hand on Lissa's back.

"It's okay. I asked you. I think this time... life, rather, saving lives, has gotten in the way." Lissa's smile looks painted on. She runs off. Kate watches her go with a sinking feeling.

***

Stacy and David sit side by side in his Bentley, saying nothing. The sun sets over the Hudson River of Lower

Manhattan. They stare at the ripples of water glistening under the glow of orange-pink streaming from the disappearing sun.

Having just left a therapy session, likely the last, the mood is somber, and the conversation has left David with a heavy heart. During the session, David finally admitted that the idea of having more children terrified him. He'd already had one wrenched from him and he didn't want to relive that heartbreak.

Stacy revealed she had already started the process of adopting one-year-old twin girls from Moldova who were born with heart defects. Bringing them to America is her dearest wish. After David's outburst in response to Stacy going behind his back, he surrendered to the reality that children were more important to her than him and he didn't want to stand in the way of her desires.

David notices Stacy twirling her emerald and diamond ring on her left wedding finger.

Her gesture alarms him. "Please don't even try to give it back. It's yours forever, Stace."

"I'll always treasure it," Stacy replies like she knows this is what he wants to hear.

"You're going to be the most amazing mom. I'm just sorry I can't—"

"I told you, David," she cuts him off. "It's okay not to be on board with my plan. You have your life. I have mine and they're no longer running along the same path."

David wants to take her hand one last time, but the deed would be pointless. He manages to say, "I will always love you."

Stacy gives a perfunctory smile. *As a friend though,*

she mouths, "Always and forever, D."

Unlike his previous relationship, he's thankful there's no bitterness or drama. Just a new chapter ahead as the old one flounders behind him, like jettisoned cargo. He's relieved but melancholy, wondering if he'll ever find a relationship that's for keeps.

***

Todd and Lissa watch TV coverage of the Boston Marathon bombings from their king-sized bed. Lissa's glass of Chardonnay is half-empty on the bedside table. The footage replays an explosion on the sidewalk near the finish line next to national flags. An ominous cloud of smoke rises above the screaming crowd and mayhem. Injured runners and spectators lie sprawled on the ground, and people rush to help them.

"Fucking hell," curses Todd. "If only I could've stopped those bastards."

Lissa keeps her eyes glued to the TV. "I keep having to remind you that you're not omnipotent."

"No, I'm not. But clearly, God is asleep on the job."

Todd's phone rings. He picks it up from the nightstand and answers, "Hey, Kate."

Lissa tries to listen but can't hear what Kate is saying.

Todd exclaims, "That's great news! Makes me feel better about Boston, which is so fucking depressing. To think that they came to America and all they can do with their newfound freedom is to radicalize online and make bombs out of pressure-cookers. I know, I know. Win some, lose some. Love you, too." Todd hangs up.

"Good news?" asks Lissa.

Todd exhales deeply as if he had been holding up the world until that phone call. "Two garbage trucks parked outside the Staples Center in downtown L.A. As the drivers climbed out, the L.A. SWAT team moved in. The bomb squad pulled up a short distance away as the army of SWAT team members surrounded them. It's like this bombing never happened. Because this time, it didn't."

Todd grabs *40 Chances. Finding Hope in a Hungry World* written by Howard G. Buffet and settles into his book.

Lissa sighs. "Sometimes, I just wish I were part of the club."

"Sorry?" replies Todd, his attention divided.

"Never mind." Lissa turns off the TV and her lamp and nestles to sleep on her side of the bed, her back to Todd.

Chapter 20

At four, Abby is obsessed with making forts. Even though her brother Jack is ten and tired of fort-building, he plays along. The twosome has created a fort using all the pillows and blankets in the living room. Abby brought every single one of her stuffed animals and dolls from her bedroom, and they seem to be enjoying the fort more than the builders.

Abby skitters to the hallway in her bare feet and retrieves her stroller, singing "This Old Man." She pushes it over to Jack, who's inside the fort, where there's barely room for him because of the toy invasion. "Dadda, push the baby!"

"I'm not your dadda, Abby," protests Jack, sighing dramatically. "I told you. He's in heaven." Jack points toward the ceiling. "Up there."

Abby's gaze follows Jack's finger and stares at the ceiling, clearly expecting to see the father she's never known. "I don't see him."

"Oh, never mind." Jack is resigned, fed up with explaining hard-to-explain things to his little sister.

Telma enters the room to check on them and queries, "Anything the matter, Jack?"

"Is my mom out of the shower?"

"Yes. You can go up," she replies.

"Come see," Abby says and grabs Telma by the hand to pull her toward the fort.

Jack bolts up the stairs. "Mom?" he asks, finding

her at the vanity in a robe with her hair wrapped in a towel.

She catches his reflection in the mirror. "Oh, hi, honey."

Jack plops on a bench by her closet, drooping from the weight of having to explain stuff he doesn't understand to his sister. He sighs. "Mom."

"What's the matter, Jacko?"

"Abby's confused about who her daddy is, where he is."

Kate's face fills with dread.

"Why don't we have a dad?" Jack asks innocently. "I mean, I know dad died, but we could have a stepdad like Tyler at school?"

Kate grins at her son as she stands. "If only it were that easy. But you make a very good point. I'll work on it. Okay, hon?"

He nods and smiles like it's a done deal. Kate sits beside her son, squeezes him tight, and kisses the top of his head.

***

The Benton house is filled with the sweet scent of vanilla cake. Stella decorates a two-layer cake on the kitchen island. The cake has a crude winding trail with a mini off-road truck like it's climbing to the top. Other frosting is sculpted to resemble boulders and patches of green grass.

Behind her, Lissa is staring vacantly at a shelf with a collection of tin men. There are three, all seemingly handmade, much like the handle on Steven's cup. She imagines a life where she and Steven can be together. Traveling the world—her performing, him directing. There are no truck cakes in that life. No little ones with pains through the night. There is a man completely in love with her and focused on her. He's not trying to save the world, just play in it.

Lissa wraps a remote-control truck at the kitchen table with blue and red paper and a bow to match. At the corner sits a balloon bouquet that features the number six.

Stella squints in concentration as she squeezes the piping bag to apply a line of icing. "Mom, when are the boys getting back from Miles's art show?"

"The exhibition runs until 4:00 PM, so they'll be back just in time for a b-day cake treat."

Stella examines the cake. "Do you think he'll like it?"

Lissa appraises her daughter's work. "Are you

kidding me? It's a masterpiece. Perfect for him. Can I help?"

"No, I've got it." Stella changes the tip of the piping bag. "What should it say, 'Leo Rocks'?"

"Sounds good to me!"

Stella grins proudly and then goes back to work, very serious about her cake decorating.

***

David and Anton are at a greasy-spoon diner within walking distance of the luxury timeshare where Angelika is staying this trip to Manhattan. They're sitting on opposite sides of a red booth upholstered in shiny red vinyl. Anton, thirteen and full of raging hormones, wears goth gear, sports a nose ring, and earrings shaped like tiny syringes. His hair is long on top, dyed blue, and shaved on both sides.

David dips his bacon into the sunny-side-up egg yolk on his plate. He takes a bite of the bacon and holds the half-eaten strip in the air as he says, "Just saying, grades matter. It's now or never. Gotta study hard if you want to get into a good college."

David is certain it'll be his connections that will get Anton accepted by a choice university but first, his son has to make the effort and apply himself to his studies.

Anton pours syrup over the stack of pancakes on his plate. He keeps pouring until the pancakes are swimming in syrup. David knows that Anton hates soggy pancakes and is making this mess just to irritate him.

"I don't know if I'm even going to college," Anton

says. "Why do you care?"

"Uh, because I'm your father," David replies. Despite this proxy war Angelika is waging against him through Anton, David slogs forward, propelled by a sense of parental duty. He senses his voice getting hard and softens his tone. "Do you think things are just going to be handed to you?" David regrets the question as soon as it leaves his mouth. Because of his trust fund, Anton will never have to work a day in his life.

Anton lets his fork drop on the floor where it clatters dramatically. "Oh God, really? You're going to tell me how to live my life? I can make a living playing computer games and stuff."

David is uncomfortably aware of the other diners staring. It's Anton playing head games, something he's learned quite well from his mother. The waitress approaches their booth with a clean fork. David scoops the other fork off the floor and gives it to her in exchange. He hands the clean fork to Anton. "With your work ethic, I highly doubt it."

Anton ignores his dad's offering. "Whatever! I hate it when you lecture me. I don't give a crap what you have to say—"

The remark triggers David and he leans across the table, fuming. "Don't ever talk to me that way. Do you hear me?"

"Or what?" Anton replies, his words dripping with disdain, "I'll talk to you however I want. It's a free country. Maybe I just won't talk to you at all." Anton slides out of the booth and storms towards the door. Once outside, he gives David the finger as he walks by the front window.

The other diners pretend they haven't been watching and return to their conversations and cell phones.

David remains still, at a loss for what to do. His heart aches in shame and rejection. He remembers Anton as an infant and warming himself on the promise of all the potential his son had. Anton would lack for nothing, and he could use every privilege as a springboard to reach success that David had not dreamed of. As an athlete. Or an inventor. A real-estate mogul. A politician. Anton's future was a highway paved with favor and advantage.

He regards Anton's swampy mess of pancakes and syrup and throws his napkin down in disgust. He sits and stares, utterly bewildered. Angelika successfully brainwashed this kid into resentment and rebellion from day one.

He retrieves his fork and dives into his son's uneaten stack of syrupy pancakes.

***

Kate stops by the Bentons' on her way to a date, wearing a new sassy black dress of linen and lace that shows off her figure. A small purse of gold lamé dangles from a shoulder chain. Lissa preps for dinner, making her special meatballs with marinara sauce.

"Oh my gosh." Kate takes a deep whiff of kitchen aromas. "Can I please skip this date and just eat here? It smells divine!"

"Of course," says Lissa. "You're always welcome!"

"Trust me, I'd much prefer the company of my niece and nephews to these losers. The problem is people aren't afraid to misrepresent themselves in their profiles!" Kate shows Lissa her phone. "Check out this profile pic from my last date." She swipes. "Now look who I actually met."

"Oh, God. He's literally two feet shorter." Lissa gapes in laughter.

"Yeah, and one guy's profile pic showed him with a full head of blond hair. When he showed up to our coffee date, he was almost bald. His excuse, the pic was from ten years ago. 'Might want to update, dude,' I thought, but I kept that to myself. I bailed as soon as was humanly possible. Oh, and guys are in the market for women ten to twenty years younger, so that means the guys interested in me would be in what, grandpa territory? They say Tinder is the place to be. It's douchebag central. But there's some hope on Match.com." Kate shows the photo on her phone.

"Tonight's date?" Lissa asks. "He is handsome. If that's really him and if he's really that tall with that much hair!"

Kate sighs and stashes the phone in her purse. "Welcome to my world."

"Where are you going?"

"Uchiko!"

"Fancy."

Stella enters the kitchen, working her arms to hold an open jar of peanut butter, a spoon, and an apple. "Hi, Aunt Kate. Cute dress!"

Kate twirls. "Thank you."

Stella covets the entire jar. Each time she takes a bite of the apple, she dips the spoon in the jar and smears peanut butter onto where she has just bitten.

Miles appears and sees Stella's peanut butter project. "Mo-om, Stella's putting her germs in the peanut butter again."

Stella stares at Miles, licks her spoon, and digs into the peanut butter.

Miles whines, "It's so gross!"

"How about this—I'll buy you each your own jars, and we'll put labels on the jars. Problem solved." Lissa samples the marinara sauce.

Miles was so focused on Stella hoarding the peanut butter that he didn't notice Kate until now. "Oh, hi, Aunt Kate!"

"Miles, my love," Kate replies.

"Nice lip gloss. What color is that?" asks Miles.

"It's new. They call it 'kissable currant.'" Kate puckers her lips. She pulls the gloss from her purse to show Miles and applies more to her lips. "Now, I'm all ready to kiss my next frog. Bye, guys!" She heads to the front door.

"Careful, it might be a toad!" Miles yells back. He grabs an apple and scurries out the other door before Kate can retort.

Lissa stirs the thick aromatic sauce, cracking up at the exchange.

***

Lissa steers her Volvo SUV through a busy neighborhood. She's dressed in a blazer, skinny black slacks with flats, and heading home from work. Today was a rough day, especially with a reluctant teenage client who claimed he didn't need counseling. He was only there because his mom had forced him to go. He sat with his arms crossed tightly over his chest, staring at the floor, answering only in monosyllabic words, if he answered at all.

What saved the day from being a total loss was a young woman making encouraging progress, processing the trauma of sexual abuse at the hands of her stepfather.

Lissa glances at the dashboard and selects a radio station playing "All of Me" by John Legend. She feels as if the song was meant for her. When she sings along with the lyrics, her mind thinks back to Steven.

They were sitting together in theater chairs, scripts in hand, talking intensely. Arms touched, not that they meant to touch; it just happened, and neither pulled away. It made for an electrifying moment, crackling with thoughts begging to be spoken. *Is it him? Is it me? Is it the possibility of being someone other than Todd's wife? Someone other than mom to Stella, Miles, and Leo? Someone in my own right.*

Digging deep and finding artistic and theatrical treasures, a spark that I didn't even know existed. Me in the spotlight, sparkling, and the audience hanging on every word.

She glances up, recoiling with horror that she has drifted into oncoming traffic. A UPS truck is barreling down the road headed straight for her. Adrenaline courses through her body, energizing her arms and legs. She swerves left, across the path of the oncoming truck, and toward a concrete pillar. *I'm going to die!*

***

David enjoys lunch with Mark, his investment banker, at the Gabriel Kreuther Restaurant in Manhattan. It's packed—not a table to spare—and busy waiters whoosh by in their crisp black and white attire, balancing glasses and plates on their serving trays.

This is one thing David loves about his second attempt at his twenties and thirties—the freedom to dine out whenever and wherever he feels like it. It beats being on the clean-up crew at home. This brings back fond memories of Kate's cooking, which was always hearty and generous. A bit like she was.

Their waiter pours champagne into flutes with a flourish as David and Mark dine on foie gras. A slender but towering Asian woman strolls by as if on a runway. Their eyes follow her as she passes. Mark raises his eyebrows and David smirks in appreciation.

Mark brings his attention back to the table, all business now. "I was reading in the *Wall Street Journal* about the big events over the past year as they relate to investing—Trump's surprise win, North Korean missile tests, global warming, and catastrophic weather. What do you make of it all?"

"Might want to look at robotic surgery, gene sequencing, and biomedical research. You wouldn't listen to me about art," David teases.

"And to think, I thought you were mad paying, what was it? $4.3 million for it. $110 Million. Man, it's like you've got a crystal ball!"

David laughs and dribbles his champagne. Mark polishes off the foie gras while David's mood shifts and he is suddenly somber. Something ominous has pierced this bubble of good humor, and clutching the flute, he stares off into the distance. He then regains his cheery self, smiles, and gets back to business.

***

Outside Uchiko, her favorite date restaurant, Kate hands her ticket to a valet attendant.

"Thanks for dinner. My treat next time," says her date dressed in a sport coat, dad jeans, and running shoes. He ducks into a blue Toyota RAV, his Uber ride home.

Kate grimaces and gives him a half-hearted wave as the Uber driver zooms off. "Trust me, there will be no next time," Kate mutters to no one.

"Uh, bad date, Ms. Kate?" asks Leroy, the valet.

Her silver Audi pulls up, and the attendant holds the door for her.

"I'm batting zero again, Leroy."

"Oh, I'm sorry. Better luck next time!"

Kate ducks into her car and sighs, relieved that her dreadful date is over. Chad was a monologuer who didn't ask even one question about her. She was tempted to drink a little too much sake to make it through his ode of self-congratulation, but she refrained because she didn't have a designated driver. Even when she yawned, he wouldn't shut up already.

She wonders if she'll ever find love again or if she is doomed for eternity to internet dating hell. She feels like she's letting Jack and Abby down by not finding a replacement dad. Who knew the landscape of available men was so dreadful? She figures there's a reason they are single. Once a woman finds a truly good man, she holds on tight and never let's go.

As Kate drives into the night, she blasts her stereo. "When a Man Loves a Woman" by Michael Bolton. The song makes Kate think of her wedding day in that other future. She and David are on the dance floor, moving together as one, David embracing her like she's the most precious gift he ever received. Even in those carefree years, she never thought so much happiness was possible.

Tears flood her eyes, smearing the colors, making her window to the world look like an impressionist painting. She switches the station to head-banging music, something to halt the memories. Kate wipes away tears and takes a deep breath of self-pity, steeling herself against the reality of her life.

***

Lissa sleeps on a slightly raised hospital bed, her head wrapped in bandages, while a nurse checks her vitals and makes notes. Monitors blink and beep all around her—a confusion of sounds from life-saving technology.

Todd is at the door with the doctor, who's reading Lissa's test results from an iPad. Todd glances at Lissa, concerned. "How bad is her head injury?"

"It looks worse than it is. The swelling will go down over the next forty-eight hours. But thankfully, there's no spinal damage or significant head trauma. The airbags did their job and absorbed most of the impact. I'm telling you, these Volvo SUVs are built like tanks, real lifesavers."

"Thank God."

"We may need to adjust her meds if the pain is

intolerable. The head and arm lacerations don't concern me. It's the cracked ribs that will bring her the most discomfort. But they'll heal pretty well. She's had a significant concussion but there's no swelling of her brain tissue. Once she's more lucid we'll start testing for the extent of head trauma."

"Thanks, Dr. Ryan. I appreciate everything you're doing."

Todd drives home so grateful that his wife is expected to fully recover from her accident. The relief brings him to tears. He arrives home to find Kate serving Stella, Miles, and Leo pizza and salad. The kids clamor for his attention.

"How's Mommy?!" Leo says, noisily slurping his Coke from a straw.

"Yeah, how's Mom?" asks Stella, who's swiping all the pepperonis from the pizza and popping them into her mouth, one by one.

"When does she come home?" asks Miles, shooting the pepperoni thief a dirty look. "Steeelllla! Don't take all of them!"

"Mom's doing okay, guys. She's sleeping now and the doctor says there is nothing to worry about." He gives a reassuring smile. "Tomorrow, we can all stop by and say hi. I'm going back tonight." Todd turns to Kate. "You're good here?"

"No problem. Mom's watching Jack and Abby. Let me set you a place at the table." Kate goes to the cupboard to retrieve a plate and cutlery while the kids start on their dinner.

Todd heads to the sink to wash up and Kate

approaches him, whispering, "This is so scary. It didn't happen last time."

"I know," he whispers back. "I wonder why she veered into oncoming traffic. Clearly, she was distracted by something."

***

Later that night, Todd finds Lissa awake and sitting up, but at an angle to protect her ribs. Todd carries a very worn stuffed bear. "Leo insisted you have Walter to keep you company."

"That is so, so sweet. Why is Walter covered in Spiderman Band-Aids?"

Todd laughs. "Leo didn't want you to feel alone in your recovery."

"What a sweetheart." Lissa takes the bear, wincing.

Todd sits beside her. "The doctor said your ribs would bother you."

"He's right about that. I can't get comfortable."

"How's your head?" Todd asks as he touches his temple.

"The staff has been asking me the same question," Lissa replies. "I spent the afternoon with them testing my hearing, my eyes, visual and color acuity, my short-term memory."

Todd studies her face like he's looking for something. "And?"

"All good." Lissa's expression turns apprehensive, seeking answers. "Did this happen before?"

"No. I'm shocked as hell. I'm just glad you're alive

and can come home in a couple of days." Todd takes her hand and kisses it. "Times like this we're reminded what's most important to us. I love you, Liss. I can't imagine life without you." Tears well in his eyes.

At that moment, Lissa realizes how much her husband loves her.

Chapter 21

Todd wears latex gloves and pecks away at a typewriter in his home office. "Damn it!" he says to no one as he makes a mistake and tries to use Wite-Out, but it goes all over the place, including his fingers. "Fucking antiquated piece of shit!" He yanks the paper out of the typewriter, wads it up, and throws it on the floor. Similar wads of paper litter his office. He feeds a new sheet and types more carefully.

The letters on his desk are addressed to MGM Resorts and the Las Vegas Police Department, warning of an impending attack. When his phone rings, Todd puts Kate on speakerphone. "I'm almost done." He types while talking and half-listening.

"Well, you're not going to believe this. Detective Manley died. Heart attack," Kate says, sniffling.

Todd freezes mid-stroke. "What the... You're shitting me?!"

"Nope."

"He wasn't all that old."

"I know. Maybe the stress of the job got to him. So I spoke to the sergeant-in-command, and he didn't take me seriously at all." Kate sighs.

"It is what it is." He jabs at the keys to finish the letter. "You know the drill. We do what we can and hope for the best."

***

David slumps on an overstuffed gray couch ladened with

colorful throw pillows. He clutches a pillow in his lap. Dr. Cowan, his therapist, sits opposite David in a black leather chair, a notepad on his lap and a pen at the ready. Cowan is balding with a closely shaven beard and sports a gray tweed jacket to give him a professorial air.

"It hit me the other night," David says. "I saw myself, my ridiculous self, from a bird's-eye view. I'd been served a gourmet dinner by my staff at my elegant dining room table with a 360-view of the city. In silence, I poured myself a glass of wine. And I thought, *Bon appetit to me.* But shit, what's the point unless you can enjoy it with someone you love. You know?"

Cowan jots in his notepad and nods. "You feel incomplete? Empty?"

"It was all right there for the taking." David shakes his head "God, I fucked up. Royally."

"What was there for the taking?"

"A beautiful relationship. The best woman ever."

"Don't be so hard on yourself."

"Trust me," David rolls his eyes at Cowan, "you don't know the half of it."

"Tell me." Dr. Cowan leans in. David thinks he's poised for a breakthrough moment.

"Kate was right there within arm's reach," David reaches to illustrate, "and well…" He lets his arm go limp.

"Kate is the woman?"

David looks away and rubs his forehead. "Well, my marriage to Angelika was all wrong from the start. Didn't stand a chance. The mistake I made was having a kid with someone I've got nothing in common with."

"Hence the struggles with your son."

"Exactly."

"Let's take a look at other past decisions that have produced unwanted results. What's curious to me is you've achieved incredible success in your business life—"

David shares a vacuous smile. "I have it all," his lips droop, "but I have nothing."

"But you do have the tools to create success in your personal life, David. Let me ask you this—if you could go back, say, the last twenty years, what would you have done differently?"

David stares at his therapist, incredulous, says nothing. A flash of hope bursts into his thoughts like a ray of brightest sunshine. It illuminates a path forward and with that visual, all the despair clouding his mind evaporates. "What a loaded question that is. If I did a 'rewind,' I wouldn't, rather shouldn't, have changed a damned thing!" He claps his hands and sits up, resolute and decidedly ecstatic.

Cowan leans away, surprised. "I don't follow."

"It's a long story." David plants both feet on the carpet and stands.

Cowan glances at a wall clock. "Our session isn't over."

"Yes, it is." David grins as he exits the office, leaving his therapist looking bewildered.

***

The Griffin School is hosting its annual art show. The student artists and their families wander the corridors and auditorium, admiring the pieces on display. The exhibition includes paintings, illustrations, photography, and ceramics. Some pieces look amateurish next to Miles's work, six in all, which are both meticulous and inspired.

Miles stands next to his abstract pastel drawing, a cubist portrait of a woman's face with her features rendered in contrasting angles and perspectives. Yet, the eyes—one a triangle and the other a square—stare judgmentally from either side of a lopsided nose and hook the viewer. Lissa snaps a photo of Todd and Miles. Miles wears eyeliner, barrettes in his shoulder-length hair, and the sleeves of his paisley silk blouse are rolled up to show off wrists crowded with colorful bracelets. Todd's arms are stiff at his sides.

Lissa steps in between her husband and son. "This is incredible. I'm so proud of you, Miles."

"Thanks, Mom." Miles beams with pride.

Kate and Jack saunter close. There are no hugs because her bestie knows Lissa's ribs are still tender. Leo is in a wheelchair tonight so he will not have to stand around. Stella is on pushing duty.

"Decided against bringing Abby?" Lissa queries.

Kate gives her a knowing look. "She wanted to come, but you and I both know she would have been bored within minutes. Sorry, Miles!"

"No bother."

Lissa glances at Leo, who is probably in the same boat. It would be so good if he became interested in visual arts. *A sedentary job is what he will need*, Lissa thinks.

"Ah well," Lissa says, "What's a nanny for if not to give you a night off?"

Why did Todd never let me get a nanny? We certainly can afford it. Between her part-time job, Leo's appointments, Stella's extracurriculars, and Miles's constant desire to go shopping, Lissa never has a minute to think.

Stella points to the portrait and jokes. "Miles, that pastel you drew of me is so amazing. I wish my nose looked that good!"

Miles turns to the drawing. "There's no way I could've made it look worse."

Even Stella laughs hard. Lissa shields Miles from being able to see Todd's face, which is anything but amused. She points at other people's art, asking questions that will get Miles talking. She knows he finds it easier to talk about the work of other artists, rather than his own.

***

The next day, Lissa takes Miles and Leo to watch Stella's swim meet. Todd had a work conflict, but when he left the house, he said to Stella, "Go get 'em, tiger!"

Why can't he be that supportive of Miles? Lissa wonders.

Stella stands on the starting block with her blue racing cap and matching one-piece. Her eyes are focused on her lane, and she shakes her arms in preparation, the gesture reminiscent of elite Olympic athletes. With the countdown, she flexes, her muscles coiled and ready. When the starting gun pops, she explodes, launching herself for the pool and slicing into the water with knife-like precision. She surfaces and begins freestyle strokes that are smooth and strong, putting her in third place out of ten swimmers.

Leo and Miles are going crazy in the bleachers, cheering her on.

Leo screams, "Go, Stella! Go, Stella! Go!"

Miles jumps up and down, pumping his arms in the air.

Lissa's hands are over her mouth, and her face is frozen in concern as if watching is excruciating.

Stella reaches the opposite side of the pool and in one graceful motion, flips and pushes against the wall. She resumes her powerful relentless cadence, gaining on her opponents. The closer the swimmers get to the finish, the more thunderous the cheering. Stella accelerates and is almost even with the lead.

The race ends and she bobs against the wall, gulping air, face flushed, and reads the clock. She smiles, and Lissa thinks she is pleased with her time. Her heart swells with pride as her daughter swims to congratulate the winner.

Lissa and Leo stand to celebrate her fabulous finish and wave their arms. Leo excitedly moves too far to the left of his bench and trips on the stairs, taking a tumble. Miles rushes to his aid. Nearby spectators crane their necks in concern.

Lissa has to climb over people to get to him. "Honey. You okay?"

"It's fine. I'm fine." Leo has banged his knee and manages to stand. Miles puts a supportive arm around him. Despite his brave face, Leo looks as if he might cry.

Miles pretends not to notice his brother's fragile expression. "Mom. Okay if Leo and I go get ice cream?"

"Sure. Great idea, Miles. And would you please get

me some water?" Lissa hands him a ten-dollar bill and sits back down. She turns her attention to Stella who's out of the pool and huddling with her coach and team. Stella looks overjoyed, but she's shivering. Lissa wants to go down there and throw a towel around her shoulders but knows that moms shouldn't meddle.

Minutes later, Miles returns with her water and a triple-decker chocolate ice cream cone.

Lissa looks about. "Where's Leo?"

"He's sulking," Mile replies, appearing dejected that his ice cream idea didn't do the trick.

"Ugh. I'll be right back." Lissa gets up and climbs down the bleachers. She heads for the concession area and spots Leo on a bench. His ice cream is splattered on the concrete like he tossed it. He's slumped on the bench, staring at the ground. "Honey, what's the matter?" She places her hand on his shoulder.

"I hate my legs. I hate my life!"

Lissa sits beside him on the bench and pats his shoulder like she used to when he was little. "I think you're perfect the way you are."

"Bull crap!" Leo scrunches his face in anger and pulls back. "Mommy. You say that all the time, to me, to Miles. But it's not true. I'm not perfect. Not with these stupid legs that don't work." His eyes well with tears. He breaks down, sobbing.

"Leo, although other people may look normal, everyone has something they're struggling with. Take Kent, the boy in your class who stutters, or Hannah, the girl who's deaf."

"I'd rather be them and not a cripple!"

Lissa winces. "Please stop using that word, sweetheart." She's crushed that Leo is so unhappy.

"Well, what would you call it? What am I?"

"A boy who is so deeply loved, appreciated, and cherished by everyone who knows him." She kisses her son and hugs him tightly.

***

There's a hive of activity as a catering crew unloads a party rental truck. A banner reads *Happy 40th Todd*. Tables and chairs are arranged around Kate's backyard. Another crew finishes erecting the stage for a band. Jack, who's fourteen, lends a hand wherever he's needed, clearly feeling like the man in charge. Kate holds a schematic, directing staff. "Keep this area clear."

Kate senses someone close behind her. She turns, startled to see David carrying a suit bag and a small backpack. "David! What are you doing here?"

"Thought I'd come early to help out."

Kate, thrown but shaking it off, says, "I think we're good. The party is, like, four hours away. Maybe you should visit with the Bentons or something?" She glances away.

"Nah. I'm here now," he replies. "I'll find things to do."

Her son walks over and shakes David's hand. "Hi, Mr. Stern. Nice to see you."

"You too, buddy. Call me David."

Kate interjects tersely, "Jack, please show David the pool house guestroom. You can leave your stuff there, I guess." She returns to her schematic as Jack and David head towards the pool house.

A few hours later, the tables are set, and the floral arrangements are done. Jack and David help with the final cutlery settings. Kate, who is nearby reading over her plans one last time, overhears them joking around.

"I almost want to place it all wrong. Put the forks over here and point the knives out. Your mother is very particular about her settings," David says with a mischievous smirk.

Jack laughs. "Yeah, she'd freak out. I guess you know her well, huh?"

"I've known your mom for decades. And then some."

Kate raises her eyebrows as she departs to slip into a flirty black dress. Somehow it feels right to choose that one.

The guests trickle in, the music starts, and a line forms at the bar. When the party is in full swing, Lissa helps Kate cajole Todd onto the deck where he, as the guest of honor, is presented with a cake on fire with candles. The crowd sings jubilantly off-key as the band plays "Happy Birthday."

Her brother tries to blow out the candles, but they keep relighting. Still, he persists until he's out of breath and the candles are at last out. The crowd cheers. Todd turns to Lissa, who's standing next to him. They share a kiss as their kids, with eww faces, quickly interrupt the gooeyness and drag them to the dance floor.

David dances with Mom, who still has some dance moves, even though they're a little old school. Jack brings Abby over to join them. David lifts Abby and spins her around. Her pigtails fly into the air and she shrieks. Kate suppresses a smile.

The night grows late, and Kate's kids are ushered inside by Telma. Jack takes one final drag from his alcopop before lobbing it into the trash can ten feet away.

"Nice one!" David congratulates him.

After saying goodnight to her kids, Kate joins the partygoers who are still rocking out to one lively tune after another. She dances with the birthday boy, her uncle, some cousins, and a couple of Todd's friends from work. She revels in the party atmosphere; the one place she feels she can really be herself. She even gets in on some karaoke action with Lissa, loosened by cocktails and the festive atmosphere.

After singing "Stayin' Alive" by the Bee Gees, she is out of breath. David approaches her. "I don't think you've ever looked more beautiful. I mean that."

Kate sips champagne, slightly amused. "When I said I forgave you, David, I did. I do... but I can't forget. So, whatever's going on in that head of yours, forget it." She clinks his champagne glass and walks away.

David watches her go, swigs his champagne, and heads toward a server with a full tray of bubbly. He takes one and toasts his glass towards Kate. "Cheers!"

At that moment, she happens to turn back and can't help but smile in appreciation.

***

David stands outside the front gate of Kate's house,

clutching flowers and a boxed cake. He buzzes the intercom, which rings, but there's no answer. He rings it again. As he turns to leave the front door opens and Abby runs out.

She's wearing pigtails and missing her two front teeth. She stops at the gate. "Hi, Uncle David."

"Hi, Abby. What happened to your teeth?"

She sticks her tongue through the hole where her teeth used to be. "The tooth fairy took them."

"How much did you get?"

"I got a bunch of dollars." And then Abby looks guilty. "But I spent it all on candy."

"Uh-oh, if you eat too much, the rest of your teeth will fall out."

She nods. "That's what Mommy says."

"Speaking of your mommy..."

"My mom said... uh, never mind. I can't let you in."

David crouches to her level. "Well, can you do me a favor and give her these?"

"Sure. But she doesn't eat cake, you know."

"She doesn't eat Bundt cake these days?"

"Noooo! She never eats junk food. Why is my mommy so mad at you?" She pouts.

"It's complicated."

Abby shrugs. "Okay." She grabs the bars of the gate and leans between them as if she's going to share a secret. She whispers, "I like cake."

"Well, then, this is for you!" David slides the box and flowers under the gate.

Abby picks them up, waves thanks, and runs off.

***

Lissa and Kate browse in KiKi Nass Boutique, a high-end women's clothing store. The racks are deliberately sparse with but a few carefully selected collections on display. The sales consultant keeps an eye on them but doesn't hover. She stands at the ready in case they need help.

Kate holds up a dusty-rose-colored silk blouse.

"I like it. It's so you!" Lissa's tone changes when she says, "Hey, guess who was over last night?"

"Oh, I don't know. George Clooney?" Kate replies, knowing full well who Lissa is referring to.

"David said, and I quote, 'Not marrying Kate is the biggest regret of my life.'"

Kate lifts a shoulder and scoffs. "Yada, yada, yada. Tell me something I don't know. All intention, no follow through. How does the saying go? 'The road to hell is paved with good intentions.'"

"You only live once. Well, in your case, twice. Why not go for it?"

Kate leans in. "Oh, let's see... Maybe because he treats me like a consolation prize. Or how about the fact that he made this go-around pretty damned miserable for me?" Kate turns back to the mirror, admiring the blouse. "This, however, cheers me up!"

***

Todd and David ride a golf cart to the fifteenth hole. They hop out and reach for their clubs.

David glances at his iPhone. "We gotta speed things up. I have to pick up a package before 5:00. A surprise for Kate."

Todd, suddenly serious, sidesteps to David and holds his gaze. "Listen, I love you, man, but if you do anything to break my sister's heart again, I will kill you. I mean it. With a nine iron, no less."

David clutches his club defensively, acting unnerved by his friend's threat. "Lucky for me, that won't be necessary. Scout's honor."

Todd's eyebrows and lips are pointed down. "I guess we'll see." He tees up and whacks the ball so hard it soars past the green, over the trees, and beyond.

David watches it until it's out of sight. He says, "I didn't know you had it in you."

Their laughter dissipates the tension, and they relax as he tees up.

***

Kate is curled up on the couch in her master bedroom, reading a book titled *God: The Human Story*, when she's interrupted by a quiet knock on the door.

Abby cracks the door open and peeks in. "Mommy, can I come in?"

"Of course, baby."

Abby hands her a jewelry box covered in light-blue velvet. "From you know who."

"Hmmm." Kate takes it, pauses, and sighs heavily. As she's about to set the box aside Abby demands, "Open it! Let's see what it is!" She claps her hands in delight.

Kate slowly opens the box and gasps. It's a replica of the necklace David gave her before, only with a much bigger diamond.

"Wow." Abby stares, entranced. "It's so sparkly!"

Tears mist Kate's eyes as she touches the necklace. "God love you, David Stern. You're one persistent guy." She simultaneously laughs and cries, her heart pulled in opposite directions.

***

Lissa mixes coconut cake batter in the kitchen while watching a soap opera on TV. She stops to take in the denouement, the moment Tess confronts Michael about his affair. Lissa switches off the TV, puts down the spoon, and repeats the actress's line, with subtle seething outrage. "Michael, I know you're lying. You don't fool me!" She gestures toward her imaginary Richard, then dramatically tears her eyes away from him, settling into disdain. *Not bad. Not bad at all.*

"And the Academy Award goes to..." The voice is deep, like that of a Hollywood emcee.

Lissa spins to see Miles watching from the door. He claps, "Bravo, Lissa Benton. Bravo."

She's all smiles as he nabs an energy bar from the pantry, tears the package open, and takes a bite as he leaves.

***

David is sitting with Kate in the balcony restaurant of a luxury hotel in Santa Monica. They enjoy the last bites of their dinner—pappardelle with chicken and pistachio-mint pesto. As they polish off their Chateau de Meursault

Chardonnay, the sun dips behind the horizon and casts a tangerine glow across the Pacific Ocean. After David signs the check, they scoot close and snicker at private jokes like teens while Nat King Cole plays in the background.

David croons, "Un-forgettable-that's-what-you-are," a little off-key.

Kate bursts out giggling. "Shh! You'll get us kicked out."

An older couple stops at their table. The man with salt-and-pepper hair and kind eyes says, "We couldn't help but notice what a lovely couple you are."

The woman is slender and elegant with shiny silver hair pulled back in an updo. "Yes, it's nice to see two people so in love. Are you celebrating anything special?"

David clasps Kate's hand. "Yes, as a matter of fact. Our first date."

"Well, I didn't expect to hear that," the woman replies with surprise. "You seem like you've been together forever!"

Kate glances at David with a knowing smile.

"I reckon there will be many more dates to come," says the man.

"I hope so." David puts his arm around Kate.

The man leans toward David. "My advice to you is"—he points at Kate—"don't let go of her." The couple walks off, arm-in-arm.

Kate turns toward David. Their noses almost touch. His blood rushes when she says, "I think we should have our first kiss right about now, Mr. Stern."

"Oh, no!" he says.

"No?" she asks, concerned.

David pulls away, stands, and hoists her to her feet. "I've got bigger plans!" He scoops her onto one shoulder. As he carries her off Kate throws her head back in glee.

Chapter 22

It's a glorious Sunday at Lake Austin, with a breeze drawing ripples across the water like invisible fingers tickling the surface. The Benton clan is usually racing in different directions to school, sporting, or social events, but today they are boating together, picnicking, and enjoying the park.

Lissa smiles at Todd as he and Leo, now eleven, row a small boat toward the shore. She knows Todd is doing the lion's share of the work, as Leo's muscles resist many of the commands from his brain. She sighs and sits at a table with the remnants of a picnic lunch. At fifteen, Miles sketches pensively under a shade tree nearby.

Her daughter Stella is a sweet sixteen, madly in love. She and her boyfriend snuggle on the park swings, all googly-eyed and holding hands. They release their hands for a swinging competition to see who can go the highest. Stella squeals each time she goes higher. Without warning, her boyfriend soars away from the swing and looks like he's coming in for a crash landing but hits the ground and tucks into a roll. Stella copies this action but stumbles. He races to catch her. Such a gallant move!

Lissa glances over at the lovebirds as they steal a kiss. *Oh, those carefree years of young love.* She chuckles and turns to peer at Miles, sketching under a tree. He's never so engrossed as when he's creating his art. It makes her heart soar to know that he found his greatest passion so early in life.

"Want a brownie?" Lissa calls out to Miles.

"Sure. Just finishing up." Miles's sketch is a self-portrait in which he portrays himself in stylized model fashion. His face is made up and he wears a skirt and midriff, which shows off his long, lean body. He admires his work, which represents him as transgender. Miles stashes his sketchpad into his backpack. He comes over to grab a brownie.

"So what did you draw? Let me guess—the lake."

He pauses between bites. "Actually, it's a self-portrait. Admittedly a little self-conscious."

"What self-portraits aren't? I mean, if you think of Van Gogh's. Totally awkward."

"If you were missing an ear, yours might be awkward, too."

They share a laugh.

Miles looks at his sketch. He's drawn hair that's longer than his, and he colored it dark pink, which matches the polish on his fingernails. He suddenly closes his sketchbook. "Mine is extra self-conscious because I find myself covering up who I am. Mom, I wish I had the courage to show my true colors."

"Miles, if there's one thing I've learned in my nearly forty years, you've got to live true to yourself. I haven't always done that. Don't make that mistake."

"Right, but your true colors aren't the colors of the rainbow." He laughs. "No offense, but you being true to yourself doesn't lead to discrimination."

Lissa sighs. "That's true. I know it's easy for me to say, but if you stick to your identity and values, you'll find your way, your path. I will always support you."

301

Miles glances up at the clouds shifting, drifting, refiguring. "Thanks, Mom."

Todd and Leo row the boat back into the landing. Leo doesn't hesitate to climb out and splash into the water. He wades and guides the boat, beaching it on the muddy shore. Todd shines with pride, then hops out to help Leo drag the boat out of the water. They head over to the table as if they sensed the brownies were out. Stella and her boyfriend converge on the picnic table at the same time. Everyone but Todd moves in on the brownies. He stands back and clearly revels in seeing his family together for a change.

***

David is throwing a football with Jack in Kate's backyard while she prepares a snack inside. What started as a friendly game of toss has turned into an all-out throwing competition, each trying to outdo the other with accompanying yelps, yahoos, and playful trash-talking.

"When I was your age, I could run past any defender. I had four touchdowns." David catches the ball and squeezes it between his hands, his thoughts fading into the past. He recalls the other Jack at fifteen, playing in a junior varsity championship game. He dodges the defensive players swarming past the blockers, aims, and throws the ball down the field, spinning in a perfect spiral and arching toward the wide receiver for a touchdown. David explodes from his seat, cheering so loudly that his throat hurts as he thinks, *Such a perfect pass. Just like I taught him.*

"Everything okay?" asks Jack.

David smiles, realizing he is gripping the ball in a pre-throw hold, staring off into space. "Yes... yes, everything's good."

He smacks the ball and cocks his arm. "Back to work." He hurls the ball at Jack, attempting but not achieving the desired spiral. The ball wobbles and Jack easily snags it from the air. David looks at his hands—*I've lost my touch*—as though they've betrayed him.

Abby runs up, her pigtails flapping and her index finger scolding David. "You're late for a very important date. Your tea is getting cold and the other guests are waiting!"

David wants another go at the ball. He's torn between that and Abby's attention. Abby it is. He looks to Jack. "You take a ten-minute break to 'recover.' Okay, buddy?"

Jack smirks and spins the ball on his fingertip. "Yeah, right. You're the one who needs to recover, old man."

Abby leads David to the gazebo with a table seated with stuffed bears.

"Well, good afternoon, friends. It's beary nice to meet you," David says, trying to fit into the toy armchair by the toy table. He loses his balance and tips over onto his back, squirming in the chair like a trapped bug.

Abby is in hysterics, trying to help him back up.

He rolls to one side, then onto his hands and knees. He wiggles loose, the chair clatters to the gazebo deck, and he stands. Stretching his back, he thinks, *this is gonna hurt later*. He looks at Abby and her bears. "Well, I didn't make a great first impression. Now, did I?"

"Oh, they don't care if you're a klutz."

***

In the early evening, Kate is busy with the kids, and David scurries around beautifying the patio and pool area. He strings lights and places floating candles and flowers in the pool. Then as he waits by the side of the pool, he notices his racing heart and sweaty palms. He chuckles. *It's like when I asked my high school crush to the prom. Play it cool. Don't let her know.*

Abby and Jack guide Kate outside, Abby trying not to giggle as they pull Kate toward David.

"Keep your eyes closed, Mommy," Abby says.

Kate toes carefully across the terrazzo, eyes shut tight.

When they stop in the middle of the patio, David gives them the signal.

Abby exclaims, "Okay, Mommy! Open your eyes!"

Kate pops her eyes open and, eyebrows raised, takes in the scene. "Ooh, what's this?" She pans from the pool to Abby, then Jack. "What are we celebrating, guys?"

David steps forward and lunges to one knee. Eyes glistening with tears, he extends one arm to offer a spectacular engagement ring, a six-carat round solitaire, which gleams brilliantly in its simple platinum band.

Kate covers her mouth. Staring at the diamond ring, the lights and the candle flames reflecting across the facets, each point of illumination sparkling like a sliver of happiness, all the pain in the past about David vanishes.

Surprise quickly turns to tears of joy, and she nods excitedly. *Yes!*

David gathers her in his arms. They share a sweet kiss. Abby jumps up and down, and Jack beams. David whirls Kate around and around as Abby yells to her brother as if he needs to be told, "Mommy's getting married!"

***

Todd finally relented and agreed to fly private using the Gulfstream G200, which David keeps in Austin. During the flight to Illinois, Todd felt both awkward and truly fortunate to be flying as the sole passenger in the luxury jet to meet with one of his long-term clients, the University of Chicago Medical. He chose to stay overnight to catch up the next day with an old friend who shares his secret about the Orb. They agreed to meet midway between Chicago and Decatur, where Howard Buffet lives. For lunch, Howard suggested Francis Italian, a popular pizza joint in the tiny town of Onargo, population 1,400.

When Todd enters the restaurant, he sees Howard already seated at a booth, wearing a uniform and sipping on a soda.

He greets his friend. "Howdy, Sheriff."

Howard beams back. "Howdy yourself," he says as Todd slides into the other side of the booth. "It's been a while—like two years since we last met."

Todd gets comfortable. "And we have less than four months 'til our journey ends."

"By the way, I ordered pizza with nothing but meat toppings. If you wanted something else, too bad."

Todd's mouth waters. "That'll do."

Howard leans across the table. "I have to say, I'm actually looking forward to not knowing what comes next."

Todd loosens his tie like he's close to the finish line of this part of his life, then reconsiders and tightens the knot. "I couldn't agree more. As much as it has been a privilege, it has been equally challenging these past twenty years. Too often I've found myself asking, is this the right way? Is this a better choice?"

"I about drove myself crazy asking the same question," Howard says, "then decided awhile back to stop second-guessing myself. All in all, I think things turned out better than we expected. We've both brought about positive changes in the world."

A server approaches the table and drops off a pizza loaded with meat. Todd orders an Arnold Palmer.

Howard's hungry gaze rakes the meal. "Best pizza in the state!"

Todd directs a stare at Howard's paunch. "Weren't you supposed to be watching what you eat this time around?"

Howard shrugs. "Well yeah, but even a lawman has to break the rules once in a while, right?" He chuckles. "You only live once!" He selects the biggest piece and bites into the cheesy-meaty goodness. His eyebrows dance to express how delicious the pizza tastes.

Todd considers this. "Yes! You only live once." He makes a mental note to give his children the very same advice, adding, "Make it your best life!"

***

Lissa spent the morning plucking flowers from her garden and sorting them for vases in her home to bring color to her life. Lately, things have seemed too easily defined, one way or the other, too black or white. She wants nuance, texture, variation. For the kitchen, she'll arrange a bouquet of yellow and orange to infuse it with a cheery feel. For the living room, a rich purple and blue scheme for depth and purpose, and for the bedroom, red and pink—the colors of passion and love.

With that thought, Lissa looks up at the shelf where now six tin men sit. She pushes back from the kitchen table, walks over, and picks up one of them. With her index finger, she traces his legs, torso, and head. She looks closely at his tin face. He is smiling, which makes her smile. Sometimes when no one is home, she lovingly rearranges the men—a salve for her yawning void. No one has noticed the collection growing on the shelf, not even when she peers up and her gaze lingers a little too long.

***

The flight from Houston to Malta is finally smooth after hours of bumpy air. At times, Kate felt like the plane might plummet out of the sky and plunge into the Atlantic Ocean like a hunted bird. She and David sit side-by-side with Lissa and Todd seated across the aisle.

Kate says to Lissa, "Oh, man, I seriously thought we might be one of those flights that vanished mid-flight and is featured on CNN for weeks."

"Shhh. Don't jinx us!" Lissa protests, "We're not down yet!"

Kate didn't get any sleep with the turbulence, but she doesn't care; her excitement supersedes fatigue as they return to the time and place where this journey began. During the countdown for departure, she, Todd, and David had many discussions about what to expect. Was there a possibility of going back a second time? Or was this time travel over, done?

No, they decided, this time around they had each learned tough lessons and, at the same time, had come out ahead. David was wealthier beyond his most outlandish dreams. He and Kate were together and much better off than in the other life. Kate and Todd had scratched the do-gooder itch and discovered that some events proceeded down channels as if destiny had to run its course. However, there was plenty of change and chaos. Kate now feels it was best to accept life as they had managed to alter it.

Kate scans the Port of Valetta as it comes into view, tankers, yachts, and cruise ships lining the harbor. From this altitude, what must be a bustling port appears tranquil, just as serene as the statuesque cathedrals, chapels, towers, and domes. She thinks about the island's history—some temples dating back to 3,700 BCE. She had read that it was once inhabited by the Knights of Malta, raided by the Ottoman forces, and invaded by France, who, in turn, capitulated to the British Empire. *Was time travel involved?*

The sky is indigo blue as the plane circles the airport and descends, coming in for a smooth landing. When they disembark through the concourse, a sign reads, *Welcome to Malta.*

After arriving at the Hotel Phoenicia and checking in, Lissa follows the others around the pool and gardens of the hotel, overlooking the ancient city and ocean.

"What do you think?" Kate prompts her friend.

"This place is spectacular!" says Lissa, twirling around for a 360 view.

Todd prances over and kisses her cheek. "Just as it was twenty years ago."

She hides a wince. The comment makes her feel like she's the butt of a joke. He takes her hand, and she tells herself that this cheerlessness is all in her head.

Strolling back into the hotel, he says, "Let's check into our room so we can recharge and enjoy it."

***

Kate is seated with David in the Hotel Phoenicia's restaurant enjoying the sunset, which casts an orange glow on the white sandstone buildings below. The streaked crisscrossing clouds appear like a painter's impatient brushstrokes. Her brother strolls over to them, a slight furrow in his brow.

Kate looks across the restaurant. "Lissa back from sightseeing?"

"She got back as I left," Todd explains, "and needed an extra moment to freshen up."

A waiter sets tall glasses frosted with moisture.

Todd asks, "What are we drinking?"

"A Batja cocktail," David answers. "It's made with liqueur from prickly pears."

After a while, Lissa plops into the empty chair between

Todd and Kate.

The waiter returns with a tray of bread and pours olive oil into a dipping bowl.

"Let me guess." David narrows his eyes at Lissa. "You toured the Hypogeum, bought a goddess statue at a store, and met Yusaf."

Kate laughs with Todd, feeling like she did when they were eight and ten, having stolen jam doughnuts from the adults' stash at a party.

Lissa raises one eyebrow. "Well, Mr. Smarty Pants, you got part of it right. Yes, to the Hypogeum, and yes, to the store. But no. No Yusaf."

"Wait." Kate reaches for the bread and stops. "What?"

"I went to the store you told me about and met a lovely woman named Alima. I didn't meet this Yusaf you all talk about."

Todd appears stunned. "Did she mention the Deheb Orb?"

"Traveling back in time?" David adds.

"No," Lissa says. "But I did buy a hand-painted Luzzo for Leo." She picks up her menu. "I'm starving!"

Kate is thrown but shakes it off as she dives into the freshly baked bread.

After a while, Todd declares, "I'd like to make a toast. To my best friend, who has stuck by me year in, year out …" He leans in and whispers, "for over twenty years now, two times over!"

"I love you, bro," David says. He holds up his hand. "Almost but not quite as much as I love your sister." He gazes at Kate with love and passion and tenderly kisses her.

Kate notices Lissa smiling at the happy couple. She glances at her brother and muses that the others mentioned how fate seemed like a meandering river, shifting and twisting, yet always moving in the same direction and arriving at the same destination.

Todd looks at David, then Lissa and Kate, his eyes brimming with tears. "To you and the gorgeous ladies at this table. I say this with every fiber of my being—you are the backbone of my life. I am who I am today because of all of you and this journey we have shared."

They clink their champagne flutes, the crystal ringing like a percussive instrument ending an arresting symphonic piece.

"Cheers!" David and Kate say in unison.

***

On a hillside just outside the city, a temple lies on an oval forecourt next to a sloping terrace. The forecourt is bounded on one side by the temple's facade. The monument's façades and internal walls are made up of orthostats, a row of large stone slabs laid on end. Two young Maltese men heave a stone slab to one side, revealing a passageway into the megalithic temple.

Lanterns flicker as Alima heads down the stone staircase with four people, their elongated shadows splaying and shimmering on the temple's ancient walls.

Alima, dressed in a white hajib and a flowy tunic, opens a door, and as a glowing golden light radiates, they move into the room. A large golden luminous orb slowly revolves atop a low elaborate stone pedestal, creating a flickering kaleidoscope of light on the stone walls. Her four guests stare transfixed at the ethereal, glowing sphere.

Alima points to a picture of a man on the temple wall. He resembles a holy man in the glowing light as though the light emanates from him. "My Uncle Yusaf would say, 'The opportunity to return to the past is to make things the way they could or should have been.'"

Yusaf decided two decades ago that Alima, his kind and soulful niece, should be his protégé. He wanted his son to fill his shoes, but it takes the wisest of the wise to do this task, so the responsibility was passed to Alima.

She ushers a man to step forward. He appears to be of Japanese descent and looks about fifty years old. Closing his eyes and inhaling deeply to steel his nerves, he lets go of his misgivings and surrenders to the forces of what could be. He steps forward, his form dissolving into the haze of light surrounding the orb.

Next, a pretty, petite brunette steps up. Unlike the other guests, who appear brittle with anxiety, she smiles at Alima, then raises her arms in a display of great confidence. "Wish me luck."

Lissa vanishes into the brilliant golden luminescence...